THE FROZEN CHILD

ROBERT J. WALKER

"And what we have here, children, is a very old item," Ms. Hemsworth said, smiling. "In fact, it's one of the oldest things in this whole museum that was made here in America. The man who made it wasn't an American, though. Can anyone tell me what country this item's maker originally came from?"

A sea of hands shot up from the kids in front of Marianne Hemsworth, and their enthusiasm made her bright, cheerful smile even broader. A pretty, vivacious woman with a head of auburn curls and piercing green eyes, she had been teaching for almost twenty years now, but not even two decades in what was becoming an increasingly stressful and difficult field had dampened her enthusiasm for education.

At the back of the group of nine and ten-year-olds, however, three boys weren't paying much attention to Ms. Hemsworth or the exhibits she was showing them in the history section of the museum. The three boys—a chubby redhead named Liam, a rake-thin boy with a shock of blond hair called Eric, and an athletic youngster with neatly combed black hair, Jeffrey, were regular troublemakers in Ms. Hemsworth's class. Jeffrey, in particular, spent more time in the principal's office and detention than most of the other students combined.

Despite the ban on phones for the field trip, Jeffrey had managed to smuggle one into the museum, and now he, Liam, and Eric were watching funny videos on the device at the back of the group, standing behind two tall girls so Ms. Hemsworth wouldn't see what they were doing.

"Guys, guys, check this out," Jeffrey said, snickering. "I watched this video last night, and I couldn't stop laughing. Just wait until you see—"

"Jeffrey!"

The boy stiffened at the sound of Ms. Hemsworth's voice calling his name. Her tone of cheerful enthusiasm had changed abruptly to one of harsh sternness, and a flush of familiar guilt heated Jeffrey's cheeks as he realized he'd been caught. Nonetheless, he tried to hide his guilt, subtly slipping the phone into the secret pocket on the inside of his jeans he'd paid his older sister to sew into them the night before.

"Uh, yeah, Ms. Hemsworth?" he said, feigning innocence with the perfect slickness of a hardened criminal.

"Don't 'uh, yeah' me, young man," she snapped. "Give me the phone."

"I don't know what you're talking about, Ms.

Hemsworth," Jeffrey said. "I don't have a phone; none of us were allowed to—"

"For the last time, Jeffrey, give me the phone," she said coldly. "Hand it over now, and I'll only make you write a few pages of lines after school. If you don't, though, the principal and your parents will hear about this."

"You'd better do it, Jeff," Eric whispered.

"Just hand it over, Jeff," Liam echoed. "You'll be in *major* trouble if you don't."

Jeffrey sighed; he knew his friends were right. He'd been skating on thin ice for a long time and was on his final warning. Breaking eye contact with Ms. Hemsworth, his cheeks now burning with fiery guilt, he reached into his jeans and took out the device.

Marianne Hemsworth marched over to Jeffrey, her slim jaw tight with suppressed wrath, and she snatched the phone away from Jeffrey and shoved it into her handbag.

"I can't believe you had the audacity to do this, Jeffrey Clarkson," she hissed, glaring with white-hot anger at the boy, who refused to meet her eyes. "After everything I had to do to organize this field trip … you're lucky I'm letting you off so easily, Jeffrey. Extremely lucky. You'll get this back after school after you've written out one hundred lines for me. Now—"

Suddenly, the entire museum was plunged into darkness. Some of the children let out shrieks of fright, while others gasped and whispered. A few laughed, thinking it was some sort of prank.

Ms. Hemsworth, however, knew it was no joke. "Stay

calm, children," she said in a reassuring tone. "It's just a power outage. The lights will be back on in a few seconds. I want everyone to just stand still exactly where you are. Nobody move, please. This will be over soon."

The power, however, did not come back on. Seconds dragged into minutes, and soon amusement and surprise turned into anxiety, and fear began to grip the group of children.

"I'm scared, Ms. Hemsworth," a girl whined, her cracking voice indicating she was on the verge of tears.

"I don't like this … I don't like this … I don't like this," a scared boy began to mutter.

"I can't see anything. I'm really scared, please help me, help me, Ms. Hemsworth," a panicking girl whimpered.

Ms. Hemsworth had left her own phone on the school bus outside, but then she remembered she had just confiscated a phone from Jeffrey. She dug around in her bag and felt relief surge through her when her fingers curled around the device. She hastily yanked the phone out and tapped the screen, which prompted a dim blaze of light from the device.

"It's okay, children, it's okay, I've got a light, see?" she said reassuringly, barely able to make out her students' faces in the inky darkness, the weak glow from the screen almost completely ineffectual against the tar-black thickness of it.

"Can't you make it brighter, Ms. Hemsworth?" a frightened girl asked. "It's still so dark, even with that light."

"Jeffrey," Ms. Hemsworth said, peering around and

shining the dim light from the screen over the children's faces.

Strangely enough, although Jeffrey had been right in front of her a minute or two earlier, he seemed to have suddenly vanished. She also thought she could detect a hint of something that smelled vaguely like a chemical of some sort in the air.

"Jeffrey, where are you? Please help me to unlock your phone, so I can use its flashlight feature."

There was no response to her request. Ms. Hemsworth shone the phone in the direction of Eric and Liam, who, like the other students, were standing in the same spot they had been when the power had gone out.

"Liam, Eric, where's Jeffrey?" Ms. Hemsworth asked sternly. "This is no time to be playing games. We need to use his phone to get some light in here."

"I, uh, I really don't know, Ms. Hemsworth," Liam said, shaking his head slowly.

Marianne could see the boy was telling the truth even in the weak glow of the light from the screen.

"What about you, Eric?" she asked. "Do you know where Jeffrey is?"

Eric shook his head, looking as perplexed as his friend. "I'm sorry, Ms. Hemsworth," he said, "but I don't know, either."

"Jeffrey!" Marianne called out. "Jeffrey, this isn't funny! Where are you? Come out! I promise you won't be in trouble, just come out, please! This isn't a game!"

There was still no response. An icy chill rushed down Marianne's spine, and a feeling of dread bubbled in the pit of her belly. She suddenly got the feeling that somehow, something terrible had happened. With a feeling of panic rising within her, she began tapping desperately on the phone screen, willing the device to somehow work. Nothing she tried, though, succeeded in getting it to unlock.

"Come on, come on, dammit," she whispered, her hands starting to tremble as she shook the device.

At that moment, the power came back on as suddenly as it had gone out, flooding the museum hall with light. Marianne let out a long sigh of relief, rubbing her forehead, and then she put on a cheerful smile and looked up at the children.

"See, everyone? I told you the power would come back on soon. All right, so everyone is … here," she said, doing a quick headcount. "Everyone except … Jeffrey."

Marianne had been sure she would be able to spot the boy as soon as she could see again, but there was still no sign of him.

"Listen up, everyone," she said, "I want you all to look everywhere in this hall and find out where Jeffrey is hiding. Do not leave this hall, okay? But please, look everywhere in the hall and find him. He's going to be in a lot of trouble when we locate him. I can promise you all that."

Despite the fact that the lights had come back on, the feeling of dread and worry within Marianne had not abated. Instead, it had only grown more severe, and she couldn't shake the feeling that something truly awful had happened.

The children searched everywhere, but there was no trace of Jeffrey, even after ten minutes. At that point, Marianne knew it was time to call security.

Four hours later, there was still no sign of the boy.

"I'm sorry, Ms. Hemsworth," the museum's head of security, an elderly but strong and fit man, said to the weeping teacher, doing his best to console her.

All the other students had been sent home with their parents at that point.

"But we've turned this place upside down, and that boy simply isn't here."

"Well, where *is* he then?" Marianne sobbed. "What could have happened to him? The lights were only out for two or three minutes! What even happened anyway? Why were they out?"

The elderly man frowned and sighed, shaking his head, his expression grim and his tone severe. "Someone tripped the power on purpose," he said. "I thought it might have been someone wanting to steal an artifact from the museum … but now I think the power was cut for a more nefarious purpose."

"What? What are you talking about? What does this have to do with my missing student?"

"Ma'am," he said grimly, "I think someone cut the power so they could kidnap that boy."

2

"Detective Lawson," the voice on the other end of the line said, "you're the police detective who solved a major kidnapping case on the East Coast a couple years ago, before you moved here, right?"

Detective Sally Lawson frowned and twirled a strand of her long, jet-black hair around her forefinger, as she often did when she was either deep in thought over something or when she was wary or suspicious of someone. And with the phone call that she had just answered, it was more a case of the latter.

"I'm sorry, who is this again?" she asked.

"Bryan Meeks," the man said. His voice had the gravelly, husky tone of a lifelong smoker.

Sally took a guess and made him out to be around seventy, which meant he was double her age. She glanced at her reflection, which shone quite clearly in the glass frame of the photo of her nine-year-old son, Derek, the light of her life. With the translucent image of her face transposed over his by her reflection in the glass, the family resemblance was clearer than ever. Derek had his mother's strong cheekbones, big brown eyes, and slightly upturned nose.

"And who are you again, Mr. Meeks?" Sally asked.

"Head of security at the museum downtown," Bryan said. "I'm sorry, I know I probably shouldn't have called your personal cellphone, but the cops who came here to speak to me weren't taking my suspicions seriously. A friend of a friend knows you and recommended I speak to you. I got your number from her. I hope you don't mind."

"Okay, I see," Sally said, still feeling a little suspicious of Meeks's intentions. "And what does my solving a prominent kidnapping case have to do with … you said there was an incident at the museum this afternoon?"

"A group of kids from a local elementary school was here on a field trip," Meeks said. "While they were in the history hall, someone cut the power. When the lights came back on, one of the kids was missing. The kid's a known troublemaker, and everyone figured he was messing around, or he ran away because he got in trouble for sneaking a phone into the museum when he wasn't supposed to. But Ms. Lawson—"

"Call me Sally, please."

"Uh, yeah, Sally, we searched high and low for almost four hours. That kid was gone. I think he was kidnapped, and I think whoever tripped the power did it so they could take the boy."

"And the officers who visited you this evening, they

9

conducted a thorough investigation of the scene? They got hold of the boy's parents?" Sally asked.

"Sure, they called the kid's parents, but he never came home. And the 'investigation' they conducted was anything but thorough. They dismissed my concerns about the kid being taken. They insisted he probably just ran away because he knew he was in trouble over the phone thing. But Ms. Law-uh, Sally, I *know* that this kid didn't run away. He was kidnapped. Before you ask, no, I don't have any proof of this … but my gut instinct, it's never wrong. And I just *know* that something terrible happened to that boy. I just … I need someone to take me seriously and get on this case right away. I've heard that the first twenty-four hours are crucial, or something like that. That's why I asked around and got your number, and that's why I'm calling you at this late hour. I'm sorry for bothering you, but—"

"No, no, it's okay, Bryan," Sally said. Her suspicion had melted away, and in its place was a concern and a driving urge to help. As Bryan had said, she had indeed solved a major kidnapping case on the East Coast a few years ago, back when she'd lived there. Before the divorce, before her life had felt like it had fallen apart.

"So, do you believe me?" Bryan asked hopefully. "Do you believe that this kid may have been kidnapped and that he didn't just run away?"

"I think you may be onto something," she said.

"Thank you, thank you," Bryan said, the relief in his voice obvious. "I've been worrying myself sick the whole evening about that poor kid."

"You did the right thing in getting hold of me," she said. "I'm going to alert my superior officer and inform them that I'm opening a kidnapping case. How soon can I inspect the scene of the crime?"

"Hell, I can let you into the museum right now if you're free," Bryan said.

"Excellent. I just put my little boy to bed, and I'm going to need to call someone to come to stay in the house with him while I'm out, just to be safe. A good friend of mine lives a few blocks away. Let me give her a call and see if she can help me. I'll call you right back, and if everything is good, I'll see you at the museum in around, say, half an hour?"

"Sounds good to me, Sally. Thank you," Bryan said.

Half an hour later, Sally pulled into the museum parking lot, which was empty aside from two other vehicles. One was a Ford truck belonging to the night guard, the other was Bryan Meeks's meticulously kept mid-80s BMW sedan.

Sally parked next to the vintage BMW and took a good look at the car as she got out of hers. The spotless state it was in told her that Meeks was a man who had an eye for detail. That alone made her more inclined to believe his claims about the missing boy having been kidnapped rather than simply running away.

Meeks was waiting for her at one of the museum's side entrances. As Sally had guessed when she had first spoken to him on the phone, he was around seventy years old. He was bald and a little overweight but otherwise appeared to be in good health for his age. His eyes were magnified to twice their regular size by the thick, coke-bottle glasses he wore.

"Ms. Lawson," he said, extending a hand to her, which she shook firmly.

"Call me Sally, please, Bryan," she said. "I'm glad to meet you."

"Sorry for dragging you out here at this hour," he said, "but like I told you, my gut instinct has been telling me that that poor boy is in trouble, and I couldn't go to bed without at least trying to get someone to help him."

"Well, I'll certainly see what I can do," Sally said.

"Follow me, please."

Bryan used his access card to unlock the side door, and Sally followed him into the museum. The side door led through a storage area full of taxidermied animals and dusty artifacts. The dim lighting in here gave the room an eerie atmosphere, and a cold shiver scurried down Sally's spine as she walked through it.

"This place can be a little creepy at night," Bryan said with a chuckle as they moved through a dark hall, illuminated only with a few soft lights on the floor. "If you hear any movement, don't get a fright or anything. It'll just be Bill Jenkins, the night security guy."

"Where are we heading first?" Sally asked.

"I figured we could take a look at the security footage from all the cameras we've got across the museum. I've already been through it myself, but as you can probably tell, my eyesight isn't exactly the sharpest. I probably missed something that maybe you'll be able to pick up.

After that, we can take a look at the history hall, which is where the boy vanished during the power outage."

"Actually, could we go take a look at the room where the fuses and power switches are first?" Sally asked.

"Oh, yeah, okay, sure," Bryan said. "This way."

Bryan took Sally through a door labeled "staff only" and flicked on a switch, illuminating a network of corridors that looked more like they belonged in an office block than a museum. The central control room was two doors down, and Bryan opened the door and flicked on the light switch in the room.

"Are these doors always unlocked?" Sally asked as she stepped into the room behind Bryan.

He shrugged. "Yeah, most doors in here are usually unlocked. This is a small museum, not the Smithsonian. We don't really have anything that's truly priceless or worth millions of dollars. The few artifacts we have that are very valuable are kept locked behind bulletproof glass displays or in the safe in the basement. We never thought of locking the control room or anything because why would anyone want to come in here and turn off the lights?"

Sally examined the switchboard. All the light switches for the various rooms and halls in the museum were clearly labeled. That, unfortunately, would have made it very easy for the kidnapper to put his plan into action.

"Is there usually someone in this room?" she asked.

"No, not usually. Only in the morning, when someone comes to turn on the lights, and then turn 'em off again at night. Once in a while, the maintenance guy comes in here to check on stuff, but mostly it's empty."

"All right. Let's go check out the history hall, where you say the boy was kidnapped."

"Sure. Let me just turn on all the lights for the hall so you can get a good look at it," Bryan said.

Bryan flipped on a few switches on the switchboard and then took Sally out of this area to the history hall, which was only a short one-minute walk away. That fact alone made her think that his theory that the boy had been kidnapped held water. It would have been very easy for the kidnapper to come in here, switch off the power, and then quickly make his way to the historic hall to carry out his crime.

Sally had been here before with her son, but it had been two years prior, and she had mostly forgotten what the museum's interior looked like. She walked around the history hall, assessing the space in terms of the possibility of a kidnapping but also pausing here and there to look at the exhibits. She had always loved visiting museums.

She soon noticed an emergency exit door tucked away in a corner near an exhibit about the Native American tribe who had lived in this area prior to European colonization.

"Where does this door go, Bryan?" she asked.

"It goes straight to the main entrance," he said.

"So if the kidnapper used this to remove the child, he would have had to have taken the boy out of the museum via the main entrance, where a whole bunch of people would have seen him doing this?"

"Yes, ma'am. I don't think he would have gone that way."

Sally frowned. "You know, he may actually have done that. If he was someone who looked like he was supposed to be there, and he smuggled the boy out inside some sort of container—a large crate, for example—nobody would have batted an eyelid. I assume large boxes and crates frequently come in and out of this place?"

"Oh, uh, yeah, of course. We're always getting deliveries and stuff, and we frequently lend artifacts to other museums in the state, sometimes even across the country. But to smuggle the child out like that, he would have had to have knocked him unconscious or something."

"He probably did, as horrifying as it sounds," Sally said grimly. "Of course, that's not the only way he could have removed the child—it's just the most likely one."

"How do you, um, how do you think he knocked the boy out?" Bryan asked.

"Probably with some sort of chemical like chloroform, especially if the kidnapper was working in the dark. It wouldn't be too difficult at all, if he knew the layout of the room well and was, say, wearing socks only to move quietly, wearing dark clothing, and perhaps using night vision goggles. Chloroform is a popular one to use, too. It acts quickly, doesn't leave many easily discoverable traces, and is very simple to apply in a hurry."

"You sure do know your stuff, Sally," Bryan said, clearly impressed.

Sally smiled. "I wish I didn't know so much about such a dark and depressing topic, but I learned a lot about the kidnapping game back when I was working on that big case on the East Coast. All right, I think I've seen enough of this room. Let's go take a look at that security footage you were telling me about."

Bryan led her out of the hall and took her to the main security office, where dozens of monitors, each connected to a different security camera in the museum, were set up all over the walls.

"Oh wow, there are a lot more monitors than I thought there would be," Sally remarked. "How many people are usually in this room watching these monitors?"

"Uh, well, usually it's just me," Bryan said sheepishly. "Sometimes, there's one other guard in here. Obviously, I can't keep an eye on all these monitors at once. It took a while for me to even notice the power had been cut in the history hall earlier. I know that having one person manning all these monitors isn't ideal, but we've had a lot of budget cuts over the last few years, and the museum can only afford to employ the bare minimum of guards."

"I see," Sally said, gazing around the room at the walls full of monitors. "Okay, well, this is going to take a lot longer than I thought, but let's focus on a few specific timeframes. I need you to pull up all of the footage from all of the monitors from, say, an hour before the school group arrived an hour after they left. If we can't find anything in that window of activity, we'll expand it."

"That's around three hours of footage on each monitor," Bryan said. "It'll take us days to check all of that."

"We can speed it up," Sally said. "Don't worry, I'm

looking for a few specific clues that I should be able to spot pretty fast. I know what I'm looking for."

"All right, well, let me start going through the recordings and finding the right timestamp for each of 'em," Bryan said, grunting as he settled his bulk into a well-worn desk chair in front of the monitor control console.

"By the way, we can't rule out the possibility that this was an inside job," Sally said.

Bryan looked up at her, an expression of surprise and shock splayed across his face. "You think someone who works here kidnapped that boy?"

"I'm just saying that it's a possibility we can't simply write off," Sally said.

"I've known everyone who works here for many years," Bryan said, "and I can tell you right away that nobody, absolutely nobody in this museum, is any sort of criminal, much less the type of person who would abduct a young child!"

"I know you probably think everyone here is perfectly trustworthy, Bryan," Sally said gently, "but if you know anything about the big case I solved back east, the man who kidnapped seven children and kept them locked up in a dark, damp basement for weeks, almost starving them to death, was a well-loved preacher, who everyone thought was a wonderful person, a pillar of his community. Not even his wife knew what he was up to—sometimes you think you know someone, and I mean, you *really* think you know someone, but in reality, you really *don't*. I don't mean to cast aspersions on your coworkers, Bryan, but we have to cover all of our bases. If I had simply believed everyone who told me that that preacher was the kindest, gentlest man in the world, I never would have saved those kids and put that monster behind bars."

He nodded slowly, looking a little crestfallen. "Well ... uh, yeah, I guess you're right. Say ... does this mean you think I'm a suspect?"

Sally didn't think Bryan had anything to do with the kidnapping—her gut instinct told her that he was perfectly innocent. Even so, she never ruled anyone out as a potential suspect, not until she was absolutely certain that they were innocent. However, she wasn't about to tell him this. Right now, it was more important to have his complete trust. She flashed him a reassuring smile. "Don't worry, Bryan, you're not a suspect."

He exhaled a sigh of relief and let out a chuckle. "Whew, you had me worried there!"

"Tell me, though," Sally continued, "is there anyone who started working here recently, someone you maybe don't know as well as you know everyone else?"

Bryan scratched his chin, which was coated with a thick dusting of prickly white stubble. "You know, there is a newish guy in the ticket office, and between you and me, I've always thought he was a bit ... weird."

"Now we're onto something," Sally said, feeling the excitement of uncovering a clue coming over her. "Tell me about this guy. And maybe bring up the footage of the ticket office, too, so we can see what he was doing during the power outage."

"William Edgar's his name," Bryan said as he brought up the footage of the ticket office. "He's maybe twenty-six, twenty-seven years old, skinny as a rail, and he's kinda slovenly about the way he dresses. Bit of a slob, if you ask me. Doesn't like to shower very much, it seems; he's often got a bit of a smell lingering around him, and his hair's always greasy. Keeps to himself, doesn't talk to anyone. But he always seemed pretty harmless, if a little weird."

As Bryan had been talking about Edgar, Sally had been watching the footage of him sitting in the ticket office. She noted that he got up, left the office, and didn't return for at least fifteen minutes.

"This right here is pretty suspicious," she remarked, staring intently at the monitor. "What time did the power go out?"

"One fifty-seven in the afternoon," Bryan replied.

According to the timestamp on the video, William Edgar had left the ticket office at one fifty-six.

"Well, well, well," Sally said. "It looks like we've just found our first suspect."

he next thing Sally did was to check the feed from the "staff only" area near the control room for the lights, but there was only one camera there, and they soon discovered it had been tampered with earlier; someone had smeared Vaseline across the lens, making the footage too blurry to make out any significant details.

They saw a smudge of a figure entering the control room a few seconds before power to the historic hall was cut, but it was impossible to tell whether it was Edgar, first because of the Vaseline smeared across the lens, and second, because the footage was in black and white, so it was difficult to tell what color clothing the figure who entered the control room was wearing.

As for the history hall, from the moment it was plunged into darkness to the moment the lights came back on, there was nothing but a black screen in terms of footage.

"We don't see William coming out with a child, though," Bryan remarked. "He just goes back into the ticket office after fifteen minutes."

"That's true, but he may have knocked out the child, hidden him somewhere in the museum, and then removed the boy a few hours later. I'm not saying he's guilty, of course, but Edgar's the only suspect we have right now, and I have to be thorough, which means investigating him. I'm going to tell my superior officer about this, and we'll question him tomorrow. Will he be in tomorrow?"

"He should be, yeah," Bryan said. "You don't want to view any more of this footage?"

Sally checked her watch. It was close to midnight. "I do, but not right now. For the moment, I want to be fresh for the investigation I'm going to open first thing in the morning. I also need to get back home so my friend can go home and get some rest. Thanks for all your help, Bryan, and for the sake of the missing boy, thank you for sticking to your guns even when my fellow officers insisted that he simply ran away. I'm certain now that boy was kidnapped … and I'm going to do everything I can to rescue him and put the person who kidnapped him behind bars. But for now, good night, and thank you for all your help. I'll see you again first thing tomorrow morning."

The next morning, Sally was up bright and early. The first thing she did was to call the head detective of her department, Detective Gareth Haxton. Haxton, a late-fifties grizzled and somewhat jaded veteran of police work, was a good cop, but he and Sally often butted heads, and rare was the occasion that they actually saw eye-to-eye on a matter. Even so, they both did their best to stay on amicable terms with each other. When he got the early morning phone call, though, Haxton couldn't pretend to be pleased.

"Thanks for waking me up half an hour before my alarm went off, Lawson," he grumbled sleepily. "This had better be good."

"Trust me, I wouldn't be waking you at this hour if it wasn't," Sally said. "Did you hear about a boy reported missing yesterday? Nine-year-old Jeffrey Clarkson disappeared during a field trip to the local museum. Do you know who investigated the initial report?"

Haxton, who was still half asleep, did his best to clear the cobwebs from his weary mind as he sat up in bed and fumbled on his bedside table for his glasses.

"Who on Earth is calling you at this hour, honey?" his wife groaned next to him. "It's not even light outside yet."

Haxton ignored her and answered Sally. "Yeah, I remember hearing about that yesterday afternoon. I believe Sergeant Walpole investigated it, him and Wachowski. I'm pretty sure they concluded that the kid ran away."

"That boy didn't run away. He was kidnapped from the museum, and I'm pretty sure it was a premeditated plan, not some opportunistic abduction," Sally said. "I did some investigating last night, and I'm certain of it. We need to move fast; that boy could be in serious trouble."

"All right, all right, give me a few minutes to wake up," Haxton muttered, heaving himself out of bed. He wasn't happy about being awake, but he trusted Sally enough to know that when she said something like this, it was to be taken seriously.

"Thanks, Gareth," she said. "I've already identified one suspect, an employee of the museum who circumstantial evidence is currently pointing to. I'm not sure if he's our man, but it certainly looks like it at this point. I want to question him as soon as we can. He's supposed to arrive at the museum at seven in the morning. We need to be there, waiting for him."

"All right, all right, I'll see you there."

Haxton met Sally in the museum parking lot a few minutes before seven. Bryan was there, too, and Sally introduced him to the head detective. Haxton started to ask Bryan a few questions about William Edgar, but before Bryan could answer most of them, he stopped and pointed at a car—a beaten-up Honda sedan that looked as if it were held together with wire and duct tape—that was about to pull into the parking lot.

"That's him, that's Edgar's car," Bryan said. "Are you guys gonna arrest him or what?"

"We're just going to ask him a few questions for now," Haxton said gruffly. "I'd appreciate it if you could step back and let us do our jobs."

"Oh, uh, yes, of course, of course," Bryan said, sticking his hands into his pockets and walking over to the side entrance.

Edgar pulled into his usual parking spot and slowly got out of his car, staring suspiciously at Sally and Haxton. The moment they made eye contact with him, they began walking toward him, making a beeline for his car. He froze halfway through getting out of his car, and Sally saw a look of pure panic flash across his pasty, narrow face.

"The scrawny son of a bitch looks as guilty as sin," Haxton muttered, his eyes locked on the target. "He'd better not try to run."

It was clear there was a furious debate raging in Edgar's mind about whether to jump back into his car and speed away or to stay, but he was so paralyzed with indecision that he simply remained stuck in place, half in his car, half out of it.

"William Edgar!" Gareth Haxton boomed, his deep voice echoing across the empty parking lot. He pulled his police badge out of his coat and flashed it at the young man. "Stay right there. My friend and I need to ask you a few questions."

Sally said nothing, but she, too, flashed her badge at Edgar as she approached. Both she and Haxton wore stony, unsympathetic expressions on their faces, and it was obvious that Edgar was intimidated. Cold sweat oozed from the pores on his forehead and all over his back, and waves of hot and cold flushed through him.

"Step out of the car, son," Haxton muttered as he approached him. "Put your hands where I can see 'em."

"Are you, am, am I ... I didn't do anything, why, what are you, I didn't—" Edgar stammered in a panic, tripping over every word that stumbled in rapid-fire out of his mouth.

"Just calm down and answer our questions, please," Sally said. "You're not under arrest … yet."

Edgar swallowed a dry gulp of fear, his prominent Adam's apple bobbing on his bent neck. He had the hunched posture and stooped shoulders of a man who spent most of his waking hours in front of a computer.

"Have you seen this boy recently?" Haxton asked, showing Edgar a printout of a photo of Jeffrey his parents had given the police the previous day.

"Uh, no, no, I haven't, I don't know who that is," Edgar muttered.

"Are you sure?" Haxton said, shoving the picture right up into his face. "Maybe you should look a little more carefully."

"Um, well, I don't know, maybe he was one of those kids who was here yesterday. Is he the, um, the boy who ran away? The one everyone was, uh, um, looking for here yesterday?"

"Well, look at that. It appears you *do* know who this is," Haxton said.

"He didn't run away," Sally added. "He was kidnapped."

Again, Edgar swallowed a dry gulp of anxiety and fear, and both detectives quietly made a mental note of this reaction.

"Uh, all right, okay," Edgar said. "Why are you telling me this?"

Ignoring his question, Sally fired a question of her

own at him. "Where were you for the fifteen minutes that the power to the history hall was cut?"

"Huh? What are you talking about? I was in the ticket office all day like I am most days," he said, now beginning to develop a little more confidence and adding a measure of defiance to his words. "What does that boy's disappearance or, uh, kidnapping or whatever have to do with me? Do you, do you people think that *I* had something to do with it?"

"We're just asking you some questions is all," Haxton said slowly, although the threat underlying these seemingly innocent words was unmistakable. "I'd appreciate it if you answered them honestly. So, tell the nice lady what you were doing in those fifteen minutes when the power to the history hall was cut, please."

"We've already seen the security camera footage, William," Sally said coolly. "We know you left your office a few minutes before the power was turned off, and you stayed out of your office for at least fifteen minutes."

"All right, if you must know, I was, I was um, in the bathroom. I have IBS, okay? I often need to go to the bathroom for … for long periods, and it can happen anytime."

"If we check the security camera footage near the staff bathrooms," Haxton said, "will we see footage of you going into the bathroom at that time? I'm warning you now, kid, lying about this will *not* go well for you, so it's best that you tell us the truth."

"The, uh, um, the security camera in that area … has

been broken for a while. You, uh, you won't see anything on it," Edgar stammered.

Haxton shot Sally a glance that she knew well; he was clearly already convinced that Edgar was guilty. As for her, though, she wasn't entirely sure. The young man was obviously hiding something and was clearly guilty of something, but she wasn't certain that his crime was kidnapping a child.

"Hmm," Haxton rumbled, staring at Edgar with an unwavering, ice-cold gaze. "Strange that you know that that particular security camera is broken … very strange. Why would someone who works in the ticket office know which cameras in the museum work and which ones are broken?"

"I … I just do," Edgar stammered. "I c-can't remember how I found out about that. I just … *did*, somehow."

"So you have no actual proof that you went to the bathroom during those fifteen minutes?" Sally asked.

"N-no, well, no! Who on Earth has 'proof' that they went to the bathroom at a certain time?" Edgar spluttered. "This is … this is outrageous! I-I don't know anything about what happened to that boy! L-leave me alone now! This, this isn't right! I'm innocent. I didn't do anything!"

"We'll be the judges of that, son," Haxton said ominously. "Now, I want to take a look in your car. Open up the trunk for me."

"Wh-what?" Edgar stammered. "N-no! You c-c-can't look in my car! You, uh, you need, uh, you don't have a warrant!"

"You're only digging yourself into a hole here," Haxton

said. "You want to show us you're innocent? Then let us look in your car."

"N-n-no!" Edgar yelled, clenching his hands into tight, trembling fists at his sides. "You c-can't, you c-c-can't!"

"This car isn't your house, and I don't need a warrant to search it, just probable cause," Haxton said gruffly, his hand moving slowly down to the grip of his pistol. "Now, William, we can do this the easy way, or we can do it the hard way … but either way, we're going to be looking inside your car in the next few seconds. Tell me, which is it gonna be? The easy way or the hard way?"

Edgar seemed to be rooted to the spot, completely paralyzed. His mouth was open, and his jaw was moving, but no words came out. Then, slumping his shoulders and almost folding over with utter defeat and misery, he let out a whimper and stepped away from his car, staring at the ground with guilty eyes.

"Sally, take a look in the vehicle," Haxton said, without once taking his eyes off Edgar. "I'm going to keep an eye on our friend here."

"Got it," Sally said.

She did a quick search of the interior of the car. It was full of junk, mostly fast food containers, disposable soft drink bottles, coffee cups, and chip packets, but nothing suspicious. Then she popped open the trunk … and when she did, she gasped.

"What is it, Sally?" Haxton asked.

"Take a look at this, Gareth," she murmured, her eyes locked on the objects in the trunk.

He stepped over, keeping his eyes on Edgar all the

while, and glanced into the trunk. When he did, his eyes widened with surprise. Then, he let out a low growl of both anger and disgust. He took out his handcuffs and marched over to William Edgar.

"Get on your knees, scumbag," he snarled. "You're under arrest for the kidnapping of a minor."

4

---

*B*ryan Meeks saw what was happening, and he rushed over to Edgar's car, where Haxton was busy putting Edgar, who was shaking and on the verge of tears, into handcuffs.

"What's going on? What did you guys find?" Bryan asked breathlessly.

"Take a look at this," Sally said, pointing into the trunk of Edgar's car.

Frowning, the old man peered into the trunk. "What's that, a bunch of comic books? I don't get what I'm supposed to be seeing here."

"Take a closer look at those 'comic books,' Bryan," Sarah said, unable to disguise the disgust in her voice. "They're not just 'comic books.' They're porn mags."

"They're just, they're Japanese manga!" Edgar protested, fighting back tears as Haxton put him in handcuffs and read him his rights. "It's, it's called yaoi manga, and it's not illegal! It's n-not illegal! I-I didn't do anything wrong!"

When Bryan examined the comic books in more detail, he discovered that one of them was open, and the pictures in it depicted a sexual act between a man and a teenage boy.

"Ugh," he muttered, recoiling in disgust. "What the hell is this?" Then he turned to glare at Edgar, who was on the ground in handcuffs. "You're a real sicko, you know that?" he growled. "Where's that boy? What have you done with him?"

"I-I didn't do anything to that kid," Edgar said, bursting into tears. "It-it wasn't me!"

"Lock this sick bastard up and throw away the key," Bryan muttered. "I can't believe I was in the same building as someone who's into sick stuff like this."

Despite the overwhelming evidence indicating Edgar was the man who had kidnapped Jeffrey Clarkson, Sally found herself doubting the young man's guilt. Her gut instinct usually informed her a suspect was guilty—it had certainly been right about the preacher on the East Coast, as it had about many other criminals she had arrested—but it just wasn't buzzing for William Edgar. As disgusting as the pornography he had in his car was, Sally now no longer believed he was the man who had abducted the boy yesterday.

However, he was their only suspect, and they had a duty to question him more thoroughly.

"Call the commissioner and organize a warrant to search this guy's house," Haxton said to Sally as he dragged Edgar over to his car. "With any luck, we'll find the kid locked up there, hopefully unharmed, and this whole thing can be over before lunchtime."

"I'll do that," Sally said. "But I'm not sure about this whole thing being over before lunchtime ... or anytime soon," she added softly.

"So what now?" Bryan asked. "You've arrested him, you guys are going to search his house ... then what, does he go on trial right away? How soon does he get tossed in the slammer?"

"Uh, it's a little more complicated than that, Bryan," Sally said. "Thank you for all the help you've given us so far, but we don't need anything else from you. If we do, though, I'll give you a call. And speaking of calls, there are a few I need to make now."

Bryan looked a little disappointed to no longer be involved in the investigation. "Oh, uh, all right," he said. "Say, though, do you want copies of the security camera footage from yesterday?"

"Actually, that would be great, thanks," Sally said. "If you could give me copies of the footage from every camera in the museum, that would be perfect."

Bryan frowned, looking a little confused. "Every camera in the museum? But don't you only need the ones that show William doing stuff?"

"I know this might seem a little strange to you, Bryan," Sally said, "but we're still not one hundred percent certain he's the right man. I mean, don't get me wrong, we're ninety percent there, but in case of that ten percent, we need all the footage, just in case we do have the wrong guy."

"You should lock him up just for having those disgusting porno comic books, even if he didn't abduct the boy, which I'm sure that he did do," Bryan said. "But sure, Sally, I'll make copies of all the footage for you from every camera. Except, of course, the one that had the Vaseline smeared over the lens."

"No, make copies from that one, too, just in case, please," she said. "And don't clean up that lens yet. We might be able to get a fingerprint or two out of the Vaseline."

"All right, I won't touch it. I'll give you a call when I've got all the copies of the footage ready for you."

"Thanks, Bryan," she said. "I'll talk to you later."

Around an hour later, Sally, Haxton, and a few other cops arrived at William Edgar's apartment. Surprisingly enough, he had given them his keys and permission to search his place, so a warrant wasn't necessary. Haxton thought he was either just plain stupid or far slyer and more cunning than they had previously given him credit for, but for Sally, it only reaffirmed her suspicions that he was actually innocent. Either way, the search would no doubt reveal the truth.

"He must be keeping the boy elsewhere," one of the cops said. "There's no way he'd let us search his place if he had the kid locked up here."

"Maybe he doesn't have the boy at all, and he wasn't the one who abducted him," Sally said.

"Have you lost your mind, Lawson?" Haxton scoffed. "You're the one who first identified him as a suspect, now you're saying he's innocent? Come on, you saw the filth he had in his car, and he openly admitted we'd find more of those disgusting comics in his house. He's a creep, through and through. He was at the scene of the kidnapping. He 'mysteriously vanished' from his office at a time that almost perfectly coincided with the boy's disappearance *and* the power outage. If all that's just a coincidence, well then, that perverted little shit should go buy himself a lottery ticket because, with those kinds of odds against him, he's bound to have a serious bout of good luck coming his way."

"I'm just saying, Gareth, that we need to keep our minds open to all sorts of possibilities here," Sally said. "And one of those possibilities is that while William Edgar is no doubt a pervert and a creep, he may not be a kidnapper on top of that."

"We'll soon find out," Haxton said as they approached Edgar's front door. "He said it was number 3A, right?"

"That's right," one of the other cops said.

Edgar lived in a run-down apartment block downtown. The entrance hall was smelly, and the cracked walls, with many chunks of plaster missing, were covered in graffiti and gang tags. Refuse bags that had clearly been piling up for weeks were sitting in one corner. A rusty bicycle chained to the stair railing had long since had both wheels and its seat stolen off it.

Edgar's apartment was on the third floor, and just as the cops were unlocking his front door, they heard the door behind them—the one across the floor from Edgar's place—open. Sally turned around and saw an elderly woman staring out at them, her eyes wide with fear.

"What's going on here?" she demanded. "Who are you people? You don't live there!"

Sally showed the old woman her police badge and explained why they were there, while behind her, Haxton and the other cops entered the apartment. Sally figured she may as well talk to the neighbor, who seemed to be the nosy type and might know something about Edgar.

"He's really quiet, and he doesn't have a wife or a girl-friend," the old lady said, staring at Edgar's front door with a sneer of disgust on her face. "He's very strange … yes, very, very strange. And not in a good way. He always has his TV turned up too loud. And it's mostly shows in some foreign language he watches, not English."

"I see," Sally said. "Have you ever seen any children entering or leaving his apartment?"

"I've never seen anyone but him go in and out of there," she said. "Oh, except for a few days ago."

This was interesting, especially considering the last few days' events, so this got Sally's attention. "Who did you see going in here?"

"There was a repairman of some sort," she said. "Which you probably don't think is very strange because there's nothing odd about a repairman coming to some-one's apartment. Except this repairman … he seemed like he was breaking into the apartment. And I know for certain that that creepy young man wasn't home; he'd left for work an hour earlier."

Sally scribbled these details down in her trusty notebook. "Can you be sure the repairman was breaking into the apartment?" she asked.

"I've never heard of a repairman picking a lock to get into a place to fix something," the old woman said. "And I watched the guy through my peephole in my door. His back was to me, so I could make out exactly what he was doing. He had some small tools, and he messed around with the lock for at least two or three minutes before finally opening the door. He was in there for around twenty minutes, then he left."

"I see. Thank you for telling me this," Sally said. "Did you inform your neighbor that his apartment may have been broken into?"

She shook her head. "Maybe I should have, I suppose … but that young man frightens me. He seems … disturbed. I thought maybe he was on drugs, that this 'repairman' was some sort of drug dealer or something. I don't know; I didn't want to get involved. You know what happens to people who stick their noses in stuff like that. Next thing you know, that 'repairman' is breaking into my apartment with a gun in his hand… No, thank you, no."

"All right, that's okay … Mrs.… Sorry, I didn't catch your name, ma'am?"

"Ms. Cossington. Anabelle Cossington," the old woman said with a smile.

"Thank you for the information, Ms. Cossington," Sally said, returning the old woman's smile. "Could you describe the repairman?"

Ms. Cossington shook her head, frowning. "You can't

see people very clearly through these peepholes," she said. "And my eyes aren't what they used to be, you know. All I can tell you is he was a white guy, probably average-sized, wearing blue coveralls and a blue baseball cap, carrying a big toolbox. His coveralls had writing on the back, some business logo, but I couldn't read it."

"Okay, thank you, ma'am. I really appreciate your help," Sally said. Now she was even more intrigued, and she was also more convinced that despite all the red flags, William Edgar wasn't their man.

What was going on with Edgar, though? Who was this mysterious "repairman" who had broken into his apartment just a few days earlier? Before Sally could seriously contemplate either of these questions, though, a triumphant shout echoed from within Edgar's apartment.

"We've got him!" one of the cops yelled. "This is it. This is the evidence we need! Edgar is the kidnapper; this proves it beyond a doubt!"

5

*S*ally rushed into the apartment. "What have you found?" she asked breathlessly.

"You might not wanna see this, Sally, since you've got a nine-year-old boy," the cop, a young man named Allen Kosinski, said to Sally as she approached him. He was standing in front of Edgar's computer, a large gaming rig that occupied a large, messy desk in one corner of his studio apartment.

The apartment was about as dirty and smelled as Sally had expected it to be, judging from how his car looked and the mess in it. The small, cramped space was full of trash, mostly takeout containers, beer cans, and food wrappers, and there was dirty laundry all over the floor. The grubby sheets on the bed smelled awful, and they looked as if they hadn't been changed in months.

"This place smells like a garbage dump," one of the cops muttered, wrinkling his nose.

"I've smelled garbage dumps that smelled a lot nicer

than this shithole," Haxton said grimly. Then he turned to face Sally, glaring at her sternly. "The idiot's got child pornography on his computer, Sally," he muttered. "That's what Kosinski is so excited about. Now you tell me: every single sign is pointing to Edgar being the kidnapper. Everything. Hell, he's even got child porn on his computer. You still think there's a chance in hell we got the wrong guy and that he might actually be innocent? Come on, Sally, the only thing that's missing is the kidnapped child himself. I hope Edgar hasn't killed the boy or something."

Sally had to admit that it seemed almost one hundred percent certain that Edgar was the kidnapper … so why was her gut instinct still telling her that he wasn't the one?

She forced herself to take a glimpse at his computer monitor, where Kosinski was standing. There were images of naked underage boys on the screen. One glimpse was all she needed to see that Kosinski was telling the truth.

"Well, he's guilty of possessing child pornography. We know that now," Sally said, "and we'll make sure he does time for that. But … I know this sounds weird, Gareth, but I just feel like he might not actually be the man who kidnapped Jeffrey Clarkson."

Haxton chuckled humorlessly and shook his head. "You and your hunches, Sally, you and your damn hunches. Well, as far as I'm concerned, we've got him. William Edgar is the kidnapper, and I'm gonna keep that son of a bitch in an interrogation room as long as it takes for him to admit that and to tell us what he did with that boy."

"Damn straight, Detective," Kosinski said, grinning. "I'll be the 'bad cop' if you wanna do the whole 'good cop, bad cop' thing."

"I have a question for you, Kosinski," Sally said before Haxton could respond to him.

"Sure, Sally, go ahead, shoot," Kosinski said.

"How did you find this child porn on his computer? Surely it couldn't have just been sitting there out in the open."

"Well, it wasn't," Kosinski said, "but it didn't take very long for me to find it. I just did a Windows search for all images on the hard drive, including hidden folders, and—"

"I mean, though, was his computer just open like that? There was no lock screen, no password?" Sally asked.

"Yeah, no password, it was just a screen saver," Kosinski said. "I clicked the mouse, and it went straight to his desktop."

That, like the thing the old woman across the hall had just told her about a 'repairman' breaking into this apartment a few days ago, made Sally suspicious. Edgar may have been a creep, but he wasn't a complete moron. She wouldn't have put it past him to have illegal pornography on his computer, but why would he have made it so easy to find? Her first impression of him had been a person who was rather paranoid. Surely, she reasoned, someone as paranoid as Edgar seemed to be would have a password to access his computer, and he would likely also have hidden his illegal pornography in password-protected folders, or he would have kept them on portable hard drives that were hidden somewhere in his filthy apartment. This was all simply too easy, too convenient.

"You got any other questions, Sally?" Kosinski muttered. "I can't believe you're defending this sick son of a bitch."

"I'm not defending him," she said. "If he's guilty, believe me, I'll be the first to celebrate when the judge gives him a few life sentences. I'm just saying, though … that we should keep our minds open to alternative possibilities."

"Whatever," Kosinski said dismissively.

They searched the rest of the apartment, but they did not find any other evidence that Edgar was the kidnapper, aside from the images on his computer. And, more importantly, they didn't find any evidence of what he may have done with Jeffrey Clarkson or where the boy might be.

"What now?" Sally asked as they walked out of the apartment.

"Now, I'm just happy to be able to breathe in air that isn't going to take ten years off of my life!" Kosinski joked, prompting a bout of laughter from the other cops.

Haxton, however, maintained an expression of grim seriousness on his craggy face. "Now, Sally, I'm going back to the station to question that sick bastard," he growled. "You have two choices. You can either help me or stay out of my way. One way or another, I'm going to find out what he did to that kid."

Sally wondered if she should tell Haxton what the old woman across the hall told her a few minutes earlier. She guessed, however, that it wouldn't make much difference to his opinion. Once Gareth Haxton zeroed in on a suspect and believed him to be guilty, he bit down like a pitbull and locked his jaws, refusing to let go. And right now, his jaws were dug into William Edgar's flesh with a bone-crushing grip.

"So, what's it gonna be, Sally?" Kosinski asked. "You gonna help Haxton twist that sick prick's wrist until he blurts out a confession?"

Sighing, Sally shook her head. "You boys go on and interrogate Edgar without me," she said. "I have other lines of investigation I need to pursue."

Kosinski rolled his eyes. "Seriously? Okay, whatever, well you go do whatever digging around you need to do. Detective Haxton and I are gonna go back to HQ and do some 'good cop, bad cop' until that perverted sack of shit gives it up."

"Good luck," Sally said. "I hope you get something out of the interrogation." She suspected, however, that they wouldn't.

She and the others left the apartment and locked it up, taking only the computer and one or two other objects away in evidence bags. Kosinski, Haxton, and the other cops headed back to the station, but Sally told them she'd meet them later. She intended to do some deeper digging into William Edgar's past, and she suspected that the deeper she dug, the more apparent it would be that whatever else he was, he wasn't the man who had kidnapped Jeffrey Clarkson.

Sally was proven right at the end of the day, but it wasn't from the research she did on William Edgar—which, incidentally, also proved to her that he wasn't the one who had kidnapped the boy. Instead, the proof came from a phone call from Allen Kosinski.

"Hey, Sally, uh, I've got some news," he said, sounding uncharacteristically sheepish.

"Oh yeah? Did you and Haxton manage to beat a confession out of William Edgar earlier?" she asked, fully expecting the answer to this question to be a solid "no."

Her prediction was correct. "No, uh, we didn't," Kosinski admitted. "The little bastard insists he's innocent. But that's not why I'm calling you."

"Get to the point, Allen," she said impatiently. "I'm busy here."

"Another child has been kidnapped."

6

This certainly wasn't what Sally had been expecting to hear. For a second or two, she was at a loss for words, unsure of how to respond. "Details," she finally said. "Give me details."

"We got a call half an hour ago, this time from the aquarium downtown. Same thing as with Jeffrey Clarkson; there was a class there from one of the elementary schools, they were on a field trip. There was a power outage—probably a deliberate cut—and in the darkness, one of the kids got taken. An eight-year-old boy named Dennis Avery."

"Dammit," Sally muttered. "I'm sorry to hear this, Allen. When did this happen, exactly?"

"A couple hours ago, around lunchtime," he answered. "The teacher and the aquarium staff spent two or three hours combing the aquarium and the neighborhood around the aquarium, but the boy was nowhere to be found. That's when they called us."

"All right," she said. "Is anyone on the scene yet? Have you spoken to any witnesses, the teacher, the other kids who were with the victim?"

"Haxton is on his way there. I figured you could meet up with him, maybe help him with talking to people at the aquarium."

"Sure, I'll do that; I'm not far away. I'll head over there right now."

At that moment, Sally was waiting outside a local karate dojo to pick up Derek from his karate classes. As she put down her phone, she saw the doors open and all the kids, dressed in their white karate gis, came walking out. Derek saw her sitting in the car and waved cheerfully. Sally was feeling down about the fact that another child had been kidnapped, but as down as she felt, her little boy's smile never failed to put her in a better mood.

Derek came running toward the car. "Mommy, Mommy!" he said excitedly as he threw open the passenger door. "I'm gonna be fighting in the tournament next weekend! Coach Paulson says he thinks I'm ready!"

"That's great, Derek! I'm so proud of you!" Sally said.

Derek blushed, but the ear-to-ear grin he wore spoke of his glowing pride. "Coach Paulson says my high kicks are looking really good," he said as he climbed into the car. "And I learned a new sweep kick today. It's super cool; you can get someone on the floor like, like, super fast!"

Sally was proud of her son, but right now, she needed to get to the aquarium to speak to whoever was there about the most recent kidnapping.

"How about we celebrate tonight with pizza, huh?" she asked Derek.

"Yeah! That sounds awesome!" he said.

"All right, great … but we're not going home just yet, okay? I have to go to the aquarium to talk to a few people about police stuff, then we'll pick up a pizza on the way back."

"Uh, the aquarium? Sure, okay, we can go there. Can I look at the sharks and stuff while you're talking to your friends?" Derek asked.

He had an interest in sharks that bordered on an obsession. Sally would usually have allowed him to wander around the aquarium unsupervised, but now that there was a predator kidnapping children—specifically boys around Derek's age, it seemed—she wasn't about to let him out of her sight, not unless he had a trustworthy adult with him.

"Well, sweetie, I'm not really going to the aquarium for fun … and the uh, the guys who are in charge of the aquarium probably don't want anyone looking at the sharks right now since it's closing time in about five minutes."

"Aww," Derek whined, his face crumpling into a frown of despair. "I wanna see the sharks! What's the point of going to the aquarium if I can't see the sharks?"

"I told you, Derek, I have to go there to talk to some people about police stuff. This isn't a trip for fun—but if you behave, I promise I'll take you to see the sharks on the weekend, okay? And if you're nice and quiet while I talk to the people I need to talk to, I'll speak to the guys in charge and see if they'll let you take a quick peek at the sharks. But only if you're real quiet and you're on your best behavior, you hear?"

Derek's frown vanished, replaced by an expression of serious earnestness, and he nodded enthusiastically. He mimed zipping his mouth shut, then pretended to lock it and toss away the key.

Sally couldn't help but chuckle. "All right, mister, you stick to that, you hear? Nice and quiet, and on your best behavior. Then we'll see if you can take a look at those sharks."

Sally drove to the aquarium, parking in a spot near the entrance, since the parking lot, which was usually full, was mostly deserted at this hour, aside from a few employee's cars, as well as Haxton's familiar police cruiser. As Sally got out of her car, she wondered whether Haxton would admit that he'd been wrong about Edgar. Merely thinking this made her chuckle; Haxton never admitted he was wrong about anything.

"What's so funny, Mommy?" Derek asked, trailing behind her, still wearing his karate gi.

"Nothing, Derek, never mind," she said, still chuckling softly. She wasn't about to rub it in when she saw Haxton, though; she knew better than to rouse his anger with his fiery temper and explosive attitude.

When they got to the main entrance, which was locked and barred, Sally flashed her police badge to one of the employees, who asked her and Derek to go around to one of the side doors so he could let them in.

The aquarium employee, an overweight young woman

with glasses and a nervous demeanor, led them past one of the huge tanks, this one filled with hundreds of neon-colored tropical fish.

"Are there any sharks in that tank, ma'am?" Derek asked, staring wide-eyed at the fish as they passed the glass walls of the tank.

"Some little ones, kid, but I don't see 'em over here," the young woman said.

"Derek, don't bug these people, please," Sally said sternly. "We're not here for fun—I'll bring you back for a nice long visit, but only if you behave, all right?"

Remembering what he had agreed to in the car, Derek clamped his mouth shut and nodded slowly. He kept his eyes on the tropical fish as they passed the tank, almost twisting his head all the way around as they moved on to a different area.

In a hallway outside one of the aquarium's theaters, they saw Haxton and two other cops talking to a middle-aged man in a crisp gray suit and a tearful, thin young man dressed in more casual attire. The middle-aged man was well-built, strong, and fit for his age and had a bald head that was so smooth and shiny that it gleamed like chrome under the hallway lights. He looked Sally and Derek up and down with a stern, almost accusatory expression on his broad, strong-jawed face.

"Excuse me, but who are you, and what are you doing here?" he asked gruffly. "Why did you let these people in?" he demanded, glaring at the chubby young employee, who cringed and withered beneath his fiery gaze.

"I'm a cop. My name is Detective Sally Lawson," Sally

said before the young woman could answer, showing the middle-aged man her police badge. "I'm here to assist Detective Haxton, who you seem to have already met. I apologize for bringing my young son along, but I only got the call about what happened earlier a few minutes ago, right as I was picking him up from karate. Don't worry, he's not going to bother anyone or get in the way; are you, Derek?"

Derek shook his head, keeping his lips sealed.

"All right, Detective Lawson," the man said stiffly. "I'm Keith Johnson, Manager of the aquarium. That gentleman over there," he said, pointing to the teary-eyed young man, "is Mr. Zachary Calder. He's the teacher who was in charge of the class when." he trailed off and glanced down at Derek, then looked up at Sally with a silent question in his eyes. Was it okay to mention the kidnapping in front of her child? Would it frighten the boy?

Sally read this unspoken question and responded accordingly. "The teacher who was in charge of the class when the incident occurred," she said. "I see. Listen, Mr. Johnson, would you mind if this young woman here took my boy around the aquarium for a few minutes?" she asked. "I'd rather not speak about the incident at this very moment … if you know what I mean."

"Uh, yes, yes, of course," he said. "Allison, please take the boy around to a few exhibits," he said to the young woman. "I'll make sure you get paid extra today for staying here after hours. Thank you."

"Go with the nice lady, Derek," Sally said to him. "And

Allison," she said to the young woman, "please don't let him out of your sight. Thank you."

"Don't worry, Detective Lawson, I'll make sure I keep him close," Allison said.

A huge, surprised smile brightened Derek's face, and his eyes sparkled with pure delight. "Wow, seriously? Can I ... can I really see some sharks?" he gasped.

"Hammerheads, tiger sharks, thresher sharks, we got all kinds of sharks in here!" Allison said enthusiastically. "Come on, take my hand, and I'll show you some of my favorites."

Mr. Johnson and Sally waited until Derek was out of earshot before they began talking about what had happened earlier. Johnson described everything that had happened that afternoon, and when he was done, he called the teacher, Zachary Calder, over.

Calder was in his mid-twenties, and he had only been a teacher for a year now. He was visibly upset about the fact that the boy had been kidnapped on his watch. He was shaken up, and he was looking dazed and pale.

"I still ... I still can't believe this happened," he said to Sally. "I ... I thought I'd done everything right. This was my first time leading a field trip, and I was so careful ... so very careful. When the power went out, I made sure to tell all the kids to sit down on the floor where they were and to stay still. I got my phone out and used the flashlight to provide some light, but it couldn't cover the whole group. I had to keep sweeping it from one section of the kids to another. And I promise you, I counted them each time I swept that light over them. But then, after maybe two minutes of darkness, I shone the light onto the group where Dennis had been sitting … and he was just gone. Gone, like that. I started yelling, calling out his name, but there was … nothing. I couldn't just leave the other kids on their own. I-I thought he might have just gone off to the bathroom or something, so I didn't go searching for him right there and then. And now I think, if only I'd done that. If I'd…"

"You didn't do anything wrong, Mr. Calder," Sally said. "The person—or people—who are involved in these kidnappings are very fast and efficient. Even if you had gone after the boy as soon as you noticed he was missing, you probably wouldn't have been able to stop them. Tell me, did any of the children near Dennis mention anything about a strange smell?"

"Uh, yeah, I think so," Calder said. "His friend, Lionel, who was sitting close to him, said he thought he heard something in the dark and smelled something weird, something like toilet cleaner, he said."

Sally nodded grimly. "Chloroform is likely what that boy was talking about. It's what the kidnappers have been using to knock their victims unconscious."

At that point, Haxton walked over to join the conversation. He gave Sally a nod of acknowledgment but said nothing to her. The tightness of his jaw said enough to her about the fact that he had been wrong about Edgar, and she had been right. Or, at least, that was what she thought.

"We already have one suspect for the other kidnapping in custody," Haxton said. "And now, with what happened here this afternoon, it looks like he might have a partner in crime."

Sally frowned but said nothing; this wasn't the time or the place to argue with Haxton. She wasn't actually very surprised that he still thought Edgar was involved; he had an immense capacity for both stubbornness and an unwillingness to admit that he might be wrong.

"We're going to need copies of all of the footage from every one of your security cameras, Mr. Johnson," she said. "And profiles of all of the employees who were on duty here today. I'm talking everyone, from the janitors to upper management."

Johnson frowned deeply. "You aren't suggesting that one of my employees was behind this, are you?"

"The other suspect was an employee of the museum where the other boy was abducted," Haxton said gruffly. "So it stands to reason that his partner may be an employee of this place, which, when the lights are off, is a very easy place to kidnap a child from, it seems."

"We're not accusing any of your employees of being involved," Sally said, her tone a lot less combative than Haxton's. "We just have to be as thorough as possible, and we have to take all sorts of possibilities into account. And one of those possibilities is that the culprit was a member of your staff."

"Especially since someone switched off the power in order to carry out the kidnapping," Haxton said. "You don't just let any Joe Schmo waltz into your power control center and start shutting things down, Johnson, do you?"

"I, uh, well certainly not, of course not!" Johnson muttered. "But speaking of this whole power situation—"

At that very moment, all the lights went out, plunging the area into the inky darkness and prompting a series of gasps and cries from everyone. As the darkness blackened everything, a wave of panic hit Sally like a speeding truck.

What if the kidnapper were still there … and what if he had just turned off the power so that he could go after Derek?

7

"Sally, where the hell are you running off to?" Haxton yelled as Sally, who had whipped out her phone and flipped on its flashlight function, ran off into the darkness.

"Derek!" she yelled as she ran, ignoring Haxton's shouts behind her. "Derek, where are you?"

Panic gushed in icy surges through her veins, and her heart was pounding with such violence in her chest that she felt as if it might shatter her ribcage. A sudden dryness filled her mouth, and anxiety pounded in her skull.

"Derek, where are you? Derek, answer me!" Sally cried as she ran, the weak glow from her puny cellphone flashlight only managing to create a small patch of illumination a few yards in front of her as she raced into the sea of darkness.

Allison and Derek couldn't have gone far, Sally

thought. They couldn't have gone too far. They had to be around here somewhere, they had to be—

Sally skidded to an abrupt halt as the light from her phone flashed over a sight that almost paralyzed her with terror: Allison's body, lying on the floor. She couldn't see the young woman's face, but the light had fallen over her legs. She was lying face-down on the floor, and she wasn't moving.

"Oh my God," Sally gasped, awash with panic. "Oh my God, oh my God."

"Mommy! I'm here!"

Relief washed over Sally the moment she heard her son's voice. Derek came rushing out of the darkness into the pool of light in front of her, and she hugged him tightly. Tears were burning the corners of her eyes, and traces of cold fear still lingered in her blood.

"What happened?" she asked, now turning her attention to Allison.

A groan came from the young woman, and her legs started to move. Another wave of relief washed over Sally as she realized that Allison was alive.

"I don't know, Mom," Derek said, his eyes wide with fear. "The lights went out, and the lady screamed, and she started running. Then I heard this, like, thump, and then I heard her fall down, and she didn't make any sounds after that. I couldn't see anything. I didn't know what to do, so I just stood by myself in the dark ... it was scary, really scary."

"You're okay now, sweetie, you're okay now," Sally said, hugging him tightly. "Stay close. I need to check that she's okay." Sally now thought she knew what had happened.

Allison had likely panicked and ran when the power went out and had hit her head on something while running, knocking herself out.

She shone her light up, and sure enough, there was a large section of steel tubing sticking out of the wall at head height, right above Allison's body. She knelt next to Allison and shone the light onto the young woman's face. She immediately saw a large lump near the top of her forehead.

Allison's eyes began to flicker open, and she let out a groan. "Wh-where am I?" Allison croaked. "Wh-wh-what happened? My h-head hurts real bad."

"You ran into a pole," Sally said gently. "You ended up knocking yourself unconscious. Don't worry, though. You're going to be okay. We need to get some ice on that lump on your head, and I think you'd better get yourself checked out by a doctor just in case. For now, though, let's just wait here until the power comes back on. I wouldn't want you to injure yourself again trying to move through this darkness."

"I'm sorry you got hurt," Derek said softly. "If I didn't ask to see the sharks, you wouldn't have been here, and you wouldn't have hurt yourself."

"Aw, it's okay, kid," Allison said, trying to force a smile onto her face. "It's not your fault I freaked out and did something stupid."

They waited for a while, and the power came back on after a few minutes. Sally helped Allison up, and then they returned to the others. When they got back, Sally found that Johnson and Haxton had disappeared. She got one of the other aquarium employees to take care of Allison, then went to speak to one of the cops.

"Where are Haxton and Johnson?" she asked.

"They went to the control room to see what happened with the power," the cop answered.

"Look after my son, please," she said to him, "I'm going to head over there myself to check things out."

"They went down the hall that way," the cop said. "I couldn't see much after that, but I heard a door open and shut, maybe around twenty seconds after they left."

Sally left Derek with the cop and Mr. Calder, and then she walked briskly down the hallway. After around twenty seconds of walking, she found herself near a door marked "staff only," so she figured this was the door Haxton and Johnson had gone through.

She tried the door and found that it was unlocked, so she went through it and found herself in a hallway. There were a number of doors in the hallway, and each of them was clearly labeled. She walked down the hallway, checking the doors.

"Hmm, 'pump control for tank one' here," she read as she passed the first door. The next was pump control for tank three, then tanks two and four, then she came to a door that said 'main lights.' She tried the door and found that it was unlocked, and when she opened it, she saw Haxton and Johnson standing in a large room full of switches, fuses, and flashing lights.

"Took you long enough," Haxton muttered.

Johnson was at least a little more polite. "Is your son okay, Detective Lawson?" he asked.

"He's fine," Sally said coolly, firing an icy glare at Haxton while she spoke to Johnson. "What happened here? What caused the power outage?"

Johnson frowned and shook his head. "I've been examining the circuit board, the fuses, and the switches for the past few minutes, and I can't find evidence that anything failed. It's just like it was this afternoon. There doesn't seem to be any explanation for why the power went out."

"And before you ask," Haxton added, "I checked the manual switches the moment we got in here, which, by the way, was when the power was still out. The manual switches were all in the 'on' position. Nobody manually shut this thing down, at least not from in here."

Sally found that to be strange. If nothing had malfunctioned, and nobody had manually flipped a switch, how could the power have gone out?

"I've called in an electrician to check things out," Johnson said to her as she was thinking about this question. "I suppose I should have called one in this afternoon, too, but after what happened, I assumed that someone manually flipped a switch in here. Now that it's happened again, though, and I'm able to see that nobody was flipping any switches, I'm honestly stumped. I have no idea what could have happened. I guess I should have called in the electrician this afternoon when it first happened."

An idea popped into Sally's head; she was starting to connect some dots here. Thinking about how William Edgar's neighbor had claimed she had seen someone breaking into his apartment just days ago, and then with the cops finding child porn conveniently located in a barely disguised folder on Edgar's computer, Sally realized that whoever was involved in these kidnappings was likely very talented when it came to computers and hacking. They had set Edgar up by planting child porn on his computer, she suspected, and, she now guessed, they may have also triggered the power outages in both the museum and the aquarium by hacking the power grids of these facilities.

"Do you have a computer network that automates any of the lights and pumps and stuff in the aquarium?" she asked Johnson.

"Yes, we do," he answered. "Actually, almost everything here is automated, and everything is under the control of a single computer system. It can all be manually overridden if necessary, though. Are you saying that you think someone might have triggered the power cuts by hacking the system?"

"That's exactly what I'm saying," Sally said. "I think in addition to having an electrician check out this room, you should get your IT guys to check the computer system to see if there's been any unauthorized access."

"I didn't even consider that," Johnson said. "But yes, yes, it makes perfect sense. In fact, one of my IT people has been warning me for some time that the system is quite outdated and vulnerable. I just, I just put off upgrading it because ... well, why would anyone want to hack it?"

"I guess this is the wake-up call you needed," Sally said.

"Please get your IT guys to check the system ASAP, and please let me know what they find. Also, please send us copies of all of today's security footage, no matter how irrelevant you might think any particular item of footage may be."

"Of course, of course, I'll make sure I do that," Johnson said.

"I think that's all I need for now. Thank you for your cooperation, Mr. Johnson," Sally said.

"I need to stay here longer to do a bit more sniffing around," Haxton said gruffly. "I'll see you tomorrow, Sally."

Sally went back to the others, picked up Derek, and left. She was glad she had made this breakthrough in realizing that the kidnappers were controlling the power remotely, but she was also more worried now about the people they were up against.

The kidnappers were clearly smarter than they had first guessed them to be—and they had already guessed that they were very smart and efficient criminals. What was more, if the kidnappers had shut down the power in the aquarium this evening, it was an even more sinister sign. If that were indeed the case, it showed that the kidnappers were watching them right now, watching them and toying with them, like cats with helpless mice.

8

Sally got a call from Keith Johnson later that night, just after Derek had gone to bed.

"You were right, Detective Lawson," Johnson said grimly. "Someone hacked our system. My IT guys spent the last few hours checking over things, and they found three instances of security breaches. The first was a few days ago, late at night. Someone got into the system and turned a few lights on and off—that was clearly a test run. They used external lights, lights that could easily be seen from the street. I'm guessing they had someone on the ground here, watching the place, to confirm whether the hack had been successful."

"Yeah, they likely did," Sally said. "When were the other two breaches?"

"This afternoon, when the boy was abducted, and this evening, when you were here."

That sent a cold chill racing down Sally's spine. There was no other reason for the kidnappers to have shut down the power this evening other than to show the cops that they were watching them and toying with them. It was a clear and unequivocal demonstration of power.

As ominous as that was, though, it also gave Sally hope. Now, in addition to knowing the kidnappers were smart and were good with computers and networks, she also knew they possessed another quality: arrogance. Like serial killers who taunted the cops who hunted them by sending clues and letters about their crimes, these kidnappers seemed to be enjoying taunting her and the other cops who were hunting them.

And if there was one thing Sally had learned about arrogant criminals, it was that sooner or later, they slipped up. When these guys did—and she was quite sure they eventually would—she would be there, waiting to pounce.

"Thank you for letting me know about all this," she said.

"No problem. I've also given your friend, Detective Haxton, some USB drives with all the footage from today from every security camera. I hope it assists you in catching the sick people behind these awful crimes."

"I hope so, too, Mr. Johnson," she said. "I hope so, too."

As worried about Sally was about the two children who were now missing, she knew there was little else she could do now, late at night. She set her alarm for an early start and got some much-needed rest.

After dropping Derek off at school the next morning, she went straight to Haxton's office. She figured at that point, he may have cooled off a little about being wrong about William Edgar. When she got to his office, she rapped tentatively on the door.

"What?" Haxton growled from within.

"It's Sally. We need to talk about the kidnapping case," she said.

"Fine."

His flat, monotone replies indicated that perhaps he wasn't quite as over the whole William Edgar thing as she had hoped he would be. She stepped in and was greeted by a glare that could have melted steel. She deflected it with a smile, though, refusing to allow Haxton's bad attitude to sour her own.

"Have you got the aquarium security footage from Johnson?" she asked.

"Yeah."

Sally sighed, resisting the urge to roll her eyes. "Listen, Gareth," she said calmly, "I get that you're a little upset about this case, but can we please just get past that and get on with our jobs?"

He locked an angry stare into her eyes. "You just wanna rub it in, don't you?"

"What are you talking about? I don't want to rub in anything," she protested.

"That bullshit with Edgar," he growled. "It was you who fingered him as the main suspect in the first place! And—"

"And I was wrong," she said. "It was my mistake. Would you like me to admit that in front of everyone here? I'll happily do it if that will allow you to get over yourself. I'll say it was all me, and you had absolutely nothing to do with it, zip, nada. How about that, huh?"

Haxton's jaw was clenched tight, as were his fists, and anger continued to simmer in his eyes. However, he said nothing and eventually looked away. Finally, he spoke.

"We're still charging that prick with possession of child pornography," he muttered.

"As we should," Sally said, "but I suspect that you'll find that an audit of his hard drive will reveal that it was planted there without his knowledge."

"What? How do you know that?" Haxton asked, now more intrigued than angry.

Sally told him about the call she had received from Johnson the previous night, about how his IT guys had discovered that the aquarium's control system had been hacked a few times, and she also mentioned how Edgar's neighbor had claimed to have seen someone breaking into his apartment a few days before the kidnapping.

"Son of a bitch," Haxton muttered. "Maybe … maybe you're right about that slimeball Edgar. Maybe he is completely innocent. We've gotta be able to do something about him possessing those disgusting porno comic books, though. We know he's guilty of that."

"Maybe, but that's about all we can get him on," Sally said, "and I suspect that the punishment for that is nothing more than a fine and maybe some community service. He's not going to see the inside of a prison cell, I can tell you that much. But anyway, forget about Edgar for now. We know he's not the kidnapper. We have to focus all our energy on finding the actual kidnappers and rescuing those kids."

"I know, I know," Haxton said with uncharacteristic humility. "You're right, Sally. Sorry I've been such a prick about all this."

She smiled. "Don't worry about it, Gareth. I know how frustrating cases like this can be. Believe me, I'm frustrated, too. Especially since it's pretty clear that these perps think they can toy with us. That's what they were doing when they hacked the aquarium control center last night when we were there: toying with us."

"Yeah, yeah, I get that now. And that brings me to another point. This whole thing, it must have been planned pretty far in advance. These guys aren't opportunists, not at all. They could have been planning this for weeks … and, what's more, they may have other operations planned."

"We know their modus operandi now, at least," Sally said. "And in light of that, I think we'd better get our people on the phone to every elementary school in the county, maybe even the whole state. We have to get them to cancel or at least postpone every field trip they've got planned, no matter how safe it might seem to be, at least until we've caught these guys. We can't afford for another child to be taken … and I have a bad feeling that these creeps are planning to do exactly that."

"I agree with you there," Haxton said. "No more field trips for anyone until these scumbags are behind bars. And although the kids they've taken so far are both of similar ages, we can't be sure that they won't try to kidnap children from a different age group, too. We'd better call kindergartens, too, maybe high schools as well."

"Yeah, yeah, you're right, we can't be too careful," Sally said. "We have to do what we can to shut down any possible opportunities these guys might have to kidnap more children."

Haxton picked up the phone on his desk. "Let me send those instructions out quick. I'll make sure that all field trips are shut down before the end of the day." He issued instructions to his juniors, and then he and Sally began to analyze the aquarium footage Johnson had given them.

"Man, there are hours upon hours of this stuff we have to get through, and at least sixteen different cameras," Haxton muttered. "We'd better go to a bigger office, get some more monitors, and rope in more people to help us comb through all this crap. Otherwise, we're gonna be here a week, even if we try to watch it all at quadruple speed."

They managed to get hold of a couple extra monitors and some young police recruits in training, to help them sift through it all. They set up the monitors in an empty interrogation room and began to comb painstakingly through the footage.

"Remember, people," Sally said to the recruits, "we're not dealing with your average dumb criminals here. These guys are smart and meticulous; you're going to have to analyze the footage carefully, or you might miss a vital clue. They're not going to let themselves be caught on camera, so we have to hope that one of them somehow made a small slipup somewhere that did get caught.

Please, pay close attention to the images. If you feel your attention start wandering, just get up and take a break instead of trying to power through it. We really can't afford to let anything slip by us."

Sally and the other cops sat down and began the meticulous task of trying to sift through the many hours of footage. The camera footage Sally was analyzing was from the main entrance to the museum. She watched as the children and Mr. Calder entered, waited for a minute or two, and were then met by an aquarium employee who led them away to another part of the aquarium.

Because it was a weekday, the aquarium hadn't been too busy. Sally watched the next hour of footage at double speed—she didn't want to blitz through it too quickly because of the risk of missing something.

A few people came into the entrance hall—mostly older people, retired folks, a few middle-aged couples, and some college students from the local campus. After around the sixty-minute mark of the footage, something caught Sally's attention. There was something odd about one man in particular. Sally zoomed in on him and then replayed the footage he was in a few times over.

"You found something there, Sally?" Haxton asked.

"I don't know," she replied uncertainly. "I think I have … but I'm not yet sure what it is."

"Who are you looking at?"

"Some older guy, probably retired, late sixties or early seventies. There's something about him, I can't quite put my finger on it…."

Haxton paused his footage, got up from his desk, and

walked over to Sally's desk. "Here, let me take a look at this guy," he said. "Maybe I'll recognize him. Is that as close as you can zoom in?"

"Yeah, that's as close as I can get it, and the resolution isn't great when you're zoomed in like this, as you can see."

They both observed the man on screen closely for a few minutes, with Sally replaying the scene over and over. However, neither of them could pick up anything particularly interesting or unique about the man. He just seemed to be another visitor to the aquarium, like all the rest of them.

Sally wondered if maybe something about his clothes was setting off something in her head. She examined them more closely. He wore a brown jacket, black pants, white tennis shoes, and a red beanie.

Then it hit her ... it was the striking red beanie she had seen before. And now, she began to realize why it seemed so familiar.

"Shit," she muttered, stopping the footage so that she could rewind back to the zero-hour mark at which she had started.

"What are you doing?" Haxton asked.

"The kid got abducted around an hour and twenty minutes into the field trip, right?" she asked.

"Yeah, that's the approximate time of the abduction," Haxton said.

"And the lights went out a couple minutes before that?"

68

"Yep. They said around five minutes before the abduction," Haxton answered.

"Dammit … this makes sense then; this makes total sense," Sally said grimly.

"What does? What the hell are you talking about, Sally?" Haxton asked.

She paused when she got to the beginning of the footage and played it for Haxton. "Watch the screen, bottom right," she said. "Then you'll understand."

Still frowning deeply, Haxton shook his head, muttered a curse under his breath, and leaned in more closely, focusing on the footage. From the bottom right of the screen, he saw an elderly man enter the entrance hall —an elderly man wearing a brown jacket, black pants, white tennis shoes, and a red beanie.

"Damn, it's the same guy!" Haxton said. "You think this is our guy?"

Sally shook her head. "Keep watching, Gareth."

Haxton continued to watch the footage, and he saw that the man in the red beanie was taking the exact same steps he had when they had first seen him. And then, just as in the later footage, a woman in a blue dress walked in behind him.

"Ah, shit," Haxton muttered when he realized what he was seeing. "It's the same footage! It's the same damn footage!"

"Looks like they hacked the security camera system, too," Sally said. "They stopped all the camera recordings for an hour and instead played back a loop of the previous hour's footage to the monitors, where the hard drives were recording."

"So essentially they completely blinded the security cameras for an hour ... and nobody knew a damn thing?" Haxton asked.

"It looks like that's exactly what they did," Sally said grimly. "If that's the case with all of the cameras, then all of this footage is as good as useless."

Haxton turned to the recruits. "All of you, stop what you're doing!" he yelled. "Pay attention now and listen to what I'm saying! I need you to compare the first five minutes of your footage with the sixty-to-sixty-five-minute sections! Check to see if they've been looped starting at the sixty-minute-mark!"

The recruits did as Haxton said, and one by one, each of them reported that the footage had indeed been looped at the sixty-minute mark.

"Those bastards have done it again," Haxton muttered when the final recruit confirmed that his footage, along with everyone else's footage, had been looped. "They've led us on a fucking wild-goose chase, and now they're laughing. These pricks, these fucking sons of bitches! They're always one step ahead of us, no matter what we do!"

Sally, however, had already started looking into an alternative solution to this conundrum ... and now, after some frantic searching on her phone's internet browser, she believed that she might have a solution.

"Not yet, Haxton, they haven't pulled the wool

completely over our eyes yet," Sally said, getting up from her chair and striding purposefully toward the exit.

"Where are you going?" Haxton demanded.

"To catch these people!" she replied. "As thorough as they were, I think there's something that I'm sure they've overlooked … and we need to go to the aquarium right now to find it. Come on, let's go!"

9

"*A*re you sure this is gonna work?" Haxton asked as they pulled into the aquarium parking lot in his police cruiser. "You really think the guys missed it?"

"I bet they did," Sally said. "Especially because it's not on the aquarium network. It's operated on a more old-school system. I know because Derek and I have used it before. It's purely coin-operated, no network connections, nothing. I'm sure of that. I know it's a long shot, but there just might be something we can use on this thing. It's worth taking a look at."

The object in question was a small photo machine outside the aquarium. There was a large statue of leaping dolphins near the aquarium entrance, and the coin-operated machine took photos of visitors standing under the leaping dolphins.

Since Sally had used the device to take pictures of her and Derek on a visit to the aquarium, she also happened to know that part of the main entrance was also captured in the machine's images. She hoped that enough people had taken photos on the day of the kidnapping that it might provide them with some clues about who the kidnappers may be.

They had called Mr. Johnson on their way to the aquarium, and Sally had explained her theory to him. The aquarium manager had been skeptical about her idea but had nonetheless agreed to help her. He was waiting for them by the statue of the leaping dolphins.

"I wouldn't get your hopes up about this, Detectives," he said to them as he walked over to the photo machine, carrying a large bundle of keys.

"We may just strike it lucky," Sally said. "This statue is a bit of a landmark, and taking a picture under the dolphins is something just about every visitor does when they visit this aquarium."

"*Used to* do," Johnson said sourly. "Many years ago, this thing was a money-spinner. Now, though, in the age of cellphone cameras, nobody wants to pay to have a machine take their photo. We used to get hundreds of photos a day taken here. Now we're lucky to get five or six if that."

"I still think it's worth a shot," Sally said. "A lot of people get photos from this machine just for the nostalgic value. And there are many older people who visit here during weekdays, retired folk whose eyes aren't good enough to get a sharply focused photo on a cellphone camera. And some of those people may have taken a photo or two yesterday during the kidnapping."

"Like I said, we can go ahead and take a look," Johnson

said, "but don't get your hopes up."

He unlocked the back of the machine and took out the memory card. "Luckily for you, while this thing isn't exactly the most modern technology, we did upgrade it to digital photography ten or twelve years ago. It still prints the photos like a polaroid, of course, but it also keeps a digital record of the shots taken."

Sally had brought her notebook computer with her, and she inserted the memory card into one of the slots and began to look for the previous day's photos, scrolling through the folders with bated breath.

"Here we go," she said as she opened the relevant folder. "Yesterday's photos."

"Each one is timestamped," Johnson said. Despite his skepticism about finding anything, he leaned in closer to the screen, and Sally could sense his hopeful anticipation.

She arranged the photos in order of time taken and quickly discovered that six photos had been taken during the period in which Dennis Avery was kidnapped. The background in which part of the main entrance to the aquarium could be seen constituted only a small section of every picture, but what was visible was clear enough to be able to make out any suspects, if any appeared at all.

In the first photo, there was nobody in the background. In the second, again, there was nobody. Sally felt her worry rising. If nothing showed up in these pictures, they were back to square one.

"Come on," she murmured softly, her eyes locked on the screen as she clicked "next." "Come on, please, show me something, anything."

There was nothing in the third picture and nothing in the fourth.

"See, I told you it was a long shot," Johnson muttered, shaking his head and sighing deeply with disappointment. "Nothing, nothing at—"

"There we go," Sally declared, her voice filled with fresh hope. "We've got one person there in the background."

Johnson pushed his glasses up his nose as Sally zoomed in. "Bah, that's just a delivery guy from the courier company," he said. "They're here almost every day, delivering this or that."

Sally was crushed to see that he was right. The man was wearing a courier company uniform and carrying a small package. Still, there was one photo left. However, this one had been taken right at the end of the kidnapping period, so she was doubtful it would reveal anything. Maybe Johnson was right, and this had all been a waste of valuable time.

Sally clicked on the final photo, and a thrill coursed through her when she saw a man in the background of the final pic. And, what was more, he was carrying a duffel bag stuffed with something large. A duffel bag that could have been holding an unconscious eight-year-old boy.

"Are you seeing what I'm seeing?" Haxton asked, leaning in closer. "That guy in the background is carrying something big."

"I'm seeing it all right," Sally said.

"Zoom in, zoom in," Johnson said eagerly. His tone had completely changed; now, he was just as eager and excited as the two cops.

While the camera was an old one, and the resolution nowhere near as crystal clear as those on modern digital cameras, it was nonetheless clear enough to make out the suspect's features when zoomed in. The man carrying the duffel bag was a lanky, pale fellow, a young man who looked like he was in his early twenties. He had a mop of curly, light-brown hair, a scraggly, patchy beard, and was wearing a red sweater and stonewashed jeans.

"You recognize this guy, Johnson?" Haxton asked. "Does he work here or anything?"

Johnson shook his head. "I've never seen him in my life. He's not an employee. I can tell you that for certain. And he's not dressed like any kind of repairman or any other contractor who may have been doing some work here—not that I have any record of any contractors doing any work here yesterday anyway. No, I think he's a visitor."

"If he arrived before the kidnappers hacked the camera and started playing that hour of looped footage," Haxton said, "we may be able to get a clearer shot of his face from some of the security footage."

Sally captured a screenshot of the zoomed-in image on her computer, and then she got out her phone and took a photo of it, too. "I'll send this to the recruits back at the station. They can go back to the footage and comb through it to see if they can find this guy."

"What if they can't, though?" Haxton asked. "If this guy we're looking at actually is one of those scumbags, we know they're smart. He would have waited until the security cameras started recording the playback loop before entering the aquarium."

"That's true," Sally said, "but we need the recruits to go through that footage with a fine-toothed comb anyway. They may not find this guy, but they might find something else we can use."

"But how do you intend to discover the identity of this particular individual?" Johnson asked.

"If the recruits don't find him on the pre-looped footage," Sally said, "and they probably won't, that doesn't necessarily mean we're out of options. For one thing, because this guy isn't an employee, he sure as hell didn't waltz into the aquarium free. He had to pay an entrance fee, either by booking online or by paying upfront at the ticket office. Either way, you'll surely have a record of him making payment. You guys don't take cash, right?"

Johnson shook his head. "No cash, that's correct. He had to either book online or pay with a credit card, so you're right; we'll have his details. The only thing is, they'll be mixed in with the hundreds of other payments for tickets yesterday."

"If you narrow the payment record window down to just two hours, I think you'll find there'll be a lot fewer details to go through."

"Hmm, yes, yes, you're right," Johnson said. "All right then, we'd best go to my office and start sorting through payment details. At the very least, you people will have a list of names to work with."

"And that's something right there, isn't it, Gareth?" Sally said.

Haxton nodded. "Even if all we have are lists of names, we can cross-reference every single name on that list against criminal records, and if that doesn't give us anything, then we can get the FBI involved and use their database, maybe dig into civilian records we wouldn't usually have access to. Either way, even a list of names will be a huge leap forward for us and should lead to us identifying the perp."

"All right, great, let's do this then," Johnson said.

They headed to his office and began to look through the payment records. Soon enough, they had a list of names to go through. Sally and Haxton took that list back to the police station, where the recruits were still combing through the footage. They began to run all the names through the criminal records system.

One of the names quickly turned up a result, and when Sally and Haxton looked at the criminal record of the man whose name turned up, Haxton curled his hands into fists of triumph.

"We've got the son of a bitch, we've got him," he growled. "It has to be him; it has to!"

Although Sally's sixth sense hadn't yet kicked in, she too was feeling quite certain about this suspect. After all, he had a criminal record for multiple counts of exposing himself to minors and had been banned from being within five hundred feet of any school or playground.

"Julian Drake, you sick fuck," Haxton growled, staring at the mugshot of the young man's wan, angular face, covered in acne. "We've found you ... and now we're coming for you."

10

The deeper they dug into Drake's records, the more convinced Haxton became that he was the kidnapper—or, at least, one of the kidnappers. Everything seemed to point to it. Drake, who was twenty-four, had first been convicted of obsessively stalking a thirteen-year-old girl when he was eighteen. He later had been convicted of exposing himself in a public park to two minors—one an eleven-year-old girl, the other a fourteen-year-old girl, on two separate counts.

He also had a long string of misdemeanor charges and other offenses he had been fined for or had done community service for. He had spent a few months in prison after being convicted of exposing himself to minors, and he had been released around six months earlier.

There was no record of his current address, though. He had been released into a halfway house, and from there, he had gone on to a relative, an aunt who had died of a drug overdose three months prior. There was no record of what had happened to Julian Drake after his aunt's overdose or where he had gone. He was unemployed, and he appeared to have very little to his name.

"He's gotta be our guy, this sick creep," Haxton muttered as he scrolled through Drake's records. "Just look at this rap sheet! If this doesn't scream 'child kidnapper,' I don't know what does."

Sally, however, was nowhere near as confident as Haxton about Drake's guilt. Although he certainly seemed to fit the bill initially, the deeper she dug, the more obvious it seemed to her that he wasn't their guy. He was a pervert, to be sure, and he seemed to be a pedophile, too, but there was one glaring detail that didn't match up.

"He's not smart, though, Gareth," Sally said to Haxton. "Take a closer look at the witness statements and reports from the officers who arrested him. These are not the actions of an intelligent man. In fact, this officer's report describes him as being 'mentally deficient,' and this one said he seems to have some sort of mental illness. And there was no subtlety about the manner in which he committed his crimes, either. His actions seem to be those of an unhinged lunatic, to be honest, a very sick and disturbed person … which is not the type of person with the sophisticated intelligence necessary to pull off the kidnappings we're investigating, not to mention the complexity of the hacking they've done."

Gareth turned to glare at her. "Really, Sally? Are we going to be getting into this again, like we did with the whole William Edgar thing?"

Sally didn't want to start an argument, but she also felt

compelled to remind Haxton that she had been right about William Edgar, even though all the signs at the time had appeared to point to him being the kidnapper.

She resisted the urge to throw this in Haxton's face, though, and instead did her best to remain calm and collected. "Gareth, I know you're eager to catch this guy and rescue those kids and trust me, I am, too, but we have to look at all the evidence as a whole. Yes, this guy is a creep who's already been convicted of preying on children, and yes, we've got footage of him walking out of the aquarium at the exact time of the kidnapping with a duffel bag that could have an unconscious child in it, but—"

"Listen to what you're saying!" Haxton said. "Right there, what you've just said, that's enough evidence right there for half the judges in this state to decide he's guilty and lock him up! Come on, Sally, stop being ridiculous. Maybe he was on drugs before, maybe that muddled his mind and made it seem like he was mentally deranged or whatever, and maybe he got clean in prison, and he's actually a very smart guy when he's not high. Did you ever think of that?"

"I'm just saying—"

"Sally, I get it, okay? I was wrong about Edgar. I admit it. But this creep, this convicted pervert who's been involved in sick sex crimes against kids, shows up at the aquarium at the very same time that a boy is abducted, and he walks out of the place literally a few minutes after the boy is taken, carrying a duffel bag that looks like it's got an unconscious child in it. What kind of lottery-winning odds are those? How the hell can this be a coincidence? I'll tell you how, Sally—it can't be. There's no way in hell that Julian Drake showed up at the aquarium at the exact time Dennis Avery was kidnapped in a coincidence. Say what you want about him being mentally deficient or a moron or whatever; he's involved. He's one hundred percent involved, and we're going to find him and arrest him and interrogate him until he admits the truth. That's the end of the story."

Sally knew Haxton well enough to understand that there would be no more arguing or debating; as far as he was concerned, the matter was closed. And although her instincts were telling her that Drake might not be the one they were looking for, all the evidence seemed to point to him being one of the kidnappers, and she couldn't ignore that. At the very least, she had to admit that it was likely that he was involved somehow. There was no way his presence at the aquarium at the exact time that Dennis Avery was kidnapped could have been a coincidence.

"All right," she said to Haxton. "I agree, we need to find Drake and bring him in, but we're going to have to hit the streets to do that. He's off the radar, and who knows where he might be holed up."

"Or if he's even still in town," Haxton said grimly. "For all we know, he might have taken the kids and crossed state lines."

"I don't know about that," Sally said. "I have a feeling that he might still be around here somewhere. Something tells me that this spate of kidnappings isn't over yet, not by a long shot."

"I'll look for any living relatives," Haxton said. "You go through his files and get a list of known acquaintances. Also, go online, see what a deep search of his name turns up."

"I'll do that," Sally said.

She and Haxton split up to go and do their research separately. When they reconvened an hour or two later, both had made a few discoveries about Drake.

"All right, so, there are no known living relatives of his in-state records," Haxton said. "He was given up for adoption at birth, raised in a series of foster homes and state institutions. The 'aunt' he lived with for a short while when he got out of prison wasn't actually an aunt. He just told everyone she was. She was an unrelated acquaintance, an older lady he'd befriended during one of his stints in a state psychiatric institution—she and Drake were in the same ward a couple years ago. It appears they had an agreement of sorts; she had court orders preventing her from buying certain medications because of her previous addictions to them, which had caused untold chaos in her life and the lives of others. Drake got hold of these meds for her in exchange for a place to crash. Needless to say, this wasn't too smart a plan. She'd been banned from buying those meds for a very good reason, and it didn't take long for her abuse of them to kill her. At that point, her apartment got repossessed, and Drake got kicked out onto the street. That's the last time we have any official records of his whereabouts."

"The internet didn't turn up much about Drake at all, aside from everything we already know about him," Sally said. "But searching our files on him did turn up a few known acquaintances, aside from the so-called 'aunt,' of course. He and this other guy, Charlie French, two years older than Drake, were busted together a few times, committing crimes together. Petty stuff, minor misdemeanors like shoplifting and graffiti, but it's enough to convince me that they were buddies."

Haxton smiled grimly and nodded. "Hmm, yeah, that seems like a close enough association to warrant getting hold of this Charlie French character. If anyone may know where Drake is hiding out, it'd be him. Let's see what a quick search of our system for information about French reveals."

Haxton did some searching, and it didn't take long for the system to turn out information about Charlie French.

"Looks like he's done more than just shoplift from some candy stores and spray paint a few letters on a wall," Sally remarked.

"Yeah … those were definitely gateway crimes into more serious stuff. Assault, arson, and an armed robbery conviction that got him a five-year sentence in the slammer. Looks like he was released after three years for good behavior—and that was only two or three months ago."

"Which is right about the time Drake got thrown out onto the street after his 'aunt' ODd," Sally said. "That's convenient timing."

"You think Drake may be holed up with French and that French might be involved in the kidnappings, too?" Haxton asked.

Sally perused French's records and nodded slowly. "If

French is involved, he's likely the brains of the operation. He seems to be pretty smart and very devious. From the description of the armed robbery case, it looks like he almost got away with it, and it was only through a very thorough investigation and shrewd detective work that he was convicted. That might explain a few things."

"Check this out," Haxton said. "French was also being investigated for a number of cybercrimes, but they never managed to convict him for any of them."

Now Sally's instincts were starting to buzz. Even though she had initially thought Drake wasn't the guy they were after, these revelations about his friend and possible partner in crime, Charlie French, were beginning to convince her otherwise.

"Do we have a last known address for French?" she asked.

Haxton did a quick search and then grinned triumphantly. "We sure as hell do. Let's go get the son of a bitch."

11

*G*iven the fact that Charlie French had previously been convicted of armed robbery, Sally and Haxton knew it would be wise to treat him as a potentially dangerous felon, so they went to his address armed, and they had backup nearby in case anything went down.

The address French was believed to be at was at a rundown apartment building downtown. The building was shabby but not nearly as bad as some of the crumbling, derelict buildings on a nearby block. His apartment was on the eighth floor. Haxton got some officers to cover the entrance and emergency exit to the building in case French tried to make a run for it, and then he and Sally went up to the eighth floor via the elevator, which creaked and groaned quite alarmingly the whole way up.

"I think I'm gonna take the stairs when we go back down," Sally said as she stepped out of the elevator. "That thing is a deathtrap ... it looks and sounds like it was last serviced in the '80s."

"Yeah, I think I might join on the stairs," Haxton said, looking uneasy. He'd always been afraid of heights, and the terrible creaking, groaning, and juddering of the elevator had shaken him up.

He and Sally loosened their pistols in their holsters as they approached French's apartment at the end of the hall. When they got to the door, they paused and listened for a while. It sounded as if someone was home; they could hear the sound of a loud TV blaring through the door.

"You ready for this?" Haxton asked as they stood on either side of French's door.

Sally gave a confident nod, so Haxton rapped on the door. "Charlie French, are you in?" he bellowed.

There was no response, so Haxton hammered on the door again, more forcefully this time. "French, if you're in there, you'd better open this door! This is the police, and if you don't cooperate, I'm gonna have a few choice words with your parole officer! We can hear that you're in there, so get your ass off your damn sofa and open up!"

"All right, all right, hold your fucking horses," said a grumpy voice, almost drowned out by the noise of the TV.

Haxton and Sally both slid their hands onto the grips of their pistols. French hadn't tried anything yet, but there was no guarantee that he wouldn't—especially if he was indeed involved in the kidnappings.

They heard several locks and deadbolts being opened

from within. The door opened a crack, just enough for French to peer out at the cops. He kept the door latched, with the chain in place so they couldn't force open the door.

He was in a grubby white T-shirt, even dirtier jeans, and looked and smelled as if he hadn't washed for a few days. A pungent odor wafted out of his apartment, and Sally wrinkled her nose in disgust. She couldn't tell if it was French or his apartment that reeked so badly—and she decided it was likely a foul combination of both.

His wavy chestnut hair was lank and greasy and hung limply around his shoulders, and his pale, chubby cheeks and flabby jaw were covered in a week's worth of thick stubble.

"What the fuck do you want?" he demanded. "I didn't do anything. You got a warrant? If you don't show me a warrant, I'm gonna slam this door in your fucking faces."

"You want me to call your parole officer and tell him about this?" Haxton growled. "We don't need a warrant to ask you a few questions. That's all we're here to do, French. We just wanna ask a few questions. Now, you can cooperate and do this the easy way, or you can keep acting like an asshole and make things a whole lot more difficult for yourself. Your choice, pal, your choice."

French was doing his best to block the cops' view of his apartment, but Sally thought she managed to catch a glimpse of a large computer rig with a number of monitors set up in the far corner of the room. French noticed her peering in that direction and scowled at her.

"All right, fine, go ahead, what do you wanna ask me?" he asked. "I haven't done anything wrong. Straight as a fuckin' arrow since I got out of the slammer. You ain't got shit on me, coz there *ain't* shit on me."

"It's not *you* we're interested in," Haxton said, even though they definitely were interested in French and considered him a suspect at this point. "We're looking for a friend of yours."

"Who?"

"Drake. Julian Drake. When did you last see him?"

"That idiot? I don't know. Maybe a couple weeks ago," French said with a shrug.

While French was speaking, Sally scrutinized him closely to see if she could tell if he was lying. She was usually very good at picking up when a suspect was being dishonest, but French's expressionless face, dead eyes, and deadpan delivery made it difficult to tell if he was spouting falsehoods.

"Oh, really?" Haxton said sourly. "Well, that's recent enough for me. Tell me, French, where can we find your buddy?"

"Why, what's he done this time?"

"That's none of your business," Haxton said gruffly. "We're the ones asking the questions here, and things will definitely go better for you if you just answer them and don't give us any attitude. So, I'm gonna ask you again, where can we find Julian Drake?"

"No idea, man," French said with a mocking sneer. "Who knows? Last I heard, he was roaming the streets like a lost ghost."

"And you're not letting this little lost puppy crash on your sofa, are you?" Haxton asked. "I don't think I need to remind you that harboring felons and fugitives from justice will get you sent straight back to the slammer."

French chuckled humorlessly. "Is that a threat, officer?" he asked mockingly.

"Are you trying to piss me off, you no-good punk?" Haxton snarled, his temper rising. "Because it's working. And I promise you, you worthless little bum, you *will not* like me when I'm angry."

"What's the computer rig for, French?" Sally asked, stepping in before the exchange between Haxton and French got too heated.

"That's none of your business," French muttered. "You people said you wanted to ask me questions about Julian, and I've told you that I haven't seen him for a few weeks, I don't know how to find him, and he's definitely not here. As far as I'm concerned, I've told you everything you need to know, and you have no right to ask me any other questions. Now, until you've got a warrant—"

"Oh, we'll get a warrant, all right, you sniveling little piece of shit," Haxton growled. "And we're gonna be watching your every move from now on. These eyes," he continued, pointing to his own eyes, "are gonna be on you like a hawk, you scumbag. I'm no idiot. I know you're hiding something. You'd better enjoy what you can of this little dump of yours because you're gonna be back in the slammer soon enough."

French flashed them a mocking smile, looking completely unintimidated by Haxton's threats. "Goodbye, officers, have a nice day," he said before slamming the door shut in their faces and bolting up all the locks.

Sally raised both eyebrows as she looked at Haxton. "What do you think, Gareth?" she asked.

"He's lying," Haxton said confidently. "He's definitely hiding something."

"I thought so, too."

"You were asking him about some computer stuff," Haxton said. "What did you see?"

"I caught a glimpse of a pretty powerful computer setup in the corner of the room," she answered. "I didn't get a very clear look at it, but I saw enough."

"You think he might be the guy who hacks the systems while Drake is on the ground, doing the dirty work?"

Sally shrugged. "I don't know, but it's definitely a possibility. Anyone who's got an operation like the one I caught a glimpse of is definitely a lot more than a simple casual user of computers. And we already know he was investigated for a number of cybercrimes, even though he wasn't convicted of any of 'em."

"The problem is," Haxton said, as they began making their way back down the hallway, "we don't have any evidence linking him to the kidnappings, aside from a shaky possible connection to Julian Drake, who we still have no location on. There's literally nothing we could get a warrant issued for."

"Hmm," Sally said, thinking. "Maybe not for the kidnapping case, but we *could* possibly get a warrant issued for something else."

"Huh? What do you mean?" Haxton asked.

"Cybercrime. Sure, it'd be, well, bending the law a little since he hasn't been charged with or even suspected of any specific cybercrimes recently, but what if we get those old investigations against him reopened? All we'd need is an anonymous tip from a concerned citizen who believes that French might be involved in something sketchy involving computers. Then we add my testimony that I saw a huge computer rig in his place … I think a warrant could be issued on those grounds. And if we then happen to find evidence linking him to the kidnappings while investigating his alleged cybercrimes… lucky us, right?"

Haxton chuckled darkly. "You know, Sally, this is why I like you. Ninety-nine percent of the time, you play everything by the book. You walk the straight and narrow with not even an inch of deviation. But when you do deviate, ever so slightly, from that road, you do it perfectly."

Sally grinned. "We both know that sometimes the law needs a little bending … just a tiny bit. And with two little boys still missing, I think it's justified."

"It sure as hell is," Haxton said. He was about to press the elevator button when he stopped his hand an inch from the button. "What am I doing? I don't wanna die in this dump. Come on, let's take the stairs."

The two cops headed down the stairs, both feeling confident that they had almost cracked the case. It all seemed to make perfect sense; all the evidence had led them here, and every clue pointed to French and Drake being the culprits, working together.

Why then, Sally found herself thinking, was there a

nagging doubt at the back of her mind that she just couldn't shake, and why was there an awful feeling of dread in the pit of her stomach, a feeling that things were about to get a lot worse rather than any better?

*I*t didn't take long to get a warrant to search French's apartment. Sally quietly asked one of her friends to call in an "anonymous tip" about French being involved in cybercrimes, and this, combined with French being out on parole, and his history of involvement in cybercrime and other crimes, was enough to motivate the issuing of a warrant.

Sally didn't feel too guilty about bending the law in this manner. Sure, she could get in a lot of trouble if it was discovered that she had asked someone to call in a fake tipoff, but her instincts told her that French was up to no good, and that was the only way for them to legally search his apartment. The end, Sally reasoned, justified the means, and if her bending of the law ended up saving the lives of the kidnapped children and putting their abductors in prison, then she didn't feel the smallest drop of guilt about it.

It was late afternoon when she, Haxton, and some

other cops returned to French's apartment building. This time they approached French's door with their guns drawn, bulletproof vests on, and three officers backing them up—two armed with M-16 rifles and one carrying a battering ram and wearing heavy body armor.

Gripping his pistol in his right hand and a search warrant in his left, Haxton pressed his back against the wall to the side of the door. He then hammered on the door with the butt of his pistol.

"French!" he barked. "Open up! We're back … and this time, we've got a warrant, so you'd best open this door in the next ten seconds, or we're gonna smash it down!"

There was no reply from within. Sally noticed she could no longer hear the TV blaring; there seemed to be nothing inside but silence.

Again, Haxton bashed on the door. "This is the last time I'm gonna say it, French! Open the door, now!"

Once more, there was no response.

"Either he's not in, or he's trying to climb out the window down the side of the building," Sally said.

"I think either of those is enough justification to bust open his door," Haxton growled. He turned to the three cops behind him and gave them a curt nod.

The three of them moved in formation, two covering the door while the one with the battering ram positioned himself in front of it. The battering ram was swung, and the impact of the heavy object on the door rattled the walls and brought down puffs of dust from the grubby ceiling. French's multiple locks were strong, but the door itself was weak, and the wood splintered. A few more hefty blows of the battering ram smashed the door open, completely demolishing it, and the armed officers charged in, with Sally and Haxton close behind them.

"Shit," Haxton muttered, lowering his pistol after a rapid initial search of the apartment.

"He's gone, and so is his computer outfit," Sally said. She walked over to the corner of the room where she had caught a glimpse of the rig before. "It was here. It was right here."

Evidence of the rig's presence could be seen by the pattern of stains on the wall and the trash and debris around it, with a perfectly clean patch on the floor where the computer and desk had been. All around that clear patch were hundreds of cigarette butts, an enormous pile of ash from an ashtray that had been hastily swept off the computer desk, and plenty of candy bar wrappers, beer cans, and fast-food waste.

There was evidence of hasty packing—a few socks and undergarments strewn in a messy trail from the closet, which was wide open, to the bed, which was unmade, its greasy, smelly sheets lying in a tangle half on the bed and half on the floor.

The sink was piled full of dishes that hadn't been washed for weeks, as well as fast food containers, many with rotting food in them—this was a major contributor to the stench that occupied the gloomy space of the apartment with the inescapable solidity of a physical presence.

"Looks like he took off in a hurry," Sally remarked as the cops conducted a quick initial search of the place.

"I'm guessing shortly after we paid him a visit earlier,"

Haxton said. "How the hell did he manage to slip past our boys on the street, though? We had two guys watching this building from the moment you and I left it."

Sally shook her head and shrugged. "I guess he knows how to get in and out of here without being noticed. That doesn't matter, though; what does is that he's gone."

"Yeah, I know. Anyway, let's see if we can find anything in this filthy dump. If he ran in a hurry, chances are he overlooked something and left something important behind. Hopefully, we can find it."

"Yeah, let's get going."

"We should have brought along some freakin' biohazard suits," Haxton muttered, wrinkling his nose. "This is one of the filthiest, most disgusting places we've searched in a while."

"Agreed," Sally said, gagging as she lifted up a t-shirt from the floor and discovered a plate of rotting food, covered in multicolored, odorous mold, beneath it.

The rancid stench motivated everyone to move quickly. They all wanted nothing more than to get out of this filthy place and suck some fresh air into their lungs, but they did their best to endure the stink and conduct the search with the appropriate amount of thoroughness.

As much as Sally knew she had to pay close attention while searching the place, the smell was getting to her so much that she could barely concentrate. With her conversation with William Edgar's neighbor in mind—the old woman who had claimed she had seen someone dressed as a repairman breaking into Edgar's apartment—an idea popped into Sally's head.

"I'm gonna go knock on all the doors on this floor," she said to Haxton. "See if French's neighbors saw or heard anything."

"I know why you're doing that," he said, coughing and almost retching as a particularly bad stink wafted into his nostrils. "You wanna get out of this dump and get some fresh air in your lungs, right?"

Sally grinned. "You saw right through me, Gareth."

Haxton chuckled. "Go on, get outta here. You might discover something by doing that anyway. I'll see you in a few minutes if this foul air in here hasn't killed us all by then."

Feeling a wave of relief wash over her as soon as she stepped out of the apartment, Sally closed her eyes and breathed in some fresh air. "Fresh" was, of course, a relative term. The whole building had a musty, slightly sour smell, but it was still far more pleasant than the stink of French's apartment.

She knocked on the door closest to French's—the one directly across the hall from his. To her surprise, someone immediately opened the door a crack, and she found herself looking at a middle-aged woman, who was peering suspiciously out at her. The woman had clearly been standing behind the door the whole time, likely watching the search operation through her peephole.

"You're one of the cops, huh?" the woman said. "What did he do, the guy across the hall? Did he kill someone? Is there a dead body in there?"

Her eyes had a slightly crazed look to them, and her disheveled appearance made Sally think she was some sort of recluse and possibly suffering from some type of mental illness. Nonetheless, she figured that perhaps the woman might have seen something.

"He hasn't killed anyone, no," Sally said, speaking slowly and calmly—she didn't want to alarm this already agitated person. "He's just under investigation for some possible computer crimes. Nothing dangerous, nothing you need to worry about."

"Oh," the woman grunted. "Well, why are you knocking on my door then?"

"I just wanted to know if you'd seen him—Charlie French, the guy who lives there—in the past few hours, or noticed anything unusual? "

"He got a new fridge maybe an hour or two ago," she said.

Sally frowned. She certainly hadn't seen a new fridge in the apartment. In fact, the only fridge in there looked like it was around twenty years old. It was discolored, covered in stains, and buzzed relentlessly as if filled with a swarm of angry hornets.

"Are you sure about that?" Sally asked.

"Yeah, one hundred percent sure," the woman said, nodding enthusiastically. "I saw the delivery guy, heard him knocking on the door across the hall. It was a big ol' fridge. They could barely get the box through the door."

"They?"

"The delivery guy and the guy who lives there, my neighbor, what did you say his name was again?"

"Charlie French," Sally said.

"Yeah, him," the woman continued. "He opened the

door for the delivery guy. They both manhandled the box until they got it inside, then they were inside for a while. Then the delivery guy left, but he took the fridge box with him again. Wheeled it away, the same way he brought it in."

Sally frowned. "You're sure about this?"

"Yeah! What, you think I'm lying? I ain't lying. You can ask anyone else on this floor. They'll tell you they saw a delivery guy with a huge fridge box here an hour or two ago. Go on, ask 'em. You'll see."

Suddenly, it hit Sally. The woman, as crazed as she looked, was telling the truth. And it made perfect sense, all of it.

"Thank you so much for your help," Sally said to the woman, smiling warmly. "You've been a great help."

She braced herself for the stench, then hurried back into the apartment. "Gareth!" she said. "I know how French got out of here without anyone seeing him!"

"Before you tell me," Haxton said grimly, emerging from French's bedroom, "you'd better take a look at this."

In his gloved hand, he was holding a small action figure, a mutant from a popular cartoon show. He walked over to Sally and pointed at a spot on the toy's leg. Written on it in permanent marker was a name that sent chills down Sally's spine.

"Oh my God," she gasped as she read the name. "Dennis Avery!"

"That's right," Haxton said. "I found this under the bed. At least one of the kidnapped boys was in this apartment."

13

"*I*f this doesn't prove that French is one of the kidnappers, I don't know what will," Haxton said grimly. "I'm sure Avery's parents will confirm this belonged to their son. I'll send them a picture of it now."

"Yeah, yeah, you'd better do that," Sally said, still stunned by the discovery of this key item of evidence.

"Gimme a minute," Haxton said. He photographed the action figure, sent the picture to Avery's parents, and then dropped the toy into an evidence bag. "All right, so, what were you saying about how French managed to escape without being seen by our boys outside?"

"The woman across the hall said she saw a large fridge being delivered here," Sally said. "But as you can see, there's no new fridge in this place."

"No … most of the appliances look like they should have been dumped ten years ago," Haxton said.

"Exactly. It was a rouse," Sally said.

"What was? This phantom fridge delivery?"

"Yes. There was no fridge; the delivery guy was clearly a friend of French's. He brought a big empty fridge box into the apartment and smuggled French and his computer outfit out in it."

"Shit," Haxton muttered. "You're probably right about that. Nobody would have batted an eye at some delivery guy with a fridge. French sure is one cunning, crafty little piece of shit. But with *this*," he continued, holding up the evidence bag with the action figure in it, "we've got the son of a bitch. Now it's just a matter of finding him."

"Considering how wily he is, that's probably going to be easier said than done," Sally said. "The first thing we need to do is to figure out whether it was a genuine delivery company that came here with the fridge box or just one of French's buddies who put on a set of cheap coveralls and used a hired van or something."

"I'd put my money on it being the latter," Haxton said. "Go ask the neighbor if she saw any logos on the delivery guy's clothes. Unfortunately, I didn't see a single security camera in this building—which doesn't surprise me much, but there may be a camera somewhere outside that might have picked up something. I'll take some of the boys down to the street and have a look around. We'll also see if there are any witnesses who might have seen something—you know, people who work around here, who have been in the same spot the last couple hours."

"All right, I'll talk to the neighbor again, and I think I'll knock on a few more doors on this floor to see if anyone else saw anything. I'll meet you downstairs when I'm done."

"Sounds good," Haxton said gruffly.

He went to round up the other police officers while Sally went across the hall to talk to French's crazed-looking neighbor. She spoke briefly to the woman but didn't get any useful information out of her. After that, she knocked on a few more doors, but either nobody was home, or none of the occupants of the apartments wanted to talk to a cop. Either way, she came up with nothing.

She headed down to the street level, taking the stairs to avoid the scarily rickety elevator. When she got to the entrance hall of the building, she checked out the room and saw that there had once been security cameras here, but that they had been ripped out of the walls and ceiling long ago, with nothing left of their former presence but a few dangling wires.

Walking out of the building, she looked up and down the street. She saw Haxton going into a nearby convenience store while two other officers were entering a liquor store on the other side of the road.

"You g-got any change, ma'am? Just a dollar or two, p-please."

This weak, gravelly rasp from a nearby pile of garbage bags immediately grabbed Sally's attention. She looked down and saw, only a few yards from the entrance to the building, an elderly homeless man sitting on a strip of cardboard between the garbage bags. Wrapped up in filthy rags, his emaciated face, which was as darkly tanned as old leather, obscured by a wild beard and a greasy tangle of hair, the old man was well-camouflaged amid the garbage and piles of litter. None of the cops had noticed him initially.

"P-please ma'am," the old man wheezed, pausing to suck on a mostly empty bottle of cheap whiskey. "I'm h-hungry, real h-h-hungry."

"How long have you been sitting here?" Sally asked, walking over to the man. "I've got a dollar for you, sure, but I can be a lot more generous if you can answer a few questions for me."

He stared up at her with suspicion in his bloodshot eyes. "Questions, huh? What kinda questions?"

She handed him a crisp dollar bill, which he snatched with his filthy hands and shoved into a hidden pocket within his tangle of rags. The donation did little to allay his suspicion of Sally's intentions.

"Don't worry," she said reassuringly, "you're not in trouble. I'm looking for someone who lives in that building over there, and I'm wondering if you maybe saw him if you've been here a while."

The old man nodded slowly, clearly not entirely convinced but indicating at least a reluctant willingness to help. "Sure," he said. "I been here. I been here all day. Where elsc you think I gotta be?" He added a toothless chuckle, lightening the mood a little and indicating that he was starting to trust Sally.

"All I want to know is if you saw a delivery company here, maybe an hour or two ago," Sally said. "A guy delivering a fridge to the building. Did you see anything like that?"

"Sure," the old man said, nodding enthusiastically. "I

seen him. Young dude, maybe late twenties, early thir-ties, I dunno. What's it worth to ya, though? A little d-donation might jog my memory a little, if you know what I m-mean … right now, the details feel a little … f-fuzzy."

Sally dug in her pocket and took out a ten-dollar bill. "Will this help you remember things a little more clearly?"

A broad smile spread across the old bum's toothless mouth, and he gave her a gummy grin, nodding eagerly. He reached out to grab the money, but Sally pulled the note back out of his reach. She felt terrible doing this, but two young boys' lives were on the line, and she needed the information this man had.

"Answers first, please," she said. "Then you get your money."

He rolled his eyes and muttered a curse under his breath. Then, however, he looked up at her and spoke. "The g-guy was driving a white van, looked pretty new. Can't r-r-remember the kind of van, sorry. But it had a logo on it, a hammer, and a lightning b-bolt. Black, on a yellow background, in a circle. Think it said something like 'Thor's Deliveries' or s-something. The delivery guy, young white guy, shoulder-length blond hair, short beard, pretty well built, maybe six-foot, six one, he had b-blue coveralls on, they had the same logo on 'em, the h-hammer and the lightning bolt. Yeah, pretty sure it was s-something like 'Thor's Deliveries,' yeah, I'm pretty sure about that."

Sally handed him the ten-dollar note. "Thank you so much for the information."

"And thank you, ma'am. That's a g-generous tip," he said with a broad grin.

Sally went and found Haxton, who was looking grumpier than usual. "You won't freakin' believe this, but not one of these damn businesses has a camera facing French's apartment building," he grumbled. "Not one! I went into every damn store, and—"

"I found something," Sally said, interrupting him before his complaints got too unbearable.

Haxton raised an eyebrow. "You did? How?"

She pointed across the street at the old homeless man, who at this point was trying to suck the last few drops of whisky out of his bottle.

"That old bum? What did he have to say?" Haxton asked.

"That he saw a guy taking a large refrigerator box in and out of French's building," Sally said. "Before you ask, no, he didn't get the van's license plate, but he did notice a logo on both the van and the delivery guy, and he gave me a pretty detailed description of the delivery guy."

"You sure he didn't hallucinate the whole thing?" Haxton asked skeptically. "He doesn't exactly look like the most reliable witness I've ever seen."

"He's an old drunk, but I don't think he's insane or hallucinating," Sally said. "He said the name of the delivery company was 'Thor's Hammer' and described the logo as being a black hammer and lightning bolt on a yellow background. Said the van and the delivery guy both had the logo on them."

"Well, there's one way to tell if he's talking out his ass

or if he really did see that," Haxton said, getting his phone out and opening his web browser. "Thor's Hammer Deliveries, huh? All right, let's take a look." Haxton punched this term into Google, and a look of surprise came over his craggy face when the results came up. "Well, I'll be damned," he murmured. "The old bum was right. Weird name aside, it's a genuine delivery company, operating locally."

"Then I guess we're going straight there to see which guy on their team matches the description given to me by the homeless guy?" Sally asked.

"Damn straight," Haxton said. "They've got their address and contact details and everything here on Google, and I know where this is; it's not far away. Maybe a fifteen-minute drive. You know where this is, right?"

"Yeah, I know how to get there," Sally said.

"Good," Haxton said. "This is the best lead we've had in quite a while. Crazy that with all this technology and all these resources we have at our fingertips, it was a tip from a crazy old wino sitting in a pile of garbage bags that led us to it!"

Sally chuckled, feeling optimistic about making some real headway in the case for the first time in quite a while. "Sometimes it's the simplest sources that make the biggest difference," she said.

"Indeed, Sally, indeed. Anyway, I'll round up the boys right away and meet you there," Haxton said. "This it … I can feel it. Finally… this is it. We've almost got 'em now."

14

*S*ally waited outside the Thor's Hammer Deliveries depot in her car for Haxton and the other police officers to arrive. For some reason, her nerves were on edge here, even though there was no obvious reason for her to feel like she was in any real danger.

The building was in a more industrial part of town, with a large diesel mechanic's workshop next to it, and on the other side, a place that sold lumber and building supplies. The depot didn't look too busy; two white vans with the hammer and lightning bolt logo were parked out front, and a much larger truck, an eighteen-wheeler, was emblazoned with the same emblem.

Haxton and the other cops showed up soon enough, and once they were all there, Sally joined them as they marched up to the front entrance of the depot.

They walked in and found themselves in an entrance

area, where a pretty, blond receptionist greeted them with a smile. "Good afternoon, Officers. How can I help you?"

"I want to talk to the manager, the owner, whoever's in charge," Haxton said gruffly.

"Certainly, sir," the receptionist said, still smiling. "I'll call Mr. Nordstrom right away. He's the manager and owner. If you'll just wait here for a minute, he'll be right out, I'm sure."

Haxton had already placed a cruiser near the back entrance to the depot, which was on another street parallel to the one out front. He also had two cruisers blocking the front entrance. He quietly sent messages to all three units, warning them to get ready in case anyone tried to make a run for it.

The owner of the company, Mr. Nordstrom, came out of some offices behind the receptionist's desk. Sally and Haxton shared a quick, subtle glance—Nordstrom didn't match the homeless man's description of the delivery guy at all.

Nordstrom was on the shorter size of average height— probably around five foot eight. He was of a stocky build, with a compact and powerful trunk and shoulders; the type of man who was naturally built for wrestling. In his early forties, he had close-cropped black hair, graying at the temples and on the sides, and his square, strong-jawed visage retained a good degree of youthful attractiveness for a man of his age. On either side of a tall, straight nose, two piercing blue eyes beneath thick black eyebrows regarded the police officers with suspicion.

Something about Nordstrom immediately got alarm

bells ringing in Sally's mind. She couldn't pinpoint it. He didn't match the suspect's description at all, but she couldn't deny that her gut instinct was telling her that there was something suspicious about this man.

"I'm Karl Nordstrom, owner and manager of the company, Officers," Nordstrom said, a tight, polite smile on his face. "How can I help you?"

"We're interested in a delivery your company made to this address earlier today," Haxton said, placing a piece of paper with French's address on the desk that separated him from Nordstrom.

"All right, let me run this address through our system," Nordstrom said. He sat down at one of the computers and punched in the address. "Yes, we delivered a refrigerator to this address earlier," he said. "The fridge was picked up from Al's Appliances, two miles from here, and then delivered to the customer at that address. The system says the delivery was successful. I'm not sure what else I can tell you about this."

"First, you can tell us who placed that order," Haxton said gruffly. "And second, you can tell us which of your people did the actual delivery. We want to talk to him."

"Okay, let me check the system," Nordstrom said, clicking with his mouse and tapping on the keyboard. "All right, well it says the order was placed by the client, a Mr. French. He contacted us to pick up the fridge from Al's; if there's a problem with the item, you need to speak to someone at Al's. All we do is arrange deliveries."

"What about the driver who made the delivery?" Sally asked. "We need to speak to him."

"The system says Pete made that delivery. You can't talk to him now, I'm afraid, because he's out on another run."

"All right, well, we'll just wait for him to get back then," Haxton said, narrowing his eyes as he stared with unabashed suspicion at Nordstrom. "In the meantime, you can tell us a little more about Pete—like what his full name is, how long he's worked for you, how much you know about him, all those juicy details, you know what I mean?"

Sally observed Nordstrom closely as Haxton spoke to him. She was sure she could see a subtle tightening of his facial muscles, almost undetectable but nonetheless visible to her eagle-eyed vision. She couldn't feel his palms, of course, but she was ready to bet that they were getting clammy about now. Nordstrom was hiding something. She was sure of it, and, what was more, she was certain that despite the ignorance he was feigning, he knew exactly why they were here and why they wanted to ask questions about this driver, Pete.

"Sure, I'll tell you guys about Pete," Nordstrom said calmly. "But tell me, has he done something? Is he in trouble? If he is, I'd like to know about it."

"We're asking the questions here, pal," Haxton said. "Why don't you just go ahead and tell us about Pete, huh?"

"All right, okay. Well, his full name is Peter Aling. He's one of our newer drivers. He's only been here for a few months. He's twenty-eight, always seemed like a good kid to me—you know, honest, reliable, doesn't give me any attitude, doesn't whine or complain or laze around like one or two of the other drivers do … I can't imagine why he'd be in trouble for anything."

"Did you run a criminal background check on him before you hired him?" Sally asked.

Nordstrom nodded. "Sure. In a business like mine, which could be torpedoed if one of my drivers stole a client's delivery, I make sure to run thorough background checks on everyone who applies for a job here. Aling came up clean; I'm sure if you people look into it, you'll find the same."

"Well, he may not be as clean as you think he is," Haxton said. "He didn't pick up a fridge earlier, and he didn't transport any appliances. Instead, he used one of your vans to transport a wanted suspect in a kidnapping case."

A look of shock came over Nordstrom's face. Sally scrutinized his expression closely, and she was sure that it was faked. Convincingly faked, yes, but faked nonetheless.

"I can't believe that," Nordstrom said with a gasp. "Pete, using my vans to transport a wanted criminal! Hold on, I need to call Al Coombs."

"Who's Al Coombs?" Haxton asked.

"The owner of Al's Appliances," Nordstrom said. "We do business with them all the time. I want to check exactly what Pete picked up from his place."

"Are you sure Aling even went there?" Sally asked. "The whole job was probably phony from the start."

"The system is showing that his van traveled there and that he picked up something from their location," Nordstrom said. "I want to find out what that was since it clearly wasn't a new fridge."

"Hold on, does the system show where he went after going to French's place?" Sally asked.

"Sure," Nordstrom answered. "It says he delivered the fridge successfully, and then he came straight back here and disposed of the empty box with the rest of our cardboard waste."

"The van didn't make any stops or detours along the way?" Sally asked.

"One stop for gas, at the usual gas station my drivers go to, around a mile from here. He stopped there just before coming back here."

"That's where French must have got out of the van," Sally said.

"Well, there certainly wasn't a fugitive from justice hiding in the back of the van when it came back here," Nordstrom said. "Another driver took the van from Pete right away for another job, and every driver has to inspect the van before setting off on a job."

Again, Sally got the sense that Nordstrom wasn't telling the entire truth here. The man was hiding something, and he was hiding it extremely well. Haxton didn't seem to think there was anything suspicious about him, and nor did the other cops. Haxton had a very particular way of looking at someone he found suspicious, a look Sally was extremely familiar with, and he definitely wasn't looking at Nordstrom in that manner.

"You got cameras in your vans?" Haxton asked.

"Yes, all of them. They run all the time, record everything."

"So you won't mind us taking a look at the footage from that van then, will you?"

"Not at all," Nordstrom said. "If you come back here, behind the desk, I'll set it up so you can take a look for yourselves. Now, if you don't mind, I'd like to call Al."

"Do that," Haxton said, "and put it on speakerphone so we can all hear, huh?"

"Of course," Nordstrom said. He dialed up Al and put the phone on speakerphone.

A receptionist answered, and Nordstrom told her who he was and asked if he could speak to Al.

"Karl," a gravelly voice on the other end of the line. "Good to hear from you, my friend. It's been too long since we had a good ol' chat. What's up?"

"We definitely need to catch up, Al, but I'm afraid that'll have to wait. This is a business call."

"All right, what's going on? Was there a problem with a delivery or something?" Al asked.

"You could say that. One of my drivers, Peter Aling, picked up a fridge from you guys earlier today—or, at least, he said he did. The order was supposed to be delivered to a guy named Charlie French. Could you just look up those details for me, please?"

"Sure thing, I'll check it out for you."

Sally and the cops listened as the sound of fingers tapping away at a keyboard came through the phone speaker. Eventually, Al spoke again.

"There are no orders this week for anyone named

French, I'm afraid. There must have been some kinda mix-up."

"Ask him if he can find out if Aling picked up an empty fridge box," Sally said.

"Can you just ask your boys in the warehouse if one of my boys came around earlier and picked up an empty refrigerator box?" Nordstrom asked.

"Yeah, sure, I'll do that," Al said. "Hold on a minute." They heard him put down the phone, and then they heard him walking away. A few minutes later, he returned. "Yes, the boys in the warehouse said a guy from your team came and picked up an empty fridge box earlier. Don't know why. It seems kinda weird. What's going on, Karl?"

"Uh, nothing, don't worry about it," Nordstrom said. "Just some irregularities we're trying to smooth out here. Thanks for the help, Al. We'll have a proper catch-up soon."

"All right, so now we all know that something fishy is going on with this Peter Aling guy," Haxton said to Nordstrom. "You need to tell us where he is right now."

"Uh, of course, of course," Nordstrom said, clicking on his mouse. "I'm tracking his journey right now." He looked up at the cops, a strange smile on his face.

"What are you smiling about, Nordstrom?" Haxton asked.

"You guys are in luck," Nordstrom said, almost smugly. "Pete's truck is about two blocks away. He'll be walking through the front door in a minute or two."

15

"*N*o, he won't, not if he sees my cruisers parked out front," Haxton said. "The son of a bitch is sure to run. You can communicate with him, right? Tell him to stop where he is right now!"

"I assure you, he won't run," Nordstrom said calmly.

Despite his veneer of cool collectedness, Sally thought she could spot a slight hint of panic in Nordstrom's eyes. It was barely detectible, but like a shark that could sniff out a drop of blood a mile away in seawater, she could pick up tiny irregularities in people's attitudes.

"And I say he will run!" Haxton said, bristling with aggression. "Get on the radio or whatever it is that you use to communicate with your people and tell him to pull over right now! Say that your system has picked up a dangerous mechanical issue with the truck or something. Do it!"

"Uh, okay, okay," Nordstrom said. "Thing is, I don't usually operate the coms controls. That's the supervisor's role. I'm going to have to go find him. I think he's in the warehouse."

Sally was sure he was stalling for time, waiting until Aling got close enough to catch sight of the police cruisers parked out front, which would give him time to pull over, jump out of the truck and flee.

"He's not going to get this done in time, Gareth," Sally said to Haxton, her tone urgent. "Tell the units outside to move out and intercept the truck before he can make a run for it."

"Yeah, that's exactly what I was thinking," Haxton said, firing a withering glare at Nordstrom. "Tell me exactly what street he's on—and don't give us any more bullshit. I know your damn software can give you that information."

"Of course," Nordstrom said. "He's coming up Long Avenue right now."

Haxton raised his radio to his lips. "All units, all units, move out to Long Avenue, I repeat, move out to Long Avenue. The suspect is moving along Long Avenue in a van with the Thor's Hammer logo on it. Intercept the van and ensure that nobody escapes from it. Detain the suspect until I get there!"

A chorus of voices came crackling through the speaker in response, and moments after this came the sound of multiple car engines revving, tires screeching and sirens wailing as the cruisers raced off to Long Avenue to intercept the van.

"I hope you get him," Nordstrom said, his voice thick with put-on sincerity that was so convincing that even Sally almost believed it. "I just can't believe that one of my trusted drivers used one of my vehicles to commit a crime … my God, if this gets out to the press, it could sink this company, this company that I built with my own hands from nothing—"

"Relax, Nordstrom," Haxton muttered. "As long as you're not involved yourself, there's nothing to worry about."

An expression of shock and indignation came over Nordstrom's face. "I've never so much as received a parking ticket or a speeding fine, Officer," he gasped. "You can check every line of my records, my entire career history, and you'll find without fail that it's clean as a whistle! I can't believe you would even hint at—"

"I told you to *relax*," Haxton growled. "You're doing the opposite. I don't like it when people don't do what I tell 'em to do."

Nordstrom gulped and nodded; Gareth Haxton could be very intimidating when he wanted to be.

Haxton raised the radio to his lips again. "Any progress to report?"

"We have the vehicle in sight," one distorted voice replied. "Two units currently moving to intercept."

"Excellent news," Haxton said.

"Moving to block off the vehicle … and we're in position."

Everyone waited with bated breath. Would Aling try to run? Would he surrender peacefully, or would he jump out of the truck with guns blazing? Since he didn't have any sort of record, it was almost more dangerous than if he was a known felon, whose behavior the cops could at least somewhat predict.

"I'm sure he won't give you any trouble," Nordstrom said. "He's—"

"With all due respect, we don't need your input at this point," Haxton said.

A few more moments of tense silence were finally broken by a voice crackling through Haxton's radio.

"The suspect is in custody," a police officer announced. "We've got him cuffed, in the back of a cruiser. He surrendered without resistance."

A broad grin of triumph spread across Haxton's face. "That's exactly what I wanted to hear, boys. Well done. Take him downtown for questioning."

"Will do. See you there."

"Well, I'm happy to see that you managed to intercept him without any trouble," Nordstrom said, smiling coolly. "If he's guilty of anything, please let me know right away because I need to fire him before word gets out to the press about whatever it was he did. And if you need any other assistance, please don't hesitate to contact me. Here's my personal number," he said, handing a business card to Haxton. "Is there anything else I can help you with?"

"No, I think we're done here," Haxton said.

Sally felt like it might be a good idea to search the premises. Although it seemed quite clear to everyone else that Nordstrom had nothing to do with the kidnappings, Sally couldn't help but feel that he was hiding something.

As they left the building, Sally took Haxton aside. "Did you notice that Nordstrom seemed to be a little off?"

"How do you mean?" he asked. "You think he's involved?"

"He might be. It did seem to me as if he may have been hiding something."

Haxton shook his head. "I didn't pick up any vibes from him. Are you sure you're not just being a little paranoid?"

"I was definitely picking up something off about him," she said. "And you know that my instincts are rarely wrong."

"All right," Haxton said, stopping. "Since we've got Aling in custody and we're already here, we may as well take a look around. I really don't think we're going to find anything, though."

"Just to be safe and to cover all our bases," Sally said.

"Sure." Haxton turned to the other cops. "You guys head on back to HQ; we'll meet you there shortly."

He and Sally then turned around and headed back into the depot building. Nordstrom was still in the reception area, talking to the receptionist. He gave Sally and Haxton a polite smile as they entered the building. The smile was broad on his lips, but the look in his eyes was cold and hard.

"Back so soon, Officers?" he said. "How can I help you."

"We believe that Aling might have hidden some contraband somewhere in the depot," Haxton said coolly.

"You wouldn't mind if we poked our noses around here a bit, would you?"

"Not at all," Nordstrom said. "In fact, I'll show you around myself. I'm always happy to give visitors a tour of my business. If you let me know exactly what sort of contraband we're talking about, I might be able to get a better idea of where Aling might have hidden it."

"We can't disclose that information to you," Sally said before Haxton could answer. "We know what we're looking for, and we can figure out where he might have hidden it."

"No problem," Nordstrom said. "Follow me, Officers."

He led them through the offices, which consisted only of three or four rooms, a bathroom, and a small kitchen, to the warehouse in the back. The warehouse was huge, and there were a number of vans of various sizes in it, as well as a few eighteen-wheelers and other trucks. Hundreds of crates and boxes were stacked all over the place.

In Sally's mind, this would be the perfect place to hide a wanted suspect, like Julian Drake or Charlie French—or, even, if it went that deep, some kidnapped children.

The moment Haxton and Sally entered the warehouse, both realized there was a major obstacle in their way. This place was simply too big for two people to comprehensively search, with all of its vehicles, crates, and boxes.

Adding to this difficultly, a few moments after they walked into the warehouse behind Nordstrom, a horrendous racket began clacking and grinding, the sound so loud that the officers had to clamp their hands over their ears. It sounded like a whole army was using jackhammers on hard concrete in here, and the large size of the warehouse created an echo and amplified the already loud sound to a skull-splitting level of decibels.

Nordstrom grabbed some soundproof earmuffs from a nearby shelf, put some on, and then handed Sally and Haxton a pair. "Put these on!" he yelled.

Despite the volume of his voice, neither of them could really hear what he was saying over the terrible noise, but his intent was clear enough. Both cops hastily slipped the earmuffs over their ears, grateful for the barrier the items created between their eardrums and the horrid noise.

"What the hell is that?" Haxton yelled.

"Ventilation system!" Nordstrom yelled back. "The compressor's on its way out! I'm getting it replaced tomorrow! Until then, we just have to put up with this noise! The system runs on autopilot. I can't shut it down!"

Haxton shot Sally a knowing glance. Conducting a thorough search of this place would be difficult enough with only two people, but now with the added obstacle of constant, earsplitting noise, it would be almost impossible to do any sort of meaningful search.

Sally realized this, and in response to Haxton's wordless message, she nodded grimly.

"How long is this noise going to go on for?" Haxton yelled to Nordstrom.

"I'm sorry, but once the system starts up, it keeps running for at least two hours!" Nordstrom yelled back. "I hope it doesn't make your search too unbearable! Like I said, I wish I could turn it off, but there's no way to do that without shutting down power to the entire site, and I can't do that!"

"Let's just do a quick search!" Sally yelled to Haxton. She wanted to do a thorough search, of course, but current conditions made it impossible.

"I'll take this section!" Haxton said, pointing at the closest section, where a large number of crates and boxes were stacked. "You take the section over there, take a look at the vehicles!" he added, pointing to the rows of trucks and vans.

Sally nodded, and as Haxton walked off to begin inspecting the rows of boxes and crates, Sally turned to Nordstrom. "Are the vehicles locked?"

"Yes, they are!" he replied.

"I need keys for all of them, please!"

"Of course! Wait here!"

Nordstrom went back into the offices to fetch the keys for the various vehicles. Sally, meanwhile, stood, waiting, doing her best to ignore the horrendous noise, which was so loud it felt as if it were rattling her insides and shaking her brain inside her skull, even with the soundproof earmuffs on.

The wait for Nordstrom to bring the keys seemed to take forever. Every second spent waiting with the hellish noise felt like extended torture, and as much as Sally wanted to conduct as thorough a search as she could under these less-than-ideal conditions, another part of her just wanted to give up and get out of here as fast as she could.

After a long wait, Nordstrom finally returned with a bunch of keys and remotes.

"Sorry!" he said with an apologetic shrug. "As you can see, we've got a ton of vehicles in here!"

"You'll have to help me with this. I don't know which key or which remote goes with which vehicle!"

"Sure!"

They went around to each truck and van, and Nordstrom unlocked them while Sally took a look inside each one. Her searches turned up nothing; it quickly became clear that all the vans and trucks were empty.

When they got to the last van, Nordstrom turned away and began heading back toward the offices.

"Hey, hold on!" Sally yelled after him. "What about this one?"

"That's a scrapped old wreck!" he said. "It can't be opened—the doors are welded shut! There's no way Aling could have gotten in there anyway!"

Sally checked the van and found that the doors were indeed welded shut. She felt suspicious about the vehicle, but the torture of the horrendous noise and the fact that all of its doors were welded shut, making it impossible to open anyway, meant that she was ready to give up her searching at this point.

Haxton was also done, and he shook his head and shrugged, shooting Sally a glance that said that his search of the warehouse had been as fruitless as hers had. They both hurried through the offices back to the reception area. Even here, the noise was deafening, and they said a hasty goodbye to Nordstrom and his receptionist before leaving.

Sally drove Haxton back to the station since his men had taken his cruiser when they had intercepted Aling.

"Man, my ears are still ringing from that damn noise," Haxton muttered.

"I know, it sounded like a warzone in there," Sally said.

"I hope this ringing stops soon. It's driving me crazy."

When they got to the station, they soon forgot about the ringing in their ears. They finally had a suspect in custody who they could question about the kidnappings.

"Where is he?" Haxton asked the moment he and Sally entered the station.

"Interrogation Room 3," the desk sergeant said. "The son of a bitch hasn't said anything, well, nothing but the whole 'I didn't go anything' bullshit. You know how it is; every asshole we drag through these doors is always innocent, right, Haxton?"

Haxton chuckled. "They sure are. Fine upstanding citizens, every one of 'em." Then he turned to Sally. "Come on, let's go grill Aling and find out where French and Drake are … and maybe even where the kidnapped kids are if we're lucky."

They went over to Interrogation Room 3, where one of the police officers who had been with them at Thor's Hammer was standing guard at the door.

"The guy you pulled out of the truck is in there, right?" Haxton asked the officer.

"He sure is, sure. Came in without a fight, but he did keep saying he didn't do anything—like every perp does."

Haxton chuckled. "We'll soon find out just how innocent this chump is."

He opened the door, but the moment he and Sally laid eyes on the man handcuffed to the table inside, they both let out a gasp of shock and dismay.

They had the wrong guy, and they knew it right away —the man handcuffed to the table was black.

16

"What's your name?" Haxton demanded, staring wide-eyed at the young black man handcuffed to the interrogation table.

"You know, man, that's the first time any one of you people has actually bothered to ask me that, and—"

"Just give me your damn name!" Haxton roared.

"Zeke Ebrahim," the young man said, cool and impassive in the face of Haxton's wrath. "Now, are you gonna tell me why you—"

Haxton slammed the door shut and turned to face Sally, his face a stormy, crimson wrath of fury. "Those idiots! Those fucking idiots!" he hissed through clenched teeth. "They arrested the wrong guy! They got the wrong fucking guy!"

"Calm down, Gareth," Sally said in a cool and collected tone, even though she too was furious about this enormous error. "I know that—"

"Calm down? You want me to calm down? I can't trust

the clowns I work with to get the right suspect, not even when he's a completely different fucking race, and you want me to calm down?"

"Gareth, the officers who picked this guy up, didn't have a physical description of Aling. They should have asked his name before throwing him into the back of the cruiser, I know, or checked him for ID—but a large portion of the blame has to be on Nordstrom. He's the one who told us Aling was in that truck, and the officers who arrested this man had no reason not to believe him."

"Shit, dammit," Gareth muttered, still consumed with anger but slowly beginning to calm down. "You're right." He dug around in his pocket and produced Nordstrom's business card. "Here, you call him. I'm too pissed to speak to that smug jerk right now, and I can't guarantee that I won't say something I'll regret."

He handed the business card to Sally and then, after giving orders that Zeke Ebrahim was to be immediately released, stormed off to find the officers who had wrong-fully arrested the young man.

Before the cop guarding the door stepped into the interrogation room to free Ebrahim, however, Sally told him to wait.

"But Haxton told me this guy has to be released right away," the cop said.

"I just want to ask him one or two questions before you do that," she said.

"All right, but you'd better hurry; the kid's been wrongfully arrested after all, and he doesn't technically have to answer anything you ask him."

"I'm aware of that. I'll be quick."

The cop gave Sally a reluctant nod, and she stepped into the interrogation room and closed the door quietly behind her.

"Oh, man, another cop?" Ebrahim muttered. "When is someone gonna tell me what's going on here?"

"What's going on here, Mr. Ebrahim," Sally said, "is that my fellow officers made a terrible mistake. You haven't done anything wrong, and when they arrested you, they thought you were someone else."

Ebrahim shook his head, smiling sourly, and let out a humorless chuckle. "Well, well, well ... look at this. I been sayin' from the get-go that I didn't do nothin', and now you people finally admit that I'm right. Well, what are you waiting for? Get these cuffs off me, and let me go! You have no right to keep me here! I'm gonna tell my lawyer about this."

"Zeke—can I call you Zeke?" Sally asked, speaking in a friendly tone and smiling warmly. "I'm Sally, by the way. Sally Lawson. I'm truly, deeply sorry about what happened."

"Don't think that some phony apology is gonna make me change my mind about telling my lawyer about this," Ebrahim said icily.

"I'm not going to try to persuade you not to take action against us," Sally responded. "If you want to do that, you can go ahead and sue us—we deserve it for what we put you through."

That took the young man off guard, and he cocked his head and frowned with confusion. "What? Are you for real? You ain't gonna try to talk me out of suing your asses?"

"No. Like I said, if you feel that that's what you need to do, you can go ahead and do it. I do very quickly want to tell you why you were arrested, though, and maybe see if you can help me with some information. This has to do with the two children who were recently kidnapped from the museum and the aquarium—did you hear about that in the news?"

"Uh, sure, I saw some stuff on social media," he said warily. "But I don't know nothin' about that. I mean, it's terrible what happened to them poor kids, but I don't know nothin' about it."

"You work with someone who might know a whole lot about it," Sally said.

"What? Who?" he gasped, his eyes widening with shock.

"Peter Aling," she said. "One of your fellow drivers. That's who my fellow officers thought they were arresting when they picked you up."

Ebrahim threw his head back and laughed. "They thought *I* was Aling? I dunno if you noticed, miss, but there's one big and very obvious difference between myself and Pete … one that only a blind man could miss if you know what I'm sayin'."

"And that's what makes our error that much more embarrassing," Sally said apologetically. "But the thing is, the officers who arrested you weren't given a physical description of Aling. They didn't know he was a white guy. Your boss, Karl Nordstrom, assured us that Aling was driving the truck that you were driving—that was why you were pulled over and brought in. We were acting on information from your boss, who was tracking Aling—who turned out to be you, instead—on the depot's tracking system."

"Shit," Ebrahim said, frowning and shaking his head. "That explains why we swapped."

Now Sally realized she had uncovered something. She narrowed her eyes and leaned in a little closer across the table. "What exactly do you mean by 'swapped,' Zeke?"

"Pete and me, we swapped trucks for that shift. I ain't never done that before, and I thought it was really weird. But Pete told me it was an order from Nordstrom, and I didn't wanna get fired, so I did it. I swapped trucks with him. I drove his truck. He drove mine. I thought it was sketchy, but hey, as long as the goods get to their destination on time, who cares who's driving, right? And I delivered his load on time, and I know Pete's a good, reliable driver, so I knew he'd get mine on time. It was bugging me the whole time, though—why would Nordstrom want us to suddenly change trucks?"

"How sure are you that Nordstrom gave the order?" Sally asked. "Can you be sure about that, or do you think maybe Peter made it up?"

Ebrahim shook his head. "I can't be one hundred percent sure," he admitted. "Pete showed me a text on his phone which looked like it came from Nordstrom, but I guess if he had really wanted to, he could have faked that."

"You didn't get any texts or messages or anything directly from Nordstrom yourself?"

"Nope, I only heard it through Pete, and he showed me that message on his phone. Nordstrom didn't tell me anything directly. By the way, what does Pete have to do with this whole child kidnapping thing? Is he involved somehow?"

"He may be. Earlier today, Peter helped one of the suspects—a man who very well may be the mastermind behind the kidnappings—flee his apartment before we could get to him."

"Damn," Ebrahim murmured, shaking his head. "I always picked up a lil' bit of a weird vibe from Pete, but I never suspected he could be involved in anything as downright evil as kidnapping children. I gotta say, that's taken me by surprise."

"If you know how to get hold of him, it would be of an immense help to us if you let us know," Sally said. "Again, I'm terribly, terribly sorry about what happened to you, and you can go ahead and contact your lawyer if you want. But also, I would personally greatly appreciate any help you could give us with tracking down Peter Aling if you know anything at all."

Ebrahim shrugged. "I'm sorry, miss, but he's just a guy I work with. We sometimes shoot the shit at work, but we ain't friends or nothin' like that. We've never hung out outside of work. I don't really know much about the guy. Shit, I don't even know where he lives. Come to think of it, though, he does have a girlfriend, some girl he tells me about all the time."

"Do you know her name? Where we might be able to find her?"

Ebrahim scratched his chin and furrowed his brow. "Lemme think, lemme think ... well she's a tattoo artist, I know that much. And she's really good, judging from the work she did on Pete. He may be a weird son of a bitch, but he's got some pretty sick ink on him."

"And her name ... can you remember her name?" Sally asked.

"Uh ... it was ... man, it's on the tip of my tongue ... Layla, yeah, that's it. Layla."

"You don't know her last name?"

He shook his head. "Sorry, but that's all I can remember about her. She's a really good tattoo artist named Layla."

"All right. Thank you so much, Zeke, and again, I'm really sorry about what happened. You're free to go now."

"Okay. I hope you guys find those missing kids."

Sally stepped out of the room and gave the cop outside a nod, indicating that he should free Ebrahim now. Instead of calling up Nordstrom to ask about the whole driver swap thing, though, she went to her desk. She suspected that Nordstrom had something to do with this, but that could wait. Right now, she had a hot lead, one that could take her directly to Peter Aling, and maybe even Charlie French as well.

"All right," she said as she sat down at her computer. "The trail's getting hot again. Let me see if I can find this female tattoo artist named Layla."

17

"I just chewed up the assholes who arrested the wrong guy," Haxton muttered as he walked over to Sally's desk. "You'd better believe that they're never going to do that again. Did you get hold of Nordstrom? What did he say about giving us the wrong info about Aling?"

Sally was listening to him, but her eyes were focused on her computer screen, and her fingers were dancing nimbly and speedily across her keyboard. "No," she said, "I haven't contacted Nordstrom yet … but I've found some info on Aling that we didn't have before."

"Oh yeah, what?"

"His girlfriend's identity. It took a bit of research, but I'm pretty sure I've found her."

Haxton leaned in closer and peered at Sally's screen, staring at the web page she was perusing. "Purple Dragon Tattoo Parlor? What's this? You getting yourself some ink?"

"This is where she works. Layla Hedges, twenty-nine years old, tattoo artist. According to Zeke Ebrahim, she's Aling's girlfriend. I checked her social media accounts, and there are recent pictures of her and Aling together, so I'm pretty sure the relationship is still on. Right now, I think she's our most solid link to where Aling might be."

Haxton noticed the address of the tattoo studio. "That ain't too far away," he said. "Maybe a half-hour drive from here. We'd best go pay her a visit."

"I think a different approach might be more successful," Sally said. "If we approach her directly, she could warn Aling, and he'll take off and run from wherever he's hiding. Let's do some discreet surveillance first, see if we can get her to unknowingly lead us to him."

Haxton smiled. "Yeah, you're right. We'll stake out the premises."

"I'm going to talk to her, too," Sally said, "but not as a cop. I'll pretend to be interested in getting a tattoo."

Haxton chuckled. "You don't think that might arouse her suspicions, Sally? You don't exactly look like the type who gets themselves covered in ink, ya know?"

"You're behind the times, Gareth," Sally said with a grin. "Everyone gets tattoos these days. And I've got a valid reason to want to get one—I've got that C-section scar on my belly from when Derek was born. Plenty of women get those covered up with pretty tattoos. I don't think she'll suspect a thing. Set up surveillance on her, of course, but let me talk to her as well."

"Sure thing. What about Nordstrom? You gonna call him?"

"I'd like to talk to him in person, gauge his reaction, take a look at his expressions. I think he's involved."

"Are you sure about that?" Haxton asked. "I didn't pick up anything from him."

"I talked to Ebrahim before he was released, and he claimed that Aling showed him a direct order from Nordstrom telling him to swap trucks with Aling, even though this was something he had never done before and wasn't in line with company policy."

"You don't think Aling could have fabricated the message to cover his own ass?" Haxton asked. "Any idiot with the tiniest drop of computer skills can create fakes with ridiculous ease these days."

"Aling may have faked the message, sure, but we can't discount the possibility that Nordstrom might be involved. It's a lot harder for him to lie convincingly in person than it is over the phone. And you know, I can't help but feel suspicious about something that happened when we were at the depot."

"What exactly?"

"The fact that his ventilation system compressor started acting up and making that terrible the minute we went into the back to search the warehouse. Didn't you find the timing a little odd?" Sally asked.

Haxton shrugged. "Well, sure, it was bad timing, but we searched the place anyway, and even though it was a quick sweep, a kidnapped child isn't exactly something we'd miss. You searched every van and truck, didn't you?"

"I did, but there was one old van with all the doors welded shut. Obviously, I couldn't search that one."

Scratching his stubble-prickly chin, Haxton thought about this for a while. "Hmm … that is kinda weird. But I'm still not convinced that Nordstrom was involved. Still, we can go there in person and talk to him. I don't mind."

"Let's do that now," Sally suggested. "Then we'll go on down to the Purple Dragon Tattoo Parlor."

They took a drive back to the depot. "Man, I hope something comes out of all this driving," Haxton muttered. "I've got a number of units all looking for Drake, French, and Aling, but those three seem to have upped and vanished into thin air."

"We'll find them soon enough," Sally said encouragingly. "And we'll get those boys back to their parents."

"I hope so," Haxton said, his countenance grim. "You know the statistics; with each day that passes in which a kidnapped kid isn't found, the chances of them being found alive drop dramatically … *extremely* dramatically."

"I know, but I have a feeling that Jeffrey Clarkson and Dennis Avery are still alive," Sally said. She wasn't just saying this to sound hopeful and to keep their spirits up; she genuinely did feel as if the boys were still alive. Her gut instinct told her this, and it was rarely wrong about such things.

After a drive that felt longer than it was, they got back to the Thor's Hammer delivery depot. When they stepped out of the car, they noticed that the horrible racket of the broken compressor had stopped. Sally shot a knowing glance at Haxton.

"Sure, it does seem a little suspicious that it's stopped

now," he said, "but then again, it wasn't running when we first got here either."

They headed into the entrance.

"Are you here to see Mr. Nordstrom again, Officers?" the receptionist asked.

"Go get him, please," Haxton said. "This won't take long."

"Of course."

She scurried into the offices and returned a few moments later, with Nordstrom following her. He had a neutral, almost unreadable expression on his face. Sally scrutinized his features and realized that it would be difficult to tell whether he was telling the truth or lying; he seemed to be one of those rare individuals who had been gifted with a natural talent for wearing a perfect poker face.

"I've been expecting you, Detectives," Nordstrom said, "although I thought that you might call instead of driving all this way."

"So you know why we wanna talk to you then," Haxton said.

"Of course. I assume it's about the fact that Aling swapped vehicles with Ebrahim?"

"Yes. Did you know about this?" Haxton asked.

"Of course not!" Nordstrom blurted, bristling with indignation. "I run this company like a well-oiled machine! Swapping vehicles with another driver is an offense punishable by firing! Aling certainly knew that, and Ebrahim should have known it as well. I had no idea that it was Ebrahim driving the truck when you people arrested him, not until he came back here and told me what had happened."

"Did you fire him since you just said it's an offense he could be fired for?" Sally asked.

"No, because he explained that Aling had somehow faked a message from me and showed it to him, claiming that it was a direct order from me. As if I would ever give such an instruction to any of my drivers! Still, the message was apparently a convincing fake, so I let Ebrahim off with a warning. However, Aling—if he's ever stupid enough to come back here—is fired. And rest assured, Detectives, if he ever is foolish enough to show his face here again, I'll get my boys to lock him up in the back of one of my trucks, and I'll call you right away."

"So, just to be clear, you had nothing to do with the whole driver swap thing, and you had no idea they'd done it until Ebrahim came back here half an hour ago?"

"Yes, that's exactly what I'm saying," Nordstrom said hotly, still indignant.

"All right, there's no need to get worked up, Mr. Nordstrom," Sally said. "We're just doing our job and being as thorough as we need to be."

"Well, I don't appreciate being treated like a suspect," Nordstrom muttered.

"Who said you were a suspect? We're just asking a few questions to clarify things."

"It sure feels like I'm being interrogated," Nordstrom said, folding his arms across his chest.

"Trust me, pal, if we were actually interrogating you, you'd know," Haxton said sourly.

"One more question, and we'll be out of your hair, Mr. Nordstrom," Sally said. "What's happened to the truck Aling was in? Your system surely tracked all of its movements from the time Ebrahim got out, and Aling got in, right?"

"Yes, of course," Nordstrom said, calming down a little. "The truck was abandoned at a gas station downtown shortly after you people arrested Ebrahim. Aling completed Ebrahim's delivery, then went on to fill up the truck with gas. He paid for it with his company card, parked the truck up at the gas station, and that's the last trace I have of him."

"Which gas station was it?" Haxton asked.

"I'll print out a map for you with the truck's entire route, from the time Aling took over to the point at which he abandoned the vehicle," Nordstrom said. "Hopefully, that will help you."

"That would be helpful, yes, thank you," Sally said. Again she scrutinized Nordstrom closely, but he was extremely difficult to read; his poker face was nigh on perfect.

Nordstrom sat down at one of the desks, tapped a few keys, and then one of the printers began to hum and whirr. Nordstrom handed the officers a few pages of printouts of Aling's route. "I hope these help. That's about all I can do for you; Aling isn't answering his phone, and I presume you already have his home address."

"All right, well, thanks for the help," Sally said. "We'll call you if we need anything else."

"Of course," Nordstrom said, smiling coldly. "And now,

Detectives, I need to get back to my office. As you may imagine, everything is a little chaotic right now, with one of my drivers unexpectedly disappearing and abandoning a vehicle. I have a lot of phone calls to make and angry clients to deal with."

"Sure thing, good luck with that," Haxton said.

He and Sally headed back to the car, examining the printouts as they walked.

"What did you think? Was he lying?" Haxton asked.

Sally frowned as she climbed into the police cruiser. "I don't know. Usually, I can tell, but with him, it's a little more difficult. He's got a really good poker face."

"Yeah, I noticed. Anyway—"

Before Haxton could continue, an urgent voice came crackling through the police radio.

"Haxton, are you there?"

"Go ahead," he said.

"You need to get downtown fast. There's been another kidnapping. Another eight-year-old boy has been abducted."

18

"Holy shit," Haxton muttered, squeezing his temples with his fingers and thumb while shaking his head. "This can't be happening … these assholes! Sons of bitches! They're snatching kids off the damn streets while we're fucking looking for them!"

"How? Where?" Sally gasped, shocked at this terrible news.

"Hold on, let me find out," Haxton said.

He radioed in the question and found out the boy had been abducted from a movie theater downtown. When they checked which movie theater, Sally noticed it was within walking distance from where Aling had abandoned his truck earlier.

"Shit," Haxton muttered as he jumped into his cruiser and fired up the motor. "Then Aling has to be one of the kidnappers, too; it must be him. Drake and French work as a team. French does all the computer stuff while Aling goes in and does the dirty work, knocking his victims out with chloroform and then smuggling them out in boxes or whatever. I guess Drake helps with that, too, or maybe did just the one time. Maybe Aling's more of the main culprit, being a delivery guy. It makes perfect sense; nobody ever looks twice at a delivery guy carrying a large box."

"Agreed," Sally said as they drove off, with Haxton stomping his foot on the gas pedal and spinning the tires in his haste to get moving, "but let's not jump to conclusions before we have more evidence."

"What? Come on, Sally, this is looking more and more obvious, so much so that it seems fucking ridiculous to deny it!" Haxton said. "Don't tell me you still think Nordstrom was involved? I mean, we saw him not two minutes ago; there's no way he could have been involved."

"Not directly, no … but he may have given the order or planned the whole thing. We don't know yet."

"You're asking too many questions, casting too wide a net," Haxton muttered. "Let's focus on catching Drake, French, and Aling right now. They're by far the most obvious suspects, and if experience has taught me anything, it's that often it *is* the most obvious suspects who end up being guilty. And in my eyes, what's just happened goes way beyond simple coincidence."

Sally knew Haxton was too worked up to argue with right now, so she didn't push it. However, she remained skeptical that Aling so obviously seemed to be the culprit. While Haxton was right about the most obvious suspect usually being the guilty one, sometimes that principle was wrong. And her gut instinct was telling her that as unlikely as it seemed, this was one of those times. Only solid evidence would tell who was right about this, though.

When they got to the movie theater downtown, they found a scene of chaos. A crowd had gathered since word had spread about what had happened, and police had had to cordon off the entrance to keep the crowd at bay.

Moviegoers, meanwhile, had had their movies cut short and had been ushered out of their respective theaters so they could be searched for the missing boy. Dozens of angry customers, upset at having their outing ruined, were gathered around the ticket office, yelling at the clerks, who were desperately trying to issue refunds and keep the irate crowd calm.

Haxton and Sally spotted Sergeant Kosinski talking to a pair of weeping adults, a portly, middle-aged couple.

"I'm guessing those are the parents of the kidnapped boy," Haxton said. "We'd better go over and talk to 'em."

Sally and Haxton introduced themselves. The missing boy was named Andy Coleman, and his parents were Paul and Elizabeth Coleman.

"I just ... I just can't believe this," Elizabeth sobbed, with tears streaming down her cheeks. Her husband, meanwhile, just stood there in silence, trembling, with a thousand-yard stare in his vacant eyes, looking utterly shellshocked. "I can't believe he's gone ... I can't ... believe ... my boy ... is gone."

"The kid went out to use the bathroom halfway through the movie," Kosinski explained to Sally and Haxton, "and he never came back. After fifteen minutes, they tried calling his phone, which was dead at that point, switched off. The father then went to the men's room to look for his son and found it was empty. That was when they called the manager. They searched all the bathrooms in this place and everywhere else. At that point, the manager shut off all the movies being screened, and then they started to search the individual theaters. When they couldn't find anything, they called us."

"Gareth, you speak to the parents," Sally said. "I'm going to go find the manager."

"Sure thing."

Sally found the manager outside. Mitch Wakefield was a tall, rail-thin rake of a man. In his late thirties, he was prematurely graying, with a full head of mostly gray hair with only a few strands of brown in it. He was chain-smoking cigarettes, and his yellowed fingers and stained teeth immediately told Sally this was something he regularly indulged in.

"Mr. Wakefield?" Sally asked as she approached him.

He dropped his cigarette onto the sidewalk, stubbed it out, and then exhaled a lungful of smoke before nodding. "Yeah, that's me."

Sally introduced herself and asked a few questions about what Wakefield and his staff had done to search for the missing boy. The topic she wanted to get onto as quickly as possible, though, was that of security cameras in the movie theater.

"Sure," Wakefield said, "we've got 'em everywhere. What business doesn't, these days? I already checked all the feeds, though. We don't have any footage of the kidnappers taking the kid out of the theater or anything. Hell, it's like the kid just vanished into thin air, like he was beamed up into a UFO by freakin' aliens or something."

"You don't have cameras in the bathrooms, do you?"

"Nope. We do have 'em just outside the bathrooms, though."

"And is there footage of Andy Coleman entering the bathroom?" Sally asked.

Wakefield nodded. "Yeah. We got that on camera. It's like his parents said, he went out to the bathroom around halfway through the movie they were watching."

"So in the footage, you can see Andy going into the men's bathrooms, but you can't see him coming out? And did anyone else enter the bathrooms after he did?"

"That's the crazy thing, the real crazy thing," Wakefield said, scratching his head vigorously, his brow furrowed deeply with confusion. "The kid never came out of the bathroom, and nobody else went in, not a single person— not a janitor, not a customer, nobody. It's like the kid flushed himself down the damn toilet or something! I don't know. Maybe I'm hallucinating or losing my mind from panicking about this situation, but I watched the tape over and over again, and that's what happened. The boy went into the bathroom, and he just never came out … and nobody entered the bathroom after him, not until his father went in when he went looking for him."

"That does sound very strange."

"Come with me," Wakefield said, jamming his cigarette pack and lighter into his shirt pocket and turning and striding toward the back door of the movie theater. "I don't know, maybe I'm going blind, or I'm crazy or something, but I want to show you the footage, just to check that I'm still sane, because this doesn't make an ounce of sense to me."

Sally followed him to the movie theater's security office. This was the third security office she'd been in in recent days, and she was now accustomed to the sight of a whole bunch of monitors spread across the entirety of a wall.

A young security guard was sitting at the control desk, and he gave Wakefield a respectful nod. He and Sally quickly introduced themselves to each other, and then Sally sat down at the table to watch the footage.

The guard played the footage from the camera outside the men's bathroom for Sally, and it was exactly how Wakefield had described it. Andy Coleman went into the bathroom, then simply never came out again. Nobody else went in after him, not until his panicking father rushed into the bathroom fifteen minutes after Andy had gone in.

"Okay, so, you're seeing this, right?" Wakefield said, shaking his head with both frustration and disbelief. "I'm not crazy, right? You're seeing what I'm seeing—the kid goes in, then he just … ups and vanishes into thin air or disappears down the damn drain or something! You saw that, right?"

Sally leaned in and peered more closely at the screen. "Play it one more time for me, please, but slow it down to half speed," she said to the security guard.

"Sure thing," he said.

They all watched the screen, keeping their eyes locked

on it as the scene played out. After Alex entered the bathroom, the security guard was about to pause the footage.

"No, let it keep playing, please, right up to the point at which Andy's father comes in," she said.

"All right," he said, and he let it play on.

"I don't get it," Wakefield said. "What are you looking for? We've already seen that nobody else enters the bathroom until the dad shows up."

With her eyes locked on the screen, Sally held up a hand to silence him; she couldn't afford to break her concentration at this point. Her focus was razor-sharp, and after a couple minutes, she finally began to nod slowly.

"What, you picked up something?" Wakefield asked incredulously. "What am I missing? Am I seeing things? Or, rather, *not* seeing things? I don't get it; I don't get it at all."

"I don't get it, either," the security guard said. "I didn't see anything, either."

"That's because you weren't looking for the right thing," Sally said. "But I know what happened now. I know exactly what happened to Andy Coleman and how he disappeared from this bathroom."

19

"Now I know I must have lost my mind," Wakefield said, shaking his head. "How does an eight-year-old boy vanish as if he freakin' evaporated like mist? What am I not seeing here?"

"Rewind to a minute after Andy enters the restroom," Sally said to the security guard, who did this. "Now, pay close attention to the lower-left corner of the screen," she said. "Play the footage, please."

They watched this section of the screen as the footage played out. After a few seconds, there was a brief flicker of light in the bottom corner of the screen as a moth flew in front of the camera.

"Is that what we're supposed to be looking at?" Wakefield asked. "A moth? Seriously? What does that have to do with anything?"

"Now fast forward to the point we stopped before this," Sally said to the guard, ignoring Wakefield. "Keep your eye on the same corner of the screen."

The guard did this, and they saw the same moth flying in the corner of the screen.

"I still don't get it," Wakefield grumbled. "So there's a moth flying around the camera, so what?"

"The moth's flight pattern is exactly the same, Mr. Wakefield," Sally said. "This tells me one thing: the footage was looped. That moth didn't fly in front of the camera a second time; if it had, its flight pattern would have been different. The odds of it having exactly the same flight trajectory are lottery winning odds. And, what's more, the kidnappers have used this exact method before. They hacked into the aquarium's computer network and looped camera footage so they wouldn't be caught on it. Someone *did* enter the bathroom right after Andy, and they knocked him out and carried him out—it's just that the camera didn't catch it because it was hacked."

"Son of a bitch," Wakefield murmured, his jaw-dropping wide open with shock. "Wait right here, I need to get hold of my IT people right away!"

"It's too late now," Sally said with a sigh. "These guys are good; they don't leave behind any traces. The only thing you can do is strengthen your network protection to stop it from happening again."

"You think they hacked all the cameras?" Wakefield asked. "The whole system?"

"Since we don't seem to have any footage of anyone carrying a child—or a child-sized package—out of the building, then yes, I assume they hacked all of the cameras. All of the cameras that would have caught them, anyway."

"Dammit, I can't believe this," Wakefield muttered, still utterly shocked. "These are some seriously devious, sneaky, sly bastards, huh?"

"Yes, they are," Sally said. "But we're going to catch them," she added resolutely. "I promise you, we're going to catch these people."

"I sure as hell hope you do, not only for the sake of rescuing those kids. This is gonna do some serious damage to the business here. Nobody's gonna want to bring their kids to a movie here knowing that they might get abducted by a couple of psychos!"

"Like I said, we're going to do everything we can to catch these people."

Just then, there was a knock on the door. "Sally, are you in there?" It was Haxton.

"I'm in here, Gareth," she answered. "Come on in."

"One of the employees saw something," he said as he opened the door and entered the room. "One of the kids selling popcorn. He saw a delivery guy from—guess which company—going in the direction of the bathrooms right around the time Andy was abducted. He was carrying a box large enough for a child to fit in, and he had the same box with him when he left a few minutes later."

"I'm guessing he matched Peter Aling's physical description?" Sally asked.

Haxton nodded. "Down to a tee," he said. "I'm almost one hundred percent certain it was Aling."

"Can I talk to the witness quickly?" Sally asked.

"Be my guest," Haxton said.

"I'll talk to you later, and thank you for your help, both of you," Sally said to Mr. Wakefield and the security guard as she left the office with Haxton.

Haxton took her to speak to the witness, a lanky teenage boy with mousy-brown hair and a bad case of acne. He was wearing thick glasses, which immediately made Sally wonder about just how accurate his sighting of Aling—if it had been Aling—had been.

Gareth introduced Sally to him, and then she began asking the young man a few questions about what he had seen, probing for finer details.

"I don't get why you're asking him all of these questions," Haxton grumbled. "We should be racing to get to Aling's girlfriend, that tattoo artist, and hoping like hell we find him at her place or that she's at least able to tell us where he is. I've already established that this kid saw Aling. I don't know what more you want from him."

"Just a few details," Sally said. "I just want to make certain."

"Fine, whatever, but make it quick," Haxton muttered.

Sally turned back to the young man. "Did you notice if the delivery guy had any tattoos on his arms?" she asked.

The teenager shrugged and looked doubtful. "Uh … I think he might have had one or two, but I don't really remember."

"And how tall would you say he was?"

"I, uh, I guess average height? Maybe a little shorter."

Sally frowned; that struck her as a little odd. The homeless man outside French's place—who Sally was sure had definitely seen Aling—had described him as being six

153

foot or six foot one. Now this kid was saying that he was on the short side of average...

"Would you say he was six foot tall?" she asked the kid.

He shook his head. "No, definitely shorter than that."

"Look," Haxton said, butting in, "the delivery guy had a short beard, shoulder-length blond hair, and some tattoos on his arms, and he was wearing coveralls with the Thor's Hammer logo on 'em, right, son?"

The teenager gulped and nodded. "Yes, sir," he said.

Haxton shook his head and glared at Sally. "See? That's all you need to know to know that it was freakin' Aling. So what if this kid thinks he was, I dunno, five foot ten, and maybe he's actually six foot? He matches the description in every other way! I think it's time to just leave it, now, Sally; we need to get our asses into gear and find Aling's girlfriend. She's the only link we've got now to find him."

Sally realized that was true, and even though she had some niggling doubts about the abductor perhaps not being Aling, she knew there wasn't much to be gained from further questioning of this young man.

"Thank you for your help," she said to him. "All right, Gareth, let's go find this girl and hope like hell she leads us to Aling."

"*A*re you still going to pretend to be a client to try to subtly extract some info out of Layla?" Gareth asked as he and Sally drove to the tattoo parlor where Layla Hedges worked. "Or should we just walk right up to her and threaten to slap some handcuffs on her wrists unless she answers our questions? Personally, with how time-sensitive everything is, I'm in favor of the latter."

"Let me try the client approach first," Sally said. "I know we're pressed for time, but if she is hiding Aling, or even if she simply knows where he is, she might send him a message or some sort of signal to run the moment she catches sight of a police badge."

"Hmm, I guess you're right," Haxton admitted, somewhat reluctantly. "But we can't waste too much time, so don't go in there and talk her ear off."

"Don't worry, I'll get to the good stuff as directly as I can without arousing her suspicions," Sally said.

While Haxton was driving, Sally did a few social media searches for people who had tagged Layla Hedges. She found a number of tattoos the young artist had done recently and picked one from around a year prior, a beautiful phoenix and flames design she had tattooed onto the thigh of a woman named Penny Hamilton, who, according to her social media profile, was the same age as Sally.

"All right, I've got my cover story ready," Sally said to Haxton. "We're around three blocks away. You can drop me here to make sure nobody in the parlor sees that I just stepped out of a police cruiser."

"You don't want me any closer?" Haxton asked. "I can't get to you right away if there's any trouble."

"I don't think there'll be any trouble," Sally said. "And if there is…" she lifted her jacket and showed Haxton that her pistol on her side, easily accessible in case of an emergency.

"All right. Well, don't take too long. If she's being evasive or wasting your time, gimme a call, and I'll come in with the badge and the handcuffs."

"Actually, I'll give you a call right now," Sally said. "I'll leave my phone on inside my pocket so you can listen in on everything that goes on."

"Good idea," Haxton said.

Sally dialed him, and when he answered and got the call started, she shoved the phone into her pocket and then got out and walked the three blocks to the tattoo parlor briskly. When she arrived, she found that it was a fairly upmarket kind of place, which came as a relief, as it made her cover story more believable. If it had been some cheap, nasty, back-alley parlor, she doubted Layla would believe someone like her could be a genuine client.

When she walked into the small, cozy space, she saw a male tattoo artist busy tattooing a full-color sleeve onto a hulking biker's left arm. Neither man looked up or acknowledged her presence, but after a few moments, a pretty young woman, covered head to toe in colorful tattoos, with shoulder-length hair dyed blood-red, emerged from the back room.

"Hi," she said, beaming a friendly, welcoming smile at Sally. "Can I help you?"

"You're Layla, right?" Sally asked, returning the young woman's smile.

"I am, yeah. What can I do for you?"

"My friend, Penny, got a beautiful tattoo here last year. I don't know if you remember her? Penny Hamilton. The tattoo was a phoenix with flames."

"Yes, of course, I remember!" Layla answered, beaming out a smile of pride. "That's one of my favorite pieces. Are you wanting something like it?"

"Yeah, I am," Sally said. "I've got some scarring on my belly from my c-section when my son was born, and I've always sort of wanted to get a tattoo to cover it up, but I've always been a little nervous about the whole thing. I don't like needles much, nor pain. But I've been seeing Penny pretty often, and every time I see the beautiful tattoo you did for her, it just makes me want to get one more. And now … well, my birthday is coming up, and I think I owe myself a very special gift this year."

"Oh, wow!" Layla said, beaming with delight. "Well, why don't we go sit down and look through a few designs, and I can talk about the whole tattoo process. It's not nearly as scary as you might think."

They sat down and chatted about tattoos, designs, and the whole process, and Sally could see she was winning the young woman over and gaining her trust. She figured it was okay to start gently probing her for information about Aling.

"The only problem I'm still not sure I can overcome is my boyfriend," Sally said. "He's not too fond of tattoos on women. You've got a lot of ink on you—what does your boyfriend think about it? You must have a boyfriend, a pretty girl like you?"

Layla chuckled softly. "I do, and thankfully he likes my tattoos. If he didn't, we'd never have hooked up in the first place, though; I can tell you that. And if he ever changed his mind about it, he'd be out on his ass in the street looking for a new place to live faster than you can say 'tattoo.' He knows how passionate I am about my ink and my art, and he'd never cross me on it."

"Ah … you're a lucky girl to have such a supportive man," Sally said. "I don't think my boyfriend would kick me out of my place if I got a tattoo, but I know he'd have to take some time to get used to the look of it."

Inside, Sally was excited, but she dared not show it. She had just managed to subtly extract some important information from Layla: the fact that Aling lived with her.

She had no doubt that Haxton had picked this up, and he was surely radioing the station to get Layla's address.

She didn't want to make things too obvious and alert Layla to the fact that she was actually probing her for information, but she needed some more details about Aling—namely, where he might hide if he was in trouble.

"It's your body, Sally, and you can do whatever you want with it," Layla said. "You don't need no damn man's permission to put some ink on your skin."

Sally chuckled. "Oh, I know, and if my boyfriend had something nasty to say about it, I'd do the same as you and kick his ass out. Only thing is, I don't think he'd really care! He's got a buddy's place he stays at pretty often … we, uh, we have some pretty big fights sometimes. He knows he's always got a place to crash when he needs one."

"If I ever kicked my man out, I don't know where he'd stay!" Layla said with a laugh. "Although, you know what, maybe I do … he's a hunter, his whole family is into it—and, go figure, I'm a vegetarian, so you can imagine how well I get on with them—but they've got a cabin up in the mountains that he goes to with his brother to shoot deer during hunting season. He'd probably just go camp out in that damn cabin and be happy to not have me nagging him about dishes in the sink and dirty socks all over the damn floor! You know what guys are like."

Sally laughed, again disguising the sense of triumph she was experiencing at having successfully extracted some additional useful information about Aling. "I sure do know, Layla. I sure do know."

Now she needed to get out of there as quickly as she could without arousing Layla's suspicions about her true intentions. She got back onto the topic of tattoo designs and pretended to be interested in a few examples Layla had shown her from the book of artwork they were paging through. After Sally had pointed out a handful she really liked, she told Layla she would think about which one she wanted and make a booking for the next few days.

She said farewell to Layla and left the studio, doing her best to avoid breaking into a sprint in her eagerness to get to Haxton. When she was a block away and out of sight of the parlor, she started running and arrived at the car breathless from the effort.

"Nice work, Sally, very nice work," Haxton said. "I've already got all the info we need from your little subtle questioning session there. I've got two units on the way to her apartment, although I doubt Aling is dumb enough to be in such an obvious place."

"And where are we headed?"

"To his brother's office downtown," Haxton said. "My bet is that Aling is hiding out in the family hunting cabin in the mountains. I called the boys at the station, and it didn't take too long to find out who his brother is. Arthur Aling. He's a bookkeeper for a small firm downtown."

"Well, what are we waiting for?" Sally asked, feeling hopeful about this new development, especially after all the setbacks and adversity they had faced in this investigation up to this point. "Let's go!"

"Damn straight," Haxton said, stomping on the gas

pedal. "With any luck, we'll find that scumbag hiding out in his mountain cabin. And if we're even luckier, we'll find all the missing kids there, too!"

"Fingers crossed, Gareth," Sally said, praying that this was finally the lead they needed, "fingers crossed."

hen Sally and Haxton arrived at the office building where Arthur Aling worked, they went straight to the floor where his firm's offices were. They headed into the reception area, where they found a bald, rotund man in his sixties having a heated argument with someone on the phone while his secretary, a nervous, mousy-looking woman in her forties, looked on helplessly.

Haxton stood in front of the main desk, folding his arms across his chest and looking imposing. Both the bald man and his secretary immediately took notice of the two detectives, especially when Haxton, stony-faced, flashed his police badge at them.

The bald man yelled a few final insults into the phone and then slammed the receiver down with such force that Sally could have sworn it rattled both the walls and the floor.

"Are you ready to say hello to us now, pal?" Haxton asked dryly.

The secretary gulped nervously and cowered—the bald man's angry outbursts were clearly a regular occurrence here—but instead of yelling, he held his breath, closed his eyes, and took a few moments to calm himself before speaking to the detectives.

"Yes, Officer?" the bald man finally said through clenched teeth, his face still glowing red with barely suppressed rage. "What can I do for you?"

"We need to speak to Arthur Aling. He works here, right?" Haxton asked.

"Yes, he does, but you can't speak to him right now, I'm afraid."

"Why not?" Haxton demanded. "Where is he?"

The man shrugged. "I was hoping you two could tell me. He got a call from someone earlier, then he got up from his desk and took off. He told Shirly here," the man said, jerking his thumb in his secretary's direction, "that he'd be back in ten minutes. That was over three hours ago. We've tried calling his home phone and his cellphone, but the man is nowhere to be found. God knows where he's gone or what he's gotten up to, but he's left me with clients breathing down my neck! I'll wring *his* fucking neck if he dares to show his face around here again, I can tell you that!"

A wave of disappointment crashed against the detectives. They had been hoping this was the last step they would have to take in order to finally corner and trap Peter Aling, but now it looked like they would have to jump a few more hurdles to get to them. They got Arthur Aling's phone numbers, address, and contact information from his boss and then left, feeling somewhat dejected but remaining determined to pursue every lead they had.

"Man, every time we get somewhere—or, rather, almost get somewhere—another obstacle gets thrown into our paths," Haxton grumbled as they headed back to his car. "I guess now our only option is to try old man Aling and see if he knows where either of his sons is. Or, better yet, he can give us directions to that hunting cabin the mountains."

"Let's split up," Sally said. "We have to go past the station anyway to get to Arthur's address and his father's address, and I can pick up my car. We can save valuable time that way."

"All right. It's a good idea since we're running out of daylight. Let's do this."

As they were driving back to the station, they got a call from the officers who had gone to Layla's place to see if Aling was there.

"There's no sign of him," the officer said. "We staked out the place for an hour, and we asked the neighbors, but he's not there, and nobody's seen him around there since he left for work this morning. We've left some plain-clothes officers in a civilian car there to maintain surveillance, but I don't think Aling is gonna be heading back to his lady's place anytime soon."

"All right, thanks for the update," Haxton said. "Another dead-end," he muttered to Sally.

"I'm not surprised, though," Sally said. "He knows

we're after him, and I'm sure he expected we'd figure out he was living with Layla pretty quickly. Still, it's worth maintaining 24/7 surveillance of her place; he might have something valuable there that he'll try to sneak back in to retrieve."

"Sure, he might," Haxton said. "I'll make sure there's at least one plainclothes unit outside her place around the clock."

When they got to the police station, Sally got into her own car and punched Aling's father's address into her navigation system. Haxton, meanwhile, headed off to Arthur Aling's address to see if he could find him there.

The father of the two missing Alings—James Aling— lived on a homestead a couple miles outside the city. By the time Sally got to his place, it was already late afternoon. Finding the gates to the property open, she drove up the long, bumpy driveway to the house, a small, cozy-looking building nestled among a number of tall trees.

Just as Sally was about to get out, two large dogs rushed out of the house and raced over to the car, barking and snapping. The look in the animals' eyes wasn't too friendly, and Sally figured it might be safer to wait in the car until their owner came out.

James Aling emerged from the house a few moments later. A tall, well-built man who carried himself with a ramrod-straight back despite being close to seventy, he had neatly-cropped, snow-white hair and a bushy, gray beard. He stared with undisguised suspicion in his eyes and an unfriendly scowl on his face as he approached Sally's car.

"You know this is private property, right?" he asked coldly as he stepped up to the driver's side window. "What are you doing here?"

Sally showed him her police badge through the window. "I need to talk to you about your sons. Could you put your dogs inside, or at least on a leash so I can get out and talk to you?"

"My boys? Peter and Arthur?" he asked, still suspicious. "Why do you need to talk to me about my boys?"

"One of them is a wanted suspect in a kidnapping case involving multiple children, and the other seems to be on the run and might be involved, too—or, at least, he's helping his brother to evade justice. I know that that's not what any parent wants to hear about their children—believe me, I have a son myself—but that's the truth, Mr. Aling."

James Aling's frown intensified. "Are you serious? My boys, involved in kidnapping children? That can't be right. That can't be right at all," he said, shaking his head. "You people are mistaken. My sons would never be involved in anything as horrible and as heinous as that."

"I hate to say it, Mr. Aling, but all the evidence we have is pointing to this being the case. I'm sorry … but it does look like your sons may be involved in kidnapping children, or at least in assisting someone else who's kidnapping children."

James opened his mouth to speak, but no words emerged. He shut it again after a few moments and nodded slowly, the look of cool anger on his face giving way to a more shocked expression, one of disbelief and sadness. He seemed to deflate, and his proud shoulders slumped. He nodded, then whistled to his dogs, who obediently came over to him.

"Come on, Rex, come on, Bluto," he muttered to the two big hounds, who seemed a lot less aggressive now that they were under his control. He wearily led them into the house and shut them in.

"It's safe to get out of your car now, ma'am!" he yelled out to Sally. "Come on over here. We can talk on the porch. The dogs can't get out, don't worry."

Although she still felt a little nervous about the possibility of the dogs somehow breaking out of the house and attacking her—Sally had always been nervous around big dogs, after being bitten by one as a small child—Sally got out and walked over to the porch, where James Aling was standing with his arms folded across his barrel-chest.

"How sure are you that my boys are involved in this … this awful crime?" he asked.

"I'm sorry, but like I said, it seems likely that Peter is directly involved. Arthur, maybe not, but it does seem that he's at least helping to keep Peter out of our hands."

"Peter's been involved in one or two minor things over the years—you know, drunk driving, bar fights, that sort of thing—and he was the kind of kid who was always getting in trouble when he grew up, but he's never been involved in anything serious. And I could never, ever picture him doing something like this. I mean, drunk driving or slugging some idiot in a bar, sure, but kidnapping children? I can't believe it. I really can't believe it."

"And what about Arthur, has he ever been involved in

any criminal activities, got into any trouble, anything like that?" Sally asked.

Frowning, with his face still crumpled into an expression that was half shock, half disbelief, James Aling shook his head. "Arthur's always been as straight as a damn arrow," he said. "Sure, his kid brother got into plenty of trouble when they were growing up, but Arthur? He was always such a good kid. Never got so much as a library fine for an overdue book. I just … I'm shocked, I just can't believe Arthur, of all people, would have anything to do with anything as horrible as this."

Sally found herself pitying the elderly man. She put herself in his shoes and wondered how she would react if police officers came to her house in twenty or thirty years and told her that Derek had been involved in such an awful crime. She knew that if such a thing happened, she would be shaken to her core.

"I don't know much about Arthur," she said, "but I doubt he's involved directly. In fact, he probably doesn't even know what Peter was doing; Peter probably just told him something vague about being in a lot of trouble and needing to lay low for a while. Arthur was probably just being a good big brother and doing what he thought was best for his kid brother."

"I see … I see," James murmured, still looking completely shocked. Then, however, his expression hardened, and his eyes gleamed like cold nuggets of iron ore. "Well," he continued, "if that younger son of mine *has* done something so stupid, so terrible, he's no son of mine, and he deserves to rot in a prison cell. I expect you came here to see if I might know where he may be hiding out?"

"That is why I came here, Mr. Aling, yes," Sally said.

"I know exactly where he's likely to be hiding out," James said. "We've got a hunting cabin in the woods. I think Peter and Arthur may have gone there."

"Could you tell me where it is?" Sally asked.

"I'll do you one better than that," James said. "I'll drive you there myself. Wait here … I'm gonna get the keys to my truck."

22

Sally waited on the porch while James Aling retrieved the keys to his truck from inside the house. For a few seconds, she wondered if he could be trusted—was he really going inside to get his truck keys, or was he actually grabbing a firearm? He was clearly a man who loved his sons fiercely, and she knew well what lengths a parent would go to to defend their offspring from any perceived threat.

She quickly pushed those thoughts out of her mind, though. Her gut instinct hadn't given her a single bad vibe about James Aling, and although his personality seemed somewhat abrasive and standoffish, there was nothing menacing or sinister about him.

James Aling returned a short while later with a set of keys in his hand. "Come on, Detective, follow me," he said, his face a mask of grim determination. "He may be a grown man, my Peter," he muttered as he strode purposefully toward the 4x4 truck parked around the side of his house, "but so help me God, if he really has been involved in something as monstrous as kidnapping children, I'll tan his damned hide until I draw blood … and only then will I turn him over to the law."

"Are you sure you want to do this?" Sally asked as they headed toward the truck. "As a parent myself, I understand the distress you're in, and—"

James held up his hand to silence her. "I don't need your sympathy," he said. "If my boy has committed a crime, I'll be the first to tell the judge to lock him up for as long as it takes. I won't be happy about it, sure, but I'll know that I've done the right thing. Blood or not, criminals deserve to rot behind bars."

"I appreciate the sentiment, but you could just give me directions to the cabin," Sally said.

James took a look at her sedan and chuckled humorlessly. "That city car of yours won't make it up to the cabin, trust me. Unless you wanna waste time going back to town to hire out a 4x4, I suggest you come with me."

"All right. Thank you for doing this."

They climbed into James's truck, an old but well-maintained vehicle from the early nineties. The motor roared to life healthily as soon as James turned the key in the ignition, and they set off, driving down a dirt road behind his property.

"I just … I can't imagine Peter doing something like this," James muttered as he drove. "I know he always gets into trouble, but it's never been anything … *evil* or *malicious*. Why would he get involved in something like this? Why?"

"We don't know what the kidnappers' motives are at this stage, so I can't answer that question," Sally said. "We're hoping that Peter will be able to shed some light on why these boys have been abducted."

"He won't be able to talk too good with a broken jaw," James growled through clenched teeth, his fingers clasping the steering wheel with a white-knuckled grip. "I'll knock his damn teeth out myself if he really was involved in this."

The drive into the mountains was a long and bumpy one, and dusk was falling by the time they reached the trailhead that led to the cabin. James parked the truck, and they got out.

"It's another hour's hike from here," he said. He grabbed two headlamps from inside the truck and tossed one to Sally. "Put this on; you're gonna need it."

Sally slipped on the headlamp, grateful for the illumination it provided against the intense, almost suffocating darkness of the mountain forest, which was coming alive with the sounds of the creatures of the night. Although she knew she was likely safer out here in the middle of nowhere than she was on city streets after dark, she was glad she had her pistol with her. As she followed James down the hiking trail, she unzipped her jacket so she had quick and easy access to the firearm.

"That damn kid has gone too far this time," James muttered as they trudged along the rocky trail, their headlamp beams blazing swathes of white light through the blanket of intensifying darkness. "If he really has done these terrible things … man, I'm gonna kick his ass. I'm gonna whip his sorry ass!"

The hike felt as if it was taking forever, and the deeper Sally got into the mountains, the more nervous and anxious she began to feel. She hadn't picked up any dangerous or suspicious vibes from James at all, but she knew that truly capable psychopaths were skilled when it came to deceiving people and lulling their victims into a false sense of trust and security. What if James Aling was in on the whole thing, working with his sons on the kidnapping operation, and he was just leading her out here to kill her?

Sally's surroundings only amplified her growing paranoia, and her heart began to thump with great, rib-rattling beats in her chest while her blood turned to ice in her veins. She forced herself to fight through this increasingly paralyzing sense of fear, using her logic to scythe through the thickening fog in her mind.

She had a gun that she could grab in the blink of an eye, and she was behind James. These two things alone already put her at an advantage. He hadn't brought any firearms or weapons with him—and she had given him a thorough if subtle visual investigation to make sure he didn't appear to have any concealed weapons on him—so if he truly were planning on trying to hurt her, he would have a difficult time doing it.

Reminding herself that she had the advantage here, Sally forced herself to calm down. She focused on her steps, on the trail, and just moving forward while leaving a respectable distance between her and James, just in case…

It felt like they had been hiking through most of the night when finally, in the distance, they saw a single light in the vast darkness of the woods.

"There it is," James said. "That's our cabin. And it looks like someone's in it."

Sally quietly took her pistol from its holder on her side and cocked the hammer. They walked cautiously down the steep, rocky path that led to the cabin. When Sally got closer to the building, she saw a simple and rustic log cabin. The drapes were drawn across the small windows, but lamps were lit up within, and smoke was curling in a lazy, undulating tower from the chimney.

Now her heart began to thump with a different sensation: excitement and anticipation. Peter Aling had to be in here, and she was about to catch him. But would she find the kidnapped children, too, or was this yet another dead-end?

There was only one way to find out.

"Here we are," James said as they walked up to the door. "You can bet your ass that one or both of my boys are in there."

"Let's go in and find out then."

23

*S*ally's heart was pounding so rapidly when James opened the door that she thought it might explode. In front of her, James stormed in, his temper flaring.

"Peter!" he roared, the vociferousness of his shout rattling the walls. "You idiot, you shit! What have you done?"

Sally came in behind him and saw Peter Aling scrambling up from the sofa he'd been lounging on, his eyes wide with shock and disbelief. A few beer cans, some full, some empty, were scattered around him on the floor, and his eyes were bleary with drunkenness.

"D-dad, what are you d-doing here?" Peter slurred, stumbling back in confusion as his father lunged for him, grabbing the collar of the plaid shirt he was wearing. "Wh-who's that?"

"Peter Aling, you're under arrest for suspicion of the kidnapping of a minor and for aiding and abetting the kidnappers of a minor," Sally said coldly, aiming her pistol at him with one hand and flashing her police badge at him with the other.

James Aling, meanwhile, shoved his son up against the wall, his fists grasping his son's shirt with a white-knuckled grip, his eyes bulging with rage as he got his face right up in Peter's.

"Kidnapping children, Peter, kidnapping innocent children?" James roared into his son's face, flecks of spittle flying from his wide-open mouth. "What the fuck are you involved in? How could you do something like this? How could my own son do something like this?"

"D-dad, I, d-don't know what you're t-t-talking about!" Peter spluttered. "I didn't k-kidnap anyone!"

"We'll let a judge decide that," Sally said, tossing a pair of handcuffs to James. "Put these on your son, Mr. Aling," she said.

"You no-good scumbag, you piece of trash, you've gone too far this time. You've gone way too far this time!" James growled, forcing his son to turn around so that he could put his wrists in the handcuffs.

"I didn't do it; I didn't k-kidnap anyone!" Peter protested.

"Charlie French did, and you helped him evade justice," Sally said. "We have evidence that you helped him to escape his apartment building in an empty fridge box. And what about Julian Drake? Do you know anything about his whereabouts?"

"Julian who? I don't know any Julians. I swear to God I don't!"

"What about Charlie French? You certainly seem to know him pretty well."

"F-French was involved in k-kidnapping kids?" Peter spluttered. "I d-didn't know, I s-swear to God I didn't know! I just th-thought he was in trouble for d-dealing weed. I th-thought that was all he did!"

"If you thought he was wanted for a relatively minor crime," Sally said, "then why were you so afraid of being caught that you switched vehicles with Zeke Ebrahim earlier? And why do we have witness reports placing you at a movie theater earlier today at the exact time that a child was kidnapped there?"

"I d-didn't—" Peter began.

"You've got a lot of explaining to do, boy!" James growled. "You'd better spit it out, and you'd damn well better tell the truth, or I'm gonna break a few of your lousy bones before I turn you over to the cops, you hear me?"

"Dad, please, I s-swear I didn't know about no kids. I didn't know! I th-thought it was just w-weed!"

Sally stepped in closer and lowered her firearm. She knew now that Peter Aling wasn't a danger to her—and, what was more, her gut instinct was informing her that he was telling the truth. Even though all the evidence appeared to point to Peter being one of the kidnappers, niggling doubts about his guilt had remained at the back of her mind, and now these doubts felt as if they were growing larger and more insistent.

"James, sit him down on the sofa, please. I'd like to ask him a few questions before we take him in."

"With pleasure, Detective, with pleasure," James growled, still fuming and burning with anger, his face red and his jaw clenched tight. He grabbed his son by the collar of his shirt and shoved him onto the sofa, kicking the empty beer cans out of the way as he did. "You damn well sit there and answer her questions, and if I think you're lying, I'll kick the living shit outta you, boy, you hear?"

"Y-yes, Dad," Peter stammered, his face pale and his eyes wide.

Sally took a seat on a wooden stool across from the sofa and fixed a cool stare into Peter's eyes. "You need to answer these questions with complete honesty, Peter," she said gravely. "As you have no doubt realized, you're in a lot of trouble. Helping me out here with some honest answers won't get you out of it, but it will lessen the amount of trouble you're in. Do you understand?"

Peter gulped and nodded slowly.

"All right, so let's start at the beginning," she said. "Why did you smuggle French out of his apartment in a refrigerator box?"

"My boss told me to," Aling said. "He s-said he owed French a favor and that French was in t-trouble with the cops for selling weed. He a-asked me to smuggle him out of the building in an empty fridge box."

"Did he arrange for you to pick up the fridge box from Al's Appliances?"

Peter shook his head. "No, I d-did that on my own. My boss—"

"Just to be clear, we're talking about Karl Nordstrom here?" Sally asked.

Peter nodded. "Yeah, Nordstrom," he said. "He just told me to find a good, sturdy box somewhere and to get it fast. And he t-told me not to let anyone know what I was d-doing. I know they always have fridge boxes at Al's, so I went there and spoke to one of my buddies, m-made it sound like it was an official job."

"Do you have any proof that Nordstrom instructed you to do this?" she asked. "Text messages, a phone call, email, anything?"

"I don't have anything. He took me out into the parking lot and made me leave my phone inside," Peter answered. "He told me all of this in person and told me not to repeat it to anyone, or I'd get fired."

"Okay, so before this, you'd never met Charlie French, and you didn't know who he was?" Sally asked.

Peter shook his head emphatically. "No, ma'am. I'd never seen French in my life before I picked him up. Didn't know who he was or what he did, except for dealing weed and him being a friend of Nordstrom's. I did think it was weird that a guy like French, living in a d-dump like that, would be a friend of my boss, who's rich and stuff, and hangs out with people at, like, golf clubs and fancy restaurants. But I got the sense that Nordstrom didn't want me asking too many q-questions, so I just did what he told me to do."

"What happened when you got to French's apartment? Was anyone else there besides him? Any children?"

Again, Peter shook his head. "No, ma'am, it was just

him. He knew what to do, and he was expecting me. I helped him get into the fridge box, he took a b-backpack with him and a box with some computer stuff in it, and then I closed up the box, wheeled it out of the building, and put it in my v-van."

"Are you sure there were no kids in his apartment?" Sally asked.

"I can't be one hundred percent certain," Peter answered. "But I can tell you that in the sh-short time I was there, I didn't s-see or hear any kids or any other people there, only French."

"Okay. Now, tell me where you took French."

"There's a gas station near the depot," he said. "Nordstrom told me to stop there and get French out. I did that, and I don't know where he w-went after that. He c-called a cab, got in, and that's the last I saw of h-him. I-I didn't know he was kidnapping kids, I s-swear to God. Seriously, I would n-never have helped him if I'd known. Nordstrom told me it was just w-weed, and since I b-buy and smoke it myself, I didn't think it was a b-big deal. But you g-gotta believe me, I didn't know anything about the kids. I swear on my life; I'll swear on anything you want me to swear on."

Sally believed he was telling the truth. However, there were still a few more details she needed to find out more about.

"All right," she said, "I believe you. But what about this whole swapping trucks with Ebrahim thing, and then running away, and what about these reports of witnesses who saw you at the movie theater shortly after ditching your truck—the same movie theater from which a child was abducted? What's your explanation for this?"

"First, I didn't go to any movie theaters, I p-promise you that. Whoever said they saw me there is straight-up lying. I got a message from Nordstrom on my ph-phone telling me to swap trucks with Ebrahim. He told me the cops were onto me and that he couldn't help me out. He could only buy me some time. He said to s-swap trucks with Ebrahim, do his delivery, then d-ditch the truck and get out of town and lay low for a while. He said I needed to keep quiet, not tell anyone, not even my g-girlfriend, where I was going. I was s-scared, so I did everything he s-said. I ditched the truck, took a c-cab to my brother's office, and asked him to d-drop me near the trailhead so I could h-hide out here for a while."

"Did your brother know why you were in trouble?" Sally asked.

Peter shook his head. "I only told him it was drug stuff."

"All right. I have one more question for you. This may not seem to be too relevant to what we're discussing, but how tall are you?"

"Uh, I'm six foot one; why?"

That was the final piece of information Sally needed. She was now convinced that someone had framed Peter for the kidnapping of Andy Coleman, and she was sure she knew who it was.

24

"I believe you," Sally said. "You weren't at the movie theater, but someone *was* who was doing their best to look like you."

Peter's face crumpled into a frown of confusion. "What? You mean ... someone was trying to frame me, to make it look like *I* was the one who kidnapped this kid?"

She nodded. "Yes, I'm pretty sure that's what happened."

"Who? And why would they have done this? Why me?" he demanded.

"The same person who's been manipulating you from the start," Sally said coolly. "Karl Nordstrom. Why? Well, clearly because you're a little gullible, Peter, and because you seem to do whatever he tells you without asking too many questions."

Peter stared at the ground with a sheepish look on his face, his cheeks aglow with embarrassment. "I uh, I guess you're right about that," he murmured.

"Don't think you're getting let off the hook, by the way," Sally said sternly. "Just because you didn't know you were aiding and abetting a couple of kidnappers, you nonetheless *did* help them—and you knew you were helping a wanted felon evade justice, even though you thought he was 'only' a weed dealer as if that isn't much of a crime."

"You hear that, boy?" yelled James, who had been stewing in angry silence throughout the questioning session. "You knew what you were doing was wrong, but you did it anyway! You're gonna take whatever punishment the law gives you, and you're gonna take it like a man. If you don't, whatever they dish out to you is gonna *pale* in comparison to what *I'm* gonna give ya, I swear to God!"

"Yes, sir," Peter murmured, his eyes downcast and his voice barely clearing a whisper.

"I could have a word with the judge and maybe get your sentence reduced to a year of community service, something like that," Sally said, "if you cooperate fully, and if we can prove you helped French to escape because you only believed he was a weed dealer, not a kidnapper. I'm not making any promises, but I'm just saying I might be able to make things go easier for you if you cooperate fully."

"I promise you I'll d-do that, ma'am," Peter said, staring at Sally with sincerity and conviction in his gaze. "You just tell me what to do, and I'll do it."

"Well, you can start by handing over your phone," Sally said. "It sounds like you at least have one or two items of evidence on there—the message from Nordstrom telling you to swap trucks with Ebrahim, for example."

Peter let out a long sigh and shook his head. "I don't have my phone. Nordstrom told me you guys would use it to track me, so I had to get rid of it. He said the safest thing was to throw it into the river outside town, so I did that."

"That's unfortunate," Sally said. "Without that message, it's going to be a lot harder to convince a judge that you were manipulated into doing what you did by Nordstrom."

"Shit … I wish I hadn't done that," Peter muttered.

"It's been done, and there's nothing we can do about that now," Sally said. "Hopefully, Ebrahim will be willing to testify that he saw a message from Nordstrom on your phone. That might work in your favor. Is there anything else that you can think of that might help to prove that Nordstrom manipulated you? Any witnesses who could corroborate what you've told me, any security cameras that might have captured footage … anything?"

"I … I really don't know, ma'am," he said.

"Okay. Well, thank you for cooperating, at least … but I'm going to have to arrest you now and take you in."

Peter sucked in a long breath and then exhaled slowly as he nodded, an expression of deep sadness and resignation coming over his face. "All right, ma'am. I understand. I'll come with you. I won't cause any trouble."

"You'd better damn well not, boy!" James growled. "And so help me, God, if you *ever* get yourself involved in anything like this ever again…"

"Trust me, Dad, I won't," Peter murmured.

They extinguished the camping lanterns and the fire in the fireplace, then James locked the cabin, and the three of them started the long hike back to the trailhead. While they were walking through the dense darkness of the forest, Sally gave Haxton a call and told him what had happened. She didn't go into detail about her theory that Nordstrom was one of the masterminds behind the kidnappings and that he had framed Peter Aling; that was a conversation she needed to have in person rather than over the phone.

The hike back to the car was a lot less tense and anxious than the hike to the cabin, but it required a lot more exertion because much of it was uphill. Finally, they reached James's truck at the trailhead. Sally felt as if it had to be around midnight, and she was relieved that her son was staying at his father's house tonight. When she checked her phone, though, she saw it was only 9 pm.

"Get in the damn truck," James growled at his son.

With his head drooping with shame, Peter climbed into the truck, sitting between James and Sally. The long drive back to James's place was silent and uncomfortable, and when they finally made it back, Sally was extremely relieved to be out of the car.

"You want me to drive him down to the station for you, Detective?" James asked.

"I don't think that will be necessary, thanks," Sally said. "You're going to cooperate, and you're not going to cause any trouble, are you, Peter?"

"I'm going to cooperate, ma'am," Peter said sincerely. "I won't cause no trouble, I promise you that."

"You'd better not," James growled, anger still simmering in his eyes. "You've already done enough dragging of our family name through the mud."

"Yes, sir," Peter murmured, wilting in the face of his father's wrath. He was sobering up now and feeling a sense of guilt and shame more intensely than ever.

"Thank you so much for your help," Sally said to James as she helped Peter, who she kept handcuffed, with his wrists behind his back, into the back of her car. "It would have been much more difficult to find that cabin without you."

James shook his head and let out a long sigh. "I'm happy to have helped, Detective, but I just wish I hadn't had to go there to pick up my son for yet another felony charge. If that boy doesn't straighten himself out after this…" he growled wordlessly and balled his hands into fists at his sides.

"Don't worry, James, I think this time he may have learned his lesson. Thanks again."

Sally and Peter drove into the city to the police station in silence, and when she finally handed him over to some of her fellow officers for processing, a wave of intense exhaustion and weariness crashed against her. For the last few hours, it felt as if she had been running off adrenalin alone, having barely had a bite to eat or a drop to drink since before lunch. Now she could finally go home and rest.

Haxton was at the police station when she brought

Peter Aling in, and Sally chatted briefly with him about her theory that Nordstrom was one of the masterminds behind the kidnapping.

"I don't know about that, Sally," Haxton said doubtfully. "But you've been right about stranger things before, so I'm not gonna write it off. So what should we do, bring him in for questioning?"

"He's very sly and very crafty, and I think we need to get some solid evidence lined up before we bring him in," Sally said. "Right now, all we've got is Aling's word against his, which isn't going to hold up in court. We also need to keep Aling's arrest secret for now; if Nordstrom knows we've got Aling, he'll quickly figure out that Aling will spill the beans about him. That'll either get him on the run, or it'll mean that he hides the kids somewhere we'll never find them. No, right now, we need to quietly, subtly investigate Nordstrom and make him think that we're still looking for Aling."

"Yeah, I think that's the best way to go about this," Haxton said. "We'll start first thing in the morning; I think we both need a good, long rest at this point."

"I agree," Sally said. "I'm beat. I'll see you first thing tomorrow, Gareth."

Sally left the station, got into her car, and set off to drive home. She was so tired that she pretty much went on autopilot, barely able to concentrate properly on the drive.

And thus, she didn't notice that a car started following her and stuck on her tail for a few miles … and she also didn't notice until it was too late when a pair of bright headlights appeared out of nowhere to her right, when a truck came blasting out of a side street at speed, hurtling directly toward her.

She was barely able to slam on her brakes, yank on her steering wheel, and let out a scream of terror before the truck T-boned her.

There was an explosive impact, a burst of blinding light behind her eyes accompanied by a percussive bang and the sickening sounds of twisting steel and shattering glass … and then everything went black.

25

"Ma'am, are you okay? Can you hear me? Are you okay? Say something, ma'am; say something!"

Sally groaned as she opened her eyes. Her head was throbbing with a sharp ache, and her mouth was filled with the metallic taste of blood. She found herself swimming in a sense of intense confusion and disorientation, and she had no idea where she was, what had happened, or how she had gotten there.

A stranger was yelling in her ear—he sounded traumatized. She still couldn't figure out what was going on, only that she was in her car. The airbag had been activated, and its gray mass in front of her face was all she could see. She reached down with trembling hands, fumbling to undo her seatbelt, and she felt broken chunks of window glass all over her lap.

"Ma'am, can you hear me?"

"I ... what happened?" Sally managed to groan.

"Thank God. Thank God you're alive!" the man said. "Hold tight, okay, don't move … an ambulance is on the way. And so are the cops. Just hang in there; the ambulance is on its way."

"Who … are you?" Sally croaked, turning her head to look up at the man.

She saw that he was an elderly black man, attired in a security guard's uniform. The gleaming, polished steel of a revolver in his hand caught her eye, and she noticed a subtle wisp of smoke curling from the barrel—the gun had recently been fired.

"I'm your guardian angel, ma'am, I'd say!" he said, smiling. "God must have put me here tonight to save your life!"

"I … don't understand," Sally groaned.

"Some car—a big truck—it just came blasting outta nowhere and T-boned you bad. I saw the whole thing from across the street there, where I was walking home from my shift at the jewelry store in the mall. I had to stay late today, y'see, because the owners was getting new stock in. They always do it late after hours, you know, to lower the chance of getting robbed. And that's why I say I gotta be your guardian angel, sent by the Lord above himself! If this had happened on any other day but today, I wouldn't have been out this late, and you'd be dead right now."

"I still … don't understand," Sally said.

"Well, after the guy in the truck plowed into you, another guy jumped out of the truck with a shotgun in his hands. He was running around to the front of your car, looking like he was gonna blast you with that shotgun right through the windshield. I didn't even think; I just reacted; I whipped out my trusty .38 and started shooting. I don't think I hit the bastard, but I did scare him off before he could pump you full of buckshot! He jumped back into the truck, and they high-tailed it outta here while I emptied my revolver at 'em."

Sally was still awash with confusion, but she understood that this stranger had saved her life from what appeared to be an assassination attempt. "Th-thank you," she managed to croak. "Thank you ... so much, sir."

He placed a hand on her shoulder and gave it a gentle, reassuring squeeze. "I'm just glad I prevented a murder tonight. Praise the Lord, ma'am, praise His name!"

"Praise the Lord, and thank you, sir ... thank you," Sally murmured, and her sentiment was genuine. Her mind was starting to become more lucid now, and goose bumps tingled all across her body as she realized just how close she had come to dying. Or, rather, to being murdered.

It was no coincidence that this had happened right after she had brought Aling in. Aling was the key to establishing Nordstrom's guilt, and clearly, Nordstrom was a far more dangerous and ruthless man than she had realized.

The wail of sirens, faint in the distance a few moments ago, became steadily louder, and soon Sally could see them flashing their bright blue and red luminescence through the night.

"They're coming down the street now, ma'am. I can

see 'em; they're almost here!" the security guard said. "You're gonna be okay. Everything's gonna be all right."

Following an extensive checkup in the hospital, Sally was discharged after a few hours. She had a few bruises and lacerations and a minor concussion but no broken bones or internal wounds. The doctor who examined her said she had been lucky. If the truck had hit her car a few inches to the right, or at a slightly higher speed or at more of an angle, her injuries would have been a lot worse, and indeed, the initial impact could have been fatal.

Haxton, who had arrived on the scene and questioned the elderly security guard, waited in the hospital for the doctors to finish examining Sally and then drove her home when she was discharged.

"You're welcome to stay at my place, Sally," Haxton said as they left the hotel parking lot. "My wife loves you, and we've got two spare beds now that the kids are away at college."

"Thanks for the offer, Gareth," Sally said, "but I'll be okay on my own."

"Sally, someone tried to kill you a couple hours ago," Haxton said, his usual abrasive tone replaced by one that was far gentler and more sympathetic. "Are you sure you're gonna okay on your own?"

"I refuse to let these scumbags intimidate me," she said resolutely.

"Well, I'm gonna get some men to stay outside your place all night," Gareth said. "You'll be protected … but I still think you'd feel safer at my house."

"I really do appreciate the offer," Sally said, "but trust me, I'll be okay."

"All right. Just know that my door is always open for ya, Sally," he said. "And I'll make sure there's a unit outside your house every night from now until this case is closed, and whoever is behind the kidnappings—"

"Nordstrom is behind them," Sally said confidently. "I'm absolutely certain of it."

"You think? I mean, he was at his business when Andy Coleman was abducted; we have irrefutable evidence of that, so there's no way we can link him to that kidnapping. As for the others, I suspect he's got some sort of solid alibi, too. I don't know, Sally, I just wasn't picking up any sort of a guilty vibe from the guy, none at all."

"Well, *I* was," Sally said, "and I'm pretty damn sure it was him who almost put a hole through my chest with a shotgun earlier."

"We'll look into that, don't worry," Haxton said. "But don't convince yourself of anything before we have the evidence to back it up … as a veteran detective, you should know this as well as I do."

"All right, Gareth, okay," Sally said wearily. A wave of sheer exhaustion had just crashed against her, and she was in no mood to be arguing now. All she wanted to do was get home and sleep.

While they drove, Haxton arranged for some cops to be stationed outside her house, and a cruiser with two men in it was already parked in her drive when they arrived. Grateful for the protection, Sally thanked Haxton again, then went over to the cops in the cruiser and thanked them for their help. After that, she stumbled inside, had a quick shower, and then flopped into bed, passing out moments after her head hit the pillow.

She felt as if she had barely slept when the piercing clamor of her alarm clock jolted her out of her deep, dreamless sleep.

"The concussion probably helped with that," Sally groaned as she struggled to get out of bed.

After she had woken up, she called her ex-husband and spoke to Derek. Although she desperately wished to be with her son, she figured it would be safer for him if he continued to stay with his father for a while, at least until she had this case wrapped up and Nordstrom behind bars. If Nordstrom was willing to kill her as well as kidnap children, she guessed that he would be willing to murder an innocent child, too.

"I'll come to see you after school, okay, pumpkin?" she said to her son on the phone. "We'll hang out later."

Both Derek and his father were okay with him staying there a while longer, and that brought Sally a measure of relief. After talking to them, she immediately called Haxton.

"How are you feeling this morning?" Haxton asked.

"Like I've been hit by a bus," she answered. "Aside from that, I guess I'm okay."

"Hit by a black Ford F-150, actually," Haxton said. "At least that's what the witness told us. And we did find a piece of broken headlamp at the scene that matches the Ford F-150 part, and there's black paint all over your car in the impact zone, so I'm pretty sure he's right."

"Have you found the truck?"

"We've had an APB out on the vehicle since the incident," Haxton said, "but we haven't found anything yet. The security guard said it had no license plates on it, so I think it's safe to assume that unless we get really lucky, we're not gonna find it."

"Yeah, I guess not. Forget about that for the moment, though. What are we going to do about Nordstrom?"

"Aling's word, although it won't exactly stand up in a court of law to convict him, is certainly enough motivation for us to at least bring him in for questioning. We can head over to the Thor's Hammer depot right away and pick him up."

"Let's do it," Sally said. "I wanna look that dirtbag in his eye … the piece of shit who drove a truck into my car and was about to pump me full of lead last night… I wanna question him myself."

"All right, you can do that," he said. "But first, let's go pick him up."

An hour later, Sally met Haxton outside the Thor's Hammer depot. She fixed a resolute stare into his eyes, which he acknowledged with a determined nod.

"You ready?" he asked.

"You bet I am," she answered.

They walked in—and as they did, the terrible cacophony from the warehouse started up. The secretary, who was scrambling to put a pair of sound-canceling earmuffs on, looked surprised to see the two detectives when they walked in.

"Hello, Detectives!" she yelled over the clanging racket. "What can I do for you?"

"Is your boss in?" Haxton yelled back.

"Yes, he is. I'll go get him," she yelled.

Both Haxton and Sally had their hands clamped over their ears to try to block the horrendous noise. Sally was half expecting Nordstrom to flee out the back, but sure enough, he emerged from the offices a few moments later, walking behind his secretary.

"Ah, Officers!" he yelled, smiling, although the look in his eyes was as cold as that of any reptile's. "What can I do for you? Perfect timing, I'm afraid—that damn compressor is acting up again, as you can hear!"

"We need to question you in connection with the kidnappings, Nordstrom," Haxton said gruffly. "You can cooperate and do this easy way, or you can make things difficult for yourself and do it the hard way. Which is it gonna be?"

From the moment Nordstrom had appeared, Sally had been staring at him with an icy, accusatory glare. For all the fury in her gaze, though, Nordstrom seemed entirely unaffected by it and showed no signs of guilt or nervousness. Instead, he was as solid and as confident as ever.

"I'll make it easy," Nordstrom said with a smile. "Obviously, we can't do it here with this noise, so I'll accompany you back to the police station. But do you mind if I bring a hard drive with me?"

"You stay here," Haxton said. "Get her to get it for you," he added, nodding in the direction of the secretary."

"Of course," Nordstrom said.

He gave his secretary some instructions, and she hurried off to Nordstrom's office, returning a few moments later with a portable hard drive in her hands. She gave it to Nordstrom, and he shoved it into one of his pockets.

"I'm ready now, Detectives," he yelled over the racket. "You can take me in."

26

*A*lthough Sally was tempted to begin questioning Nordstrom as soon as he got into the back of Haxton's cruiser, she waited until they returned to the station. She wanted to make him sweat, but despite all her subtle attempts to intimidate Nordstrom, he remained calm and unflappable.

That irked her greatly, but she didn't show it, keeping up an attitude of cool detachment in his presence. She was, at this stage, completely convinced of Nordstrom's guilt. Haxton, however, appeared to still be on the fence about the whole thing.

They got Nordstrom into one of the interrogation rooms, with Sally and Haxton sitting on one side of the table and Nordstrom, who was smiling coldly with his arms crossed defiantly across his chest, on the other.

"I'm ready when you are, Detectives," he said calmly. "Let's get this ridiculous shitshow over with so I can get back to work."

"First question," Sally said. "Do you know Julian Drake and Charlie French?"

Nordstrom's poker face was perfect as he answered this question. "I've never met either of those people in my life."

"Really?" Haxton asked, leaning in closer and transfixing Nordstrom with a withering glare. "Your employee, Peter Aling, swears on his life that you gave him the order to smuggle Charlie French out of his apartment in a refrigerator box before we could raid the place. He also says you ordered him to change trucks with Zeke Ebrahim so we wouldn't be able to catch him."

Nordstrom shrugged. "He's lying," he said casually. "There's no way in hell he has any proof to back these ridiculous claims up. I didn't tell him to do any of those things. As far as I was concerned, Peter Aling was engaged in regular deliveries on the day all of that happened."

"So you didn't tell him to pick up French and then change trucks with Ebrahim?"

"How many times do I have to tell you that I didn't, Detective?" Nordstrom asked with a sneer. "Now, if you don't have any proof to back up these fantasies of yours, I suggest you move on to a different set of questions."

"Fine. Where were you last night at around 10 pm?" Haxton asked.

"At home," Nordstrom answered.

"Do you have evidence to prove this?"

"I certainly do," Nordstrom answered smugly. He calmly set the portable hard drive down on the table between them. "All the evidence I need to prove my complete innocence is on here."

"What is this?" Sally asked, barely able to keep the venom out of her voice.

"Have you never seen a portable hard drive before, Detective?" Nordstrom asked with a mocking sneer. "They're very useful items, I assure you—"

"Don't be a jackass, Nordstrom," Haxton growled. "She's asking what's on it."

"Security camera footage from my home last night," he answered smugly. "I've included everything from the time I arrived home from work yesterday evening until the time I went to bed, which was around midnight last night. You'll see that the footage is all timestamped, and the TV shows in the background were freshly aired last night. You can check with the relevant TV stations if you want."

Sally glared coldly at him, but she picked up the hard drive.

"Well, Detectives?" Nordstrom asked. "Is there anything else you'd like to ask me?"

"Do you own a black Ford F-150 truck?" Sally asked. "Or do any of your friends or family members own one?"

"No," he answered, his smile cold and tight.

Sally scrutinized Nordstrom's face. He was a smooth liar—but nonetheless, she was certain she was picking up signs that he wasn't telling the truth.

"Are you sure about that?"

"I said no, and yes, I'm sure about that," he answered.

Sally figured that even if he had braced himself for the

impact, he would have had at least some minor injuries from smashing into her car the night before.

"How's your neck feeling, Nordstrom?" she asked.

He chuckled. "What a strange question, Detective," he said. "I thought I was being questioned by two police officers, not a doctor."

"Just answer the damn question," Haxton growled.

"My neck is perfectly fine, as is the rest of my body," Nordstrom answered, shrugging. "I don't see what that has to do with anything."

"You know exactly why I'm asking the question," Sally said icily, her eyes aflame with cold wrath. "If your neck is so healthy, I guess it won't be much of a problem for you to turn it all the way left, looking over your shoulder, then all the way right, correct?"

"You really are wasting my time now, Detectives," Nordstrom said. "I don't see why—"

"Do it," Haxton growled.

"Fine," Nordstrom said. He turned his neck all the way to the left and then did it again to the right.

Sally observed him closely for any signs that he might be concealing some pain. She thought she picked up a subtle tensing of his body when he had to turn his neck to the right, but he appeared to be as skilled at hiding his pain as he was at lying in her eyes. She wasn't able to conclusively determine whether he was hiding his pain or not, but it seemed to her that he was experiencing some discomfort, although he was masking it incredibly well.

"Are you satisfied now that my neck functions like that of any normal human being?" Nordstrom asked.

"Do you own a shotgun?" Sally asked.

Nordstrom chuckled again and shook his head. "I don't see what relevance that has in terms of what I'm being questioned about. But no, I don't own any shotguns. I have a .45 caliber pistol at home, and that's the extent of it when it comes to firearms."

"We're going to need you to provide solid proof of where you were on these dates, and at these times," Sally said to him, pushing a list of dates and times across the table to him. These were the dates and times of each of the kidnapping events.

"Oh, you'll find all the proof you need for this on the hard drive," Nordstrom said.

"You didn't even look at the list I just gave you," Sally said. "How do you know that you have alibis for dates you're not sure about—unless you already know what time and date each child was kidnapped ... and tell me, Nordstrom, how on earth would you know that unless you were involved?"

If Sally thought she had gotten Nordstrom with that question, she was mistaken.

"I'm a big fan of being as thorough as a man can be, Detective," he said coolly. "There's over two weeks of footage on that hard drive, twenty-four hours for each day from both my home and my business. I don't know exactly when these kidnappings started, but I do remember reading the first news report about that child who was abducted from a museum field trip. And that was around a week ago, or less; I don't know, I can't quite remember. But since you said you'd be questioning me about these kidnappings, I figured I'd better be as thorough as I could be and cover all my bases. So go on, why don't you start looking through that footage right now? You might want to get a team on it, considering there are 336 hours of footage on there, actually, six times that if you consider the fact that there are six camera feeds. But I assure you, you'll find that I have an alibi for any time point you may consider within the last two weeks."

Haxton shot Sally a worried glance. If what Nordstrom was saying about the footage were true, they would have nothing on him at all. Unless evidence could be found that he had instructed Aling to swap trucks with Ebrahim or other evidence came to light that linked Nordstrom to Drake and French, there was no way they could link him to the kidnappings or to the attempt on Sally's life.

"We'll take a good look at the footage," Haxton said.

"Please do," Nordstrom said. "And now, unless there are any other questions you want to ask me, I'd like to get back to work."

Sally was fuming; her gut instinct was screaming out that he was guilty, but if his alibis really were as solid as he was claiming, there was little more they could do at this stage. Haxton looked at Sally, and, with her jaw clenched, she nodded.

"You can go now," Haxton said reluctantly. "But don't think you're off the hook, pal. You'd best stick around; don't go out of town, and you'd better not even think of leaving the state."

"I wouldn't dream of going anywhere right now,"

Nordstrom said smugly. "I have way too much work to cover to even think of taking an afternoon off." He stood up, his mocking smile broadening. "Well, Detectives, it's been a nice little chat, but I really must get going. If you need to speak to me again, you know where to find me."

Without another word, Nordstrom walked briskly out of the room.

After he had left, Haxton turned to Sally. "What do you think?"

"I think he's guilty."

"And if his alibis are as strong as he's saying they are?"

Sally sighed. "Then I don't know, but I know he's guilty, Gareth, I just do. You know my gut instinct; it's never wrong about these sorts of things."

"You say that, Sally," Haxton said with a weary sigh, "but nobody's infallible, and there's a first time for everything. I think—and it pains me to say this, it really does—but maybe, just maybe, you're wrong about this suspect."

2 7

Sally was incensed at this comment, but she restrained herself from reacting with anger, for the logical part of her mind understood that Haxton was right. Aside from what Aling had told them, there was no evidence against Nordstrom, and Sally was certain he wouldn't have handed over all the security footage so willingly unless it proved his apparent innocence. Regardless of how guilty she felt she knew Nordstrom was, proving it with evidence that would convince a judge was another matter entirely. And just because he could prove where he was didn't mean he wasn't involved, just that he wasn't present at the scene of the crime. But Sally held her tongue.

"We'll see about that," was all she could say to Haxton without completely losing her temper. "But we can't afford to mess around here, Gareth. Three kids are still missing, and every day that goes by without finding them … you know what that means."

"I know, I know," he said grimly. "The chances of finding any of 'em alive just keep getting smaller. Don't worry, Sally, I don't intend to sit on my ass here. All I'm saying is that you need to accept that despite what your gut instinct might be telling you, maybe Nordstrom isn't involved."

"What about what Aling said? He said the message to swap trucks came directly from Nordstrom, as did the order to sneak French out of his apartment inside a refrigerator box."

Haxton shrugged. "Who knows, Sally? Aling could be lying to cover his own ass. It's the first thing half these perps do when we get 'em into in interrogation room. You, of all people, should know that. They're willing to throw anyone under the bus if it means that they get to keep their own asses out of the slammer."

Sally sighed. The anger was still seething within her, but she did her best to calm it. "I know, Gareth, I know … it's just that my gut instinct was telling me so strongly that Aling was innocent and that Nordstrom was guilty."

"I get that. I really do," Haxton said. "I mean, sometimes my own gut instinct is seriously strong about a suspect's guilt or innocence … but often, it's just plain wrong. Don't get so wrapped up in your gut instinct that you lose sight of the fact that *evidence* is the bottom line. I'm saying this to you not only as a fellow detective but also as a friend, Sally. I know last night was a frightening and traumatizing experience, too, even if you can't remember much of it. And maybe you feel okay physically, but the doctor *did* say you have a mild concussion, and even minor head injuries can seriously affect your judgment and your cognitive abilities."

Anger flashed across Sally's eyes, and it burned hotly in her cheeks. "What are you trying to say, Gareth?" she demanded. "That you think that I'm wrong about Nordstrom because I've got fucking brain damage or something, that I'm making all of this up like some hallucinating junkie or something?"

"No, no, that's not what I'm saying at all," Haxton said cautiously, regretting his earlier choice of words. "I'm just saying … maybe you're not at the top of your game at this very moment, after having been in a pretty major car wreck a couple hours ago. Maybe you need some time to rest and recover for a little. You've been burning the candle at both ends on this case for a while now, and that, combined with what happened last night … look, I'm not trying to criticize your capabilities, Sally. You and I both know you're one of the best, no, no scratch that, *the* best detective on this squad. Seriously, you are. But everyone goes through rough patches, no matter how good they are."

Anger continued to simmer in Sally's core, but she knew Haxton was probably right. She had been pushing herself extremely hard since the kidnappings had started, and she had barely had any time to rest or recuperate since then. And with someone—perhaps Nordstrom, or perhaps someone else, she was now willing to concede—attempting to kill her the night before, maybe she wasn't in the best mental space to be making judgment calls.

"All right," she muttered. "Fine, maybe you're right."

Admitting this felt like admitting defeat, like acknowledging weakness, and she hated to do either of those things. However, she had to acknowledge that Haxton had a point.

"Why don't you take the rest of the day off, Sally?" Haxton suggested. "I'll put a team together to go through the footage Nordstrom just gave us, and I'll make sure they go through every reel with a fine-toothed comb."

"Make sure they look for signs of looping, like what was done by French, or whoever hacked the security camera networks in the museum, the aquarium, and the movie theater."

"Of course, of course," he said. "And I'll interrogate Aling again, myself this time, to see if he really is telling the truth about not knowing anything about the kidnappings."

"I don't think that's necessary," Sally said. "I already—"

"I know you did, but we have to be thorough here," Haxton said. "I do think it would be helpful to at least talk to him again. I'm not saying he's guilty—I'll let the evidence make that call—but maybe there's something you missed when you spoke to him. Maybe he'll remember some detail that'll prove to be important. Who knows? I just think it's a good idea to talk to him again."

"All right, you do that then," she said.

"You go home and rest. It's Friday; hang out with your son when he gets home from school, have some fun, just try to get your mind off of all this crap for a while."

"But those kids are still out there, Gareth, and—"

"And you wearing yourself down to a nub isn't going

to help us find them any faster," Haxton said. "*They* need you to rest as much as you need it."

Sally drew in a deep sigh, which she released slowly from her lungs, and then, finally, she nodded. "Okay," she said. "You're right. You're absolutely right. I do need some time to rest and relax. I'll take the day off and try to get my mind off everything. But if you find anything—and I do mean anything at all—you need to call me right away, okay?"

Haxton chuckled. "Sure. I'll keep you updated. But seriously, go home now; get some rest. Then you can come back and attack this case with more energy than ever, with a mind that's sharper than ever, you feel me?"

"I understand, Gareth, I get it. Don't worry, I'm going. I'll see you later."

Sally left the police station, but she didn't drive home. Instead, when she was a few blocks away, she pulled over to make two phone calls. The first was to her ex-husband, Simon. Although they were divorced, their separation had been an amicable one, and they were on good terms. Sally considered Simon a close friend rather than an ex-husband. They shared parenting duties fairly and rarely argued over Derek.

"Hey, Sally, what's going on?" Simon's familiar voice asked through the speaker as Sally sat in her idling car and watched the traffic on the busy street zooming by.

"I'm taking the day off work," she said.

"Ah. Is that because of what happened last night? How are you feeling about that today, by the way? When I heard about it last night, I was rocked to my core. I barely slept. I'm worried about you, Sally."

"You didn't mention anything about it to Derek, did you?"

"No, of course not. I just told him you were very busy at work like you asked me to."

"Thanks, Simon. I appreciate that. And don't worry about me, I'm fine."

"You wanna spend some time with him today when he gets back from school?" Simon asked.

"That's why I'm calling, yeah. I'll come by when he's there and maybe stay for dinner if that's okay?"

"Sure, no problem."

"Great, thanks. I'll see you this afternoon," Sally said.

She hung up and then dialed another number. This one was the number of a man she spoke to far less frequently. The phone rang for a while, and then a gruff, gravelly voice answered.

"Ant's Radio Hut, how can I help?"

"Anthony, it's me, Sally Lawson."

"Well, well, it's been a while, Detective Lawson. It's been quite a while. Let me guess, you're after some specialty equipment?"

"That's right."

"Another off-the-books surveillance operation, huh?" Anthony asked.

"Correct. I need the same stuff I used last time."

"That's gonna take a few hours for me to put together. I'm not sure if I have all the requisite parts here in my shop. How soon do you need it?"

"I need that stuff by tonight, if possible," Sally said.

Anthony let out a low whistle. "I'm not sure I can have it ready that soon."

"There are lives on the line here, Ant," she said. "Children's lives. And every day that passes without finding them gets us closer to the point at which it's unlikely that we'll find them alive at all."

"Damn ... so this isn't just your usual drug dealer bust, huh?" Anthony asked.

"Not at all. This is serious—deadly serious. Please, I need that stuff as quickly as you can put it together."

"All right, all right, I have some buddies I can get the parts from. I'm having a pretty quiet day at the store here, so I should have a few hours free to put the equipment together. And while I'm happy to help find missing kids, I don't want to get in any trouble with your cop buddies. Same deal as ever, right?"

"Yes, strictly cash, no receipts," Sally said. "Tell me how much it'll all cost, and I'll have the cash ready for you."

"I'll give you a call with the total later," Anthony said. "And we'll meet at the usual spot in the park to do the exchange. I'll let you know when it's all ready."

"Thanks, Anthony. I owe you one."

Sally hung up, stuck her phone into her handbag, and then gripped the steering wheel of her car—a replacement rental since her own vehicle had been pretty much totaled when the truck had smashed into it the previous night— and then she let out a long sigh. She glanced up into the rear-view mirror, and the reflection she saw was a face that was tight with grim determination.

She knew Nordstrom was guilty, no matter how watertight his alibi appeared to be. And since there was no way she could legally conduct the kind of investigation that would prove her theory about him, she had to go off the books.

Sally had no intention of resting on her night off. Instead, she was putting together a plan to conduct an unauthorized surveillance operation, one that she would put into action that very night.

28

*W*hile Sally was spending time with Derek that afternoon, she got a call from Haxton.

"Hey Sally, I'm really sorry to bother you while you're taking time off, but you did want me to keep you updated about the case."

"Of course, Gareth. Thanks for calling. What's up?" she said.

"Well, I put together a team to go over the footage that Nordstrom gave us. I had two people for every camera stream, just to make sure nobody missed a single thing. You know, two pairs of eyes being a lot better than one, when the mind wanders or when there are distractions and stuff, ya know."

"Sure. And what did your team find?"

"Nothing at all," Haxton said. "Nordstrom's alibis are beyond watertight, Sally. He was in his office during every kidnapping—the museum, the aquarium, and the movie theater. And he wasn't making calls to anyone during the kidnappings, he wasn't sending messages on his phone, nothing, he was just doing paperwork in his office."

"Was he on his computer?" Sally asked.

"Not much. He was mostly working with actual paper, on his desk, with a pen … old-school style. A few times, his secretary brought him some more papers, but she just scribbled some stuff on 'em and filed 'em. There's really nothing at all we could pick up. No evidence of any looping of the footage, either, like there was with the videos at the kidnapping sites. And believe me, we looked for evidence of it."

"What about the footage from his house?"

"I've got a team going through that as well right now," Haxton answered. "But it's looking like it's gonna be about as fruitless an investigation as the one we conducted on the office footage. So far, we haven't seen him do anything at his home but walk around, eat, scratch his ass, and watch TV. And he seems to spend most of his time at work, anyway. I don't know, Sally … I understand that your instincts about this guy are strong, but … maybe you just need to let go of the idea that he's involved. Everyone's gut feeling can be mistaken once in a while."

Sally disagreed, but she wasn't going to waste time arguing with Haxton about this now, so she changed the subject. "Okay. Well, thanks for updating me, anyway. How did your second interrogation of Aling go?"

"I'm thinking he's a very good liar. He maintains his innocence, and he insists Nordstrom told him to pick up French and swap trucks with Ebrahim. Even though, very conveniently, he doesn't have any evidence to back up these claims. But yeah, he insists he knows nothing about French and nothing about the kidnappings. I'm keeping him a the holding cell ... I'll try to interrogate him again tomorrow. Maybe use a different approach. I'll get him to crack eventually and make him tell us the truth about him and French, and Drake, too."

"All right," Sally said. She knew that Aling wouldn't "crack" because he was innocent, and there was no way to get an innocent man to admit to committing a crime he had nothing to do with. However, she wasn't going to get into an argument with Haxton over this at this point. "Thanks for updating me, Gareth," she said. "I appreciate that. I hope you have a good Friday night. Talk soon."

"You too, Sally ... take it easy, okay? Just try to rest and relax, like the doctors said you should."

"Sure, I'll do that."

Of course, she had no intention of doing any of that. After dinner, she said goodbye to her son and Simon and then set off for the downtown park, where she would meet up with Anthony to get hold of the equipment for her unauthorized surveillance of Nordstrom.

When she arrived at the meeting spot—a secluded area near the duckpond—Anthony was waiting there. She recognized his short, rotund form in the shadows as soon as she caught sight of a presence there.

"Here you go, everything you need is in there," Anthony said, handing her a small gym bag. "Took me a few hours to put together. I hope it helps find those missing kids."

Sally handed him an envelope with cash in it. Anthony trusted her; he didn't need to count the money. He stuffed the envelope into one of his pockets, gave her a nod and a quick smile, and then he turned and walked off briskly, melting into the dark shadows beneath the trees.

After heading back to her car, Sally briefly checked the bag's contents. In it were night vision binoculars, a thermal vision camera, a directional listening device that allowed the user to listen in on conversations that were well out of range of normal earshot, and a few bugs that could be installed inside a house. There was also a GPS tracker that could be surreptitiously fastened to the underside of a car with a magnet and two tiny cameras that could be hidden inside someone's house and used to spy on them.

Using any of this equipment to conduct surveillance on someone without official authorization could land Sally in very hot water. Indeed, it was not only a risk for her in terms of getting punished, but it also put the investigation itself at risk. At best, evidence obtained by such means couldn't be used in court, and at worst, it could get the case dismissed by the judge, even if it was clear the defendant was guilty. Sally knew that she had to proceed with extreme caution here.

She had to assume that Nordstrom knew what car she was driving—after all, he had known where and when she would be driving and what car she had been driving when he had ambushed her and tried to kill her. Thus, before she had come here, she had returned her rental car, and, in order to throw off anyone who might be following her, she had taken a series of buses and cabs to get to another car rental place, where she had used Simon's credit card to pay. She had borrowed it earlier, saying that she needed to pay some extra bills from Derek's school.

Thus, now that she was on her way to Nordstrom's place, she was at least somewhat confident that he—or whoever he was paying to follow and track her—wouldn't know where she was.

Nordstrom lived in an upscale suburb just outside town. His house—a large, expensive property that wasn't quite a mansion but wasn't far off from being one—was located on a leafy avenue, lined with mature trees with thick foliage. Beneath each of these large trees in the avenue was a thick patch of shadow, and there was one right outside Nordstrom's house. It was a perfect spot to park for the surveillance operation.

Sally wasn't planning on using any of the items that would require her to get inside Nordstrom's house just yet—only if this initial surveillance operation made it clear that he was hiding something big. For the moment, she was content to simply observe him through her night vision binoculars and eavesdrop on him using the directional listening device.

His house was completely dark, and it didn't look like anyone was home. His car wasn't parked in the drive either, so Sally—a veteran of many surveillance operations—got her equipment set up and settled in for what could be a long wait.

After around an hour, though, in her rear-view mirror, she saw a pair of car headlights coming down the street.

She slid down in her seat so her head wasn't visible through the windows, and then she waited with bated breath as the car approached. She could hear the vehicle slowing down as it got closer to her, and by the time it passed her car, it had almost stopped.

Although she was tempted to pop her head up to look, she resisted the urge. She was thankful she did, for she heard the car pulling into Nordstrom's drive. After she heard the sounds of the car engine shutting off, the door opening, and someone getting out, she raised her head a little so she could peek over the dashboard.

And when she did, a surge of excitement fluttered within her—it was Nordstrom. He appeared to be alone, and he walked up his drive to his house without looking around or behind him.

"Now the tables are turned, you son of a bitch," Sally whispered into the dark car as she observed him through the night vision binoculars. "Now it's *me* who's tracking *you.*"

Once he was inside his house, the binoculars weren't much use because all of his drapes were shut. A few lights came on in the house as he moved around. Sally took this opportunity to turn on the GPS tracker and then hurry over to Nordstrom's car to attach the device to the vehicle.

She knelt down to stick the magnet to the underside of his car—a late model Toyota SUV—but just as she was about to do this, she heard the sound of another vehicle coming down the road. It was close, and it was slowing down. It seemed to be coming directly toward Nordstrom's property.

"Oh shit," Sally gasped.

There was no way she could get back to her own car now without being seen, and when she glanced down Nordstrom's drive at the street, she could see the blaze of the car's lights on the street. It was about to pull into this driveway, and she was stuck here out in the open, with nowhere to run and nowhere to hide.

The operation was about to be blown before it had even really started, and Sally was about to find herself in some deep trouble.

29

There was nowhere to hide … except for one place. Sally scrambled under the SUV, only barely managing to squeeze herself under the car when the vehicle pulled into the driveway behind the Toyota.

Sally's heart was pounding in great, booming thumps in her chest, and she was buzzing with adrenalin. She held her breath; in the still silence of the night, she felt as if even the sound of her breathing could give away her presence.

She couldn't see much from here, but she could hear everything clearly enough. Someone got out of the car and walked right past her. She was tempted to exhale a sigh of relief. It seemed her presence hadn't been noticed, but she felt as if breathing audibly right now might give her away, so she kept on holding her breath until the man was well away.

It had been a man—his shoes and pants, which was all she had been able to see of him—had made that clear enough. Sally listened with bated breath as the stranger knocked on Nordstrom's door. The silence of the night, which had been a terrible threat to her just moments earlier, was now something she could see as an ally.

However, her hopes of using this vantage point to eavesdrop on whatever conversation Nordstrom and the man were about to have were quickly dashed. She heard the door open, and no words passed between the two men. Sally heard the man enter Nordstrom's house, and then the door closed behind him.

Wasting no time—she knew the man might emerge from the house in mere moments—she hastily attached the magnetic GPS tracker to the underside of Nordstrom's SUV, and then she hurriedly scrambled out from under the car and dashed back to her own vehicle, with her pulse racing and adrenalin still tingling in her veins.

As she ran silently back to her car, she took a quick look at the visitor's vehicle. It was a newish Lexus sedan, black. She made a quick mental note of its license plate and punched the numbers into her phone to keep a record of it as soon as she was back in her own vehicle.

"All right," she whispered breathlessly to the darkness inside her car, "that was a close call, a very, *very* close call, but I'm okay ... I'm okay."

Although the night vision binoculars weren't of much use at the moment, Sally figured the thermal imaging camera would be. It was a higher spec, more sensitive model than most civilian models—thanks to Anthony's tinkering with it—and it could pick up heat signatures through walls.

She set it up and saw the heat signatures of two figures standing inside Nordstrom's house near the front door. Interestingly enough, the figures were exactly the same size. Whoever this was, he was pretty much a physical match of Nordstrom.

Now that Sally had established the men's positions with the thermal imaging camera, she was able to set up the eavesdropping device, which would only work if it was pointed in exactly the right direction—the direction from which the sound was coming.

She slipped on her headphones and aimed the device's satellite-dish-shaped antenna at the position of Nordstrom and his friend, revealed by the thermal imaging camera.

Although the device was powerful and accurate, the fact that there was a closed door and solid walls between Sally and her targets made it difficult to hear clearly—as did the fact that Nordstrom had music playing in the background.

Nonetheless, Sally did her best to listen in on what Nordstrom and his buddy were talking about.

Nordstrom was speaking, but because of the music in the background and the faintness of the sound of his voice, blocked by the door and the walls, Sally was only able to pick up fragments of what he was saying.

"… can't fail again, because … and if that happens, you know."

"… need to move the merchandise … almost found it … serious fucking trouble."

Sally tried to fine-tune the device to get it to pick up

their conversation more clearly, but all of the dials were already maxed out; as frustrating as it was, this was as good as it was going to get.

"… bitch is breathing down my fucking neck, and," Nordstrom muttered.

Sally was quite sure he was talking about her.

"… take care of her … make sure your alibi is even more solid … trust me, we've got this, brother."

Sally was now certain the men were discussing her, and she was also sure what they meant when they were talking about "taking care of her." They had tried to "take care of her" the night before, and she was sure they wouldn't mess it up again a second time.

"… can't keep the merchandise where it is … too risky."

She wondered whether this "merchandise" they talked about was the kidnapped children. It was more than likely, she thought.

The sound of their voices became fainter, and when Sally checked the thermal imaging camera, she saw they had gone deeper into the house. Now it was almost impossible to make out a word of what they were saying. Sally waited a while longer, wondering if she should stick around or whether she should take off now. Although her car was largely hidden where it was parked, if Nordstrom or his friend noticed it and came to check it out and found her there, who knew what the men would do. They had already proved that they were more than willing to kill her.

As much as Sally wanted to wait and try to do some more surveilling of Nordstrom's place, she was feeling increasingly worried about the risk of getting caught by him or his friend. After a minute or two of agonizing over the decision, she decided to leave. She had already seen and heard more than enough to prove that Nordstrom was up to something shady. She hoped that this would be enough to convince her superiors to authorize an official surveillance operation.

She started up the car and drove away quickly, simultaneously relieved and disappointed to be abandoning her task.

When she was a couple miles away, she pulled into a gas station so she could park for a while and call Haxton. She knew he wouldn't be happy about what she had done, but she had to tell him what she had discovered.

When he answered his phone, his hoarse voice and somewhat confused tone made him sound as if he had just woken up. "Sally, what's going on? Are you okay? Jeez, what time is it?"

"It's not that late, Haxton," she said. "But that's not the point. Don't worry, I'm okay. I've got some news about the investigation."

"News? What news?"

"I ... I did something that I maybe shouldn't have, Gareth," she said cautiously. "But it yielded some good results."

"Huh? What are you talking about? I don't like the sound of this."

Sally had known that he wouldn't be happy about what she had done, but she had to tell him everything. "I knew you wouldn't be too pleased to hear this, but I did some surveilling of Nordstrom's place tonight."

"What? Are you insane, Sally?" Haxton yelled. Now he was as awake as if someone had doused him with a bucket of ice water.

"I know you're mad, Gareth, but hear me out—"

"Sally, what the hell do you think you're doing? You could have put the entire investigation in jeopardy! If Nordstrom had caught you, or, hell, if *anyone* had caught you—"

"I know how serious the consequences would have been," she said calmly. "Look, just forget about what could have happened for a second, and let me tell you what did happen, okay?"

"I still can't believe you just did that, Sally," Haxton muttered, fuming. "But fine, whatever, go ahead and tell me what you discovered. Jeez, you're supposed to be resting, *resting,* you freakin' maniac, *resting,* not conducting unauthorized and frankly *illegal* surveillance operations!"

Ignoring these remarks, Sally got straight to the point. "A friend of Nordstrom's came to visit him while I was there. I didn't get a good look at the guy, but I did catch his license plate. We need to run it through the system and find out who he is."

"Okay, so, a friend came to visit him on a Friday night," Haxton muttered sourly. "Last I checked, it wasn't illegal for people to have friends over at their houses."

"This guy wasn't just some drinking buddy of his, Gareth," she said. "He's someone who I'm almost certain is involved in the kidnappings."

"And what makes you say that?"

"I didn't hear their entire conversation, but they talked about moving merchandise, getting in trouble if they were discovered, and needing to 'take care of' a certain 'bitch'— and that 'bitch' they were talking about is me."

"It could just be some business associate of Nordstrom's," Haxton said.

"A 'business associate' who happens to come and visit late on a Friday night? That's kind of a weird time to be having a business meeting with a business associate, wouldn't you say?"

Haxton sighed. "All right, all right, maybe you're onto something … maybe. But for God's sake, you need to quit this Batman shit and do things through the official channels, Sally! Even if Nordstrom is our guy, doing what you did could get the entire operation flushed down the damn toilet."

"I understand that; believe me, I do," Sally said. "It just felt as if everyone had completely written off Nordstrom as a suspect … and I couldn't let him off the hook like that; I just couldn't. Not when my gut feeling about his involvement in this whole thing is so strong."

"We'll talk about this in the morning," Haxton said. "Right now, I need you to promise me that you're going straight home and that you're gonna get some damn rest. No more of this vigilante shit, you hear me?"

"All right, all right. I'm going home now."

"I want you to swear to me, on the life of your son Derek, that you're going to go straight home and rest,"

Haxton said sternly. "I mean that, Sally. I want you to swear this to me."

"I swear that—"

"On Derek's life, Sally. I'm serious here, dead serious," he insisted.

"I swear on Derek's life that I'm going to go straight home and get some sleep," Sally said. "There, are you happy now?"

"I ain't happy, no, but that'll do. Now go home, Sally, and get some damn sleep."

Sally smiled; although Haxton was angry, she had expected him to be, and he hadn't blown up with too much explosiveness. And although her unauthorized operation had been extremely risky, she had pulled off one of her main aims, even though she hadn't managed to get any solid evidence against Nordstrom: she had got the sights of her fellow investigators back on him.

"We're onto you, Nordstrom," she murmured as she drove off to return the rental car, feeling exhausted but vindicated. "We're onto you."

30

Sally did what she had promised to Haxton, and after returning the rental car, she went home—where there was a police cruiser parked out front to keep watch over her—and went straight to bed. Her head was still feeling a little fuzzy from the concussion, which helped her fall asleep quite quickly. Again, she had a long and dreamless sleep and only woke up when her alarm clock roused her the next morning.

She didn't waste any time in continuing the investigation. As soon as she'd had a shower and gotten dressed, she gave Haxton a call.

He answered in a more amicable tone than that with which he'd spoken to her the previous evening, although he didn't hide his annoyance with her at having gone behind his back to conduct an unauthorized operation.

"Well, well, if it isn't the renegade," he said when he answered. "I hope you got a better night's sleep than I did after you woke me up in the middle of the night."

"I slept like a baby, Gareth," Sally said, "and now let's cut the crap. Are you at the station yet?"

"Just got here, yeah, and I'm brewing myself a strong pot of coffee, which I sure as hell need after last night."

"Didn't I just ask you to cut the crap? Come on, cut me some slack, I said I was sorry, and I know what I did was wrong."

"Yeah, yeah," he muttered. "All right, forget about it. Why are you calling? What is it that can't wait until you get here yourself and talk to me in person?"

"Did you run Nordstrom's friend's license plate through the system yet?" she asked eagerly.

"Not yet, Sally, not yet. Sheesh, hold your damn horses. Some of us are still trying to wake up here!"

"Can you do it now, please?"

"All right, all right, I'll do it, just give me a minute to sit down."

Haxton sighed, settled down at his desk, and typed the license plate into the system.

"Hey, Sally," he said, "are you sure you gave me the right license plate number?"

"Positive." She read it out to him again.

"Yeah, that's what I put in. What kinda car was it?"

"A Lexus sedan. Black, pretty recent model," she answered.

"Well, the system is showing that that license plate is for a Pontiac that was scrapped over thirty years ago."

"I knew it," Sally said. "I told you there was something fishy going on with Nordstrom. Do you still think he's got nothing to do with the kidnappings, that he's totally innocent? If so, why does he have some guy with false license plates coming to visit him, talking about trouble if they don't move merchandise and 'take care' of the 'bitch' who's 'breathing down their necks,' huh?"

"All right, all right, I'll admit that this is starting to sound pretty suspicious," Haxton said. "Come down to the station, and we'll figure out how to proceed."

"I'll do that. I'll see you soon."

Sally headed down to the station, but just as they were about to sit down and start discussing things, an important email arrived in Haxton's inbox, and the subject of it immediately grabbed their attention.

WANTED SUSPECT CHARLIE FRENCH—POSITIVE ID ON TWO COUNTS

"Whoa, looks like we've had a breakthrough," Haxton exclaimed. He opened the email from an old friend of his who was now a sheriff in a neighboring state, and he and Sally read eagerly through its contents.

Hey there, old buddy,

I'm passing on this news to you as soon as it's come to me. I just received these images from a local Greyhound bus office in our state. These are some very clear images, and I'm pretty sure they show wanted felon, Charlie French, purchasing tickets. We contacted the ticket office as soon as we got these photos, but they have no record of anyone named Charlie French buying any tickets there. That's not a surprise; we can be pretty sure he's using some form of fake ID. Anyway, what the ticket office was able to tell me from the timestamp of the video, is that around the time French was captured on camera, they sold tickets to New Mexico, Arizona, three to Texas, and two to

California. So French could be headed to any of those places, but I'd guess that maybe Arizona or New Mexico could be it, considering the fact that he may be intending to illegally hop the border into Mexico.

Let me know if there's anything else I can help you with.

PS... You still owe me a beer!

Jeb

THEY EXAMINED the attached images from the Greyhound office's security cameras, and both Sally and Haxton were certain that they were looking at Charlie French.

"We need to get hold of that ticket office and cross-reference the names of every passenger that bought a ticket around the timestamp of the images," Sally said. "We'll soon be able to figure out whose names are real and whose name is fake."

"And then we'll know which ticket French bought," Haxton said. "I'll call the ticket office right now."

"If we can catch French, we'll be leaps and bounds closer to wrapping this whole case up," Sally said excitedly. "He could lead us to Julian Drake and anyone else involved, including Nordstrom."

"Yeah, we've got that toy belonging to Dennis Avery that we found in his apartment; he's got no way to weasel his way out of this … if we can catch him. And considering he took the bus last night, depending on where he went, he could be mighty close to getting across the border. If that happens."

231

"We'll never see him again," Sally murmured softly. "And without him."

"The whole case could fall apart. And we may never see those kids again, either."

"One good thing about this, though," Sally said, "is that French clearly didn't have the kids with him. So at least we know that he's not smuggling them out of the country or anything. The kids must still be here, hopefully in this town, or at least this county."

"There is, of course, another possibility," Haxton said darkly. "One that we can't rule out, I'm afraid … and that's the possibility that French didn't take the kidnapped children with him because they're already dead and buried in an unmarked grave."

A surge of intense emotional pain cut through Sally's core. It was so fierce, so sudden, that she almost doubled over. But as quickly as it had slashed at her, it vanished, replaced by a fresh sense of courage and determination. She shook her head. "No, Gareth, those kids are still alive. And that's not just wishful thinking … I *know* they're still breathing; I *know* their hearts are still beating. I don't know for how much longer … but I know that for now, they're still alive. I know you still aren't convinced that Nordstrom is involved, but he and his buddy were talking about moving the 'merchandise,' and I don't think they would be using that term to describe dead children. Those kids are alive, but the clock is ticking. The need to find them is now more urgent than ever."

"You don't need to remind me," Haxton said. "I'll get on the line to the ticket office now."

While Haxton called the Greyhound office, Sally went to get some case files. While she did that, she suddenly remembered the GPS tracker she had put on Nordstrom's car.

"Damn, how could I have forgotten about that?" she murmured to herself. "Must be this concussion, making my memory fuzzy."

Now, though, she regretted not putting it on Nordstrom's friend's car. She cursed herself for committing this oversight and wasting what was surely a valuable opportunity. Nordstrom wasn't likely to drive anywhere suspicious in his own car, but his mysterious associate, whose car had fake plates on it, would surely be driving to important locations—including, very possibly, the place where they were keeping the kidnapped children.

"I can't believe I didn't think of that," Sally muttered, feeling like kicking herself.

"Didn't think of what?" Haxton asked as he put down the phone. He had overheard her mutterings.

She told him about the GPS tracker she had put on Nordstrom's car and the opportunity she had wasted by not attaching it to Nordstrom's friend's vehicle instead.

"Don't beat yourself up about it," Haxton said with a shrug. "Your adrenalin was surging, your heart was racing, you were worried about being caught—as you should have been, considering the fact that you could have blown this whole operation—so you weren't in the right headspace to be making snap judgments."

"I know … I just wish I'd done it."

"Does the GPS tracker record movements as well as tracking them in real-time?" Haxton asked.

"Yeah, it does," Sally answered.

"It might be worth checking out where Nordstrom's been then," Haxton suggested. "Sure, he's very smart and thorough, and I doubt he'd be stupid enough to go anywhere suspicious in his own vehicle ... but you never know."

"You're right. I doubt he went anywhere that would get him in trouble between late last night and now, but I'll check, and I'll keep checking."

At that moment, an email came through from the Greyhound office.

"Here it is," Haxton said, "the list of people who bought tickets during the timeframe French was seen at the office."

"Send me the lower half of the list. I'll check those names, and you check the names from the top half of the list. We can get it done faster like that."

"I've already forwarded you the email. Let's get busy."

Sally hurried over to her computer and got started on checking the list. She ran each of the names through the state driver's license database and quickly found that one of the passenger's names wasn't registered. She ran the name through another few databases and found that it wasn't on any of them.

"I'm pretty sure I've got him," Sally announced.

"Good, because it seems that everyone on my list is legit," Haxton said.

"It looks like he's got a fake ID with the name

Bartholomew Korhonen," Sally said. "And, more importantly, he used it to buy a ticket to Albuquerque, New Mexico. He's going to try to get across the border into Mexico, I think."

"Let me check the Greyhound schedule to find out when that bus is supposed to get there," Haxton said, his fingers dancing hastily across his keyboard. "It's a very long drive, and with any luck, the bus hasn't arrived yet. If that's the case, we can get hold of our compatriots in Albuquerque and have men waiting to arrest that sick son of a bitch the moment he steps off that Greyhound."

"Let's hope so, Gareth, let's hope so."

"Dammit," Haxton muttered, shaking his head. "We're just too late. The bus arrived there literally half an hour ago. Man, if we'd just gotten to the office a little earlier this morning."

"That's okay, that's fine," Sally said. "Even though he managed to get off the bus, he's still got a long way to go to get to whatever spot he's hoping to sneak across the border at. And he's still in Albuquerque somewhere right now. Get their PD on the phone and have them put out an APB for him—both with his real identity and his fake identity."

"I'll do that. With any luck, we can stop him before he gets to the border."

"I'll get hold of the border patrol there," Sally said, "and inform them that a wanted felon is intending to illegally cross the border in the next day or two. It won't be long before every law enforcement officer in New Mexico is on the hunt for French. We'll get him, Gareth, we'll get him."

After Sally got off the phone to the New Mexico Border Patrol, she opened the app on her phone that was linked to the GPS tracker she'd put on Nordstrom's car. She wasn't expecting to find anything of interest on it, but she was surprised to see that he had gone somewhere at two o'clock in the morning.

She checked the location on a map, and when she did, she went straight over to Haxton, triumph blazing brightly in her eyes. "We've got him, Gareth, we've got him," she said.

"What? What do you mean?"

"Nordstrom," she said. "My tracker shows that at around two in the morning, he drove somewhere he had no reason to be driving."

"All right, and where exactly was this?" he asked.

"A condemned tower block downtown, a known hangout spot for drug dealers and gangs ... now tell me, why would a supposedly respectable businessman from a wealthy suburb drive to the most dangerous and sketchy part of town at two o'clock in the morning? There's no way he had any legitimate reason to be there, Gareth. You and I both know that; we know it well."

"You're damn right about that," Haxton said. "And you're right about something else you said: we've got him now. Let's get a warrant for his arrest arranged, and then go pay him a little a visit with a solid pair of handcuffs."

"Hold on," Sally said. "How are we going to justify a warrant for his arrest? Remember, my GPS tracker isn't exactly authorized."

"Shit, yeah, I'm getting ahead of myself here," Haxton said. "All right, well, he used his own car, which has legit license plates, so all we have to do is find some evidence that places his car there last night."

"A witness would be okay, I think," Sally said. "And, even better, some security camera footage from somewhere around there."

"Yeah. Let's take a drive down to the 'hood and see what we can find. All we need is one little item of evidence or one witness willing to testify that they saw Nordstrom there in the early hours of the morning."

They got their things together and got some backup—although the two of them were both fearless officers, they knew it was risky to go into such a dangerous area on their own. Kosinski and another cop got into a cruiser and accompanied them downtown.

The journey there was uneventful, but when they arrived in the rundown neighborhood, an acrid smell polluted the air, and a pall of smoke blanketed the area.

"Ah, smell that!" Kosinski remarked sourly as he stepped out of his cruiser, gripping his pump-action shotgun. "Nothing like the smell of burning tires in the morning, huh?"

The buildings on this block—including the one Nordstrom had visited the night before—were all crumbling ruins, half-collapsed and condemned, covered in graffiti. Burned-out shells of wrecked cars lined the street, and tent camps where homeless people and junkies lived were sprawled out everywhere, including an entire "tent city" under a nearby freeway overpass. Homeless people pushed around shopping carts full of junk, drunks and junkies lay passed out in drug and alcohol-fueled stupors on the sidewalks, and destitute people were gathered around fires in alleys, warming their shivering hands on this chilly morning by the flames that writhed from burning tires and trash.

As experienced as a cop as Sally was, she couldn't help but feel vulnerable and intimidated in an environment like this, especially seeing every pair of eyes here regarded her and her colleagues with an unfriendly and often hateful gaze. Cops were neither popular nor welcome in a neighborhood like this.

"I feel like I could pick up a dozen different diseases just by standing here," Kosinski muttered. "Let's do whatever it is we gotta do as fast as possible, and then get the hell outta here."

"What's the exact spot Nordstrom drove to?" Haxton asked, surveying his surroundings with a steely gaze, his hand resting on the grip of his pistol, which was loose in its holster, ready to whip out at a moment's notice.

"That building over there, according to my GPS app," Sally said, pointing at a huge, crumbling wreck of an apartment building two blocks over.

"Then that's where we're going," Haxton said. "Let's do this."

They left the cruisers and walked toward the massive building, moving briskly and staying alert. A few people hurled abuse at them, and almost everyone glared at them with disgust, distrust, or plain hatred in their eyes, but nobody attempted to cause any trouble. A few men—drug dealers, from the look of it—took off at a sprint as soon as they caught sight of the cops, but the officers weren't interested in them—at least not on this occasion.

When they got to the building, they had a look at its surroundings. Many of the stores across the street from the building were either burned-out shells, gutted by fire or slow rot over the years, or were boarded up, but a few businesses were still open. They were the usual sorts of businesses one could expect to find in a location such as this one: loan sharks, liquor stores, and a small convenience store. All of them had bulletproof glass windows and heavy-duty security. And, luckily for the cops, all of them had security cameras all over the place, too.

"Let's split up to get this over with as quickly as we

can," Haxton said. "Sally and I will do the liquor store and the loan shark. You two check out the convenience store."

"Got it," Kosinski said. He and the other cop crossed the street and headed over to the convenience store while Sally and Haxton entered the liquor store.

A short, slim Indian immigrant in his fifties regarded the two cops with suspicion as they walked into the store. He was positioned behind a thick screen of bulletproof glass, where most of the more expensive liquor was kept on shelves. The shelves in the front of the store only contained the cheapest hooch.

"Did you find robbers?" he asked, scowling.

"I'm sorry, sir, but we're not here about a robbery," Sally said.

"Useless!" the man spat. "Two men robbed my store with guns, pointing guns at my wife, and we can see them on the cameras, all these cameras!" he said, pointing at the security cameras all around the store. "You people came here last week. You told us you would find these men! And now you say you know nothing!"

"I'm sorry you got robbed, pal," Haxton said dryly, "but robberies ain't our department. We're here investigating something else entirely. We need to take a look at your security camera footage from last night."

"Last night? Why last night?" he demanded. "We didn't get robbed last night! When are you going to catch the men who robbed us. When?"

"I'll, uh, make sure my team gets right on it," Haxton muttered, sensing that he needed to at least pretend to offer something in exchange for this man's cooperation.

"I'll tell the captain to put a few more men on the team, all right?"

"I want those men caught and punished!" the man insisted. "This is the fifth time we've been robbed this year! Five times, five times we've had guns pointed at us!"

"We'll make sure the robbery team takes this as seriously as it should be taken, sir," Sally said calmly. "But please, we need you to help us out here. Three young children have been kidnapped, and your cameras may have picked up evidence we can use to catch the men who abducted these kids. Do you have any children, sir?"

Still scowling, the man nodded. "Three," he muttered. "This store is putting them through college in this country ... or, at least, it *would be* if it didn't get robbed all the bloody time!"

"I'm very sorry about the robberies, sir, and I assure you, we'll do everything we can to catch the robbers and make sure it doesn't happen again," Sally said. "But right now, if you could help us find these missing boys, I'd be extremely grateful."

The man let out a long, slow sigh, shook his head, and muttered a curse in his native tongue. However, after that, he nodded. "Fine, you can look at the footage. Come this way."

He unlocked a series of security doors and steel gates and let them into the back of the store. His wife, a plump, nervous-looking woman, was in the backroom, watching a Bollywood show on a small TV. Her husband rattled off a rapid-fire stream of instructions to her in their native language, and she nodded demurely and beckoned to the detectives to enter the room.

"She will show you the footage," the man said. "I need to watch the store."

His wife, who barely seemed to speak any English, showed the detectives two old, dusty computers in the corner and then turned on the monitors. Each screen showed a feed from one of the cameras—one outside the store, the other inside the store. She sat down and got the footage into playback mode and then backtracked it to midnight the previous night.

"We only need to see this one," Sally said, pointing at the monitor showing the outside of the store.

The woman seemed to understand, and she nodded and stepped back, gesturing to Sally that she should take a seat at the computer, which Sally did. The woman went back to her TV show and allowed the detectives to do what they needed to do, uninterrupted.

Haxton came and stood behind Sally, and both of them locked their eyes on the screen as they began to scrutinize the footage.

"He went out at 2 am, you said? Fast forward to around twenty after two," Haxton suggested. "It would have taken him at least twenty, maybe thirty minutes to get here. We already know he was here. All we need is some visual evidence, then we can get that arrest warrant."

Sally did this, and both of them focused intently on the screen. They played the footage, which gave a clear view of the street and a little of the derelict building, in fast forward. Since it was a recording of around two in the morning, there wasn't much going on. A few cars came past, but Sally didn't slow down—she would recognize Nordstrom's vehicle right away.

And then, at the 2:47 mark, she saw it and immediately switched to slow motion.

"That's him. That's the bastard," Haxton muttered. "I'm sorry I doubted you before, Sally. Now I know this guy is a crook."

They watched in suspense as the car slowed down and pulled up next to the sidewalk in front of the derelict building.

"That's it. We've got a shot of his license plate in this frame," Haxton said.

"We need a little more than this, though," Sally said. "Keep watching. Let's see what he does here."

"I know, I was just saying."

On the screen, Nordstrom seemed to wait in his car. They saw a small rectangle of illumination in front of him —he was phoning someone. He appeared to talk on the phone for a few minutes, and then he sat and waited. They couldn't see his face clearly in the grainy footage, but it was obvious enough that it was him.

After a minute or two, a young man who clearly appeared to be a gang member or drug dealer—probably both—emerged from the dilapidated building. He looked up and down the street, scoping his environment out for threats or cops, or both, and then walked over to Nordstrom's car, at which point Nordstrom rolled down his window. The young man handed Nordstrom a brown paper bag, and Nordstrom took it and handed him what appeared to be a wad of cash. The young man flipped through the bills, nodded, and then jogged back into the darkness of the condemned building. At that point, Nordstrom drove off.

"I don't know if this has anything to do with the kidnapping," Haxton said, "but it's pretty damn obvious that Nordstrom is involved in something illegal. I know the guys in the other department working on the drug problem are trying to take down a number of drug dealers who work out of this building. We could tie Nordstrom to that case; it'll provide a valid reason for us to get both an arrest warrant and a search warrant for his home and business premises. Using the search warrant, we could find evidence to link him to the kidnappings."

"And find the missing kids, too, hopefully," Sally said.

"Yeah, let's hope so," Haxton said. "Anyway, get your USB and make a copy of this recording. We've got what we need. Let's get back to HQ and get some arrests issued for this son of a bitch."

$\mathcal{W}$ hen Sally, Haxton, and a number of other cops pulled up outside Nordstrom's house in their police cruisers, with the sirens wailing and the lights blazing their dazzling red and blue luminescence into the leafy suburban afternoon, Sally couldn't deny that she was feeling both a sense of triumph and vindication.

She had an arrest warrant in one hand and a search warrant in the other, and with Haxton and other armed policemen flanking her, she strode confidently up to Nordstrom's door and knocked on it.

"Karl Nordstrom, this is the police! Open up, now!" she yelled.

His car was parked in the drive, and according to her GPS tracking app, he hadn't gone anywhere today, so there was no reason to think that he might not be at home. Speaking of that particular device, Sally intended to quietly and surreptitiously remove it from his car after he had been taken downtown. For now, though, she was focused on getting him into a pair of handcuffs and shoving him into the back of a police cruiser.

After a few moments, the door opened a crack, and she saw Nordstrom's familiar face peering suspiciously out at her. He was dressed in a bathrobe and was barefoot.

"What do you want?" he demanded gruffly. "Have you come here to grasp at some more straws? If you people don't quit harassing me, my lawyer—"

Sally held up the arrest warrant in front of his face, grinning smugly. "We've got a lot more than 'straws' to grasp at, Nordstrom," she said. "Can you read what's on this warrant? You're under arrest. And we have a warrant to search your house. I'm going to need you to step outside, with your hands where I can see them, nice and slow."

"What?" Nordstrom spluttered, his eyes bulging with shock and disbelief as he read the warrant. "This can't be possible … this is … this is bullshit! You can't arrest me!"

"We can either do this the easy way or the hard way, Nordstrom," Haxton growled menacingly. "And trust me when I say that, I really, *really* don't think you're gonna enjoy the hard way."

"This is preposterous!" Nordstrom gasped. "You can't arrest me! What are you arresting me for? You can't just go around arresting innocent people. This isn't, this isn't fucking Nazi Germany!"

"So, it's the hard way then, huh?" Haxton asked coldly.

"You can't do this! You can't!" Nordstrom yelled.

Haxton stepped aside and gave the other officers a

nod. Two burly cops shoulder-barged their way through the half-closed door, knocking Nordstrom to the floor, and they swiftly pounced on him, pinning the struggling man's arms behind his back and clamping handcuffs around his wrists while Haxton read him his rights.

While the cops and Nordstrom were on the floor, Sally stepped over them and walked calmly into his house, conducting a quick cursory examination of the place. When she wandered into his living room, she saw lines of a suspicious white powder lined up on his glass coffee table, along with a rolled-up hundred-dollar bill. There was also other drug paraphernalia scattered around the living room.

"We can add possession of numerous illicit Schedule 2 substances to your charge sheet, Nordstrom," Sally said, tasting a little of the white powder and discovering that it was, as she had suspected cocaine. "Get him out of here, boys."

Once Nordstrom had been bundled into the back of a cruiser and taken away, Sally, Kosinski, and Haxton started a more thorough search of his property.

"Kosinski, you take the garage and the exterior of the property," Haxton said. "Sally and I will search the house."

"Sure thing," Kosinski said.

"All right, Sally," Haxton said. "Let's hope our little stunt pays off. We aren't going to be able to keep him in custody for longer than a night, even with all these drugs in here. It's pretty clear he's a user, not a dealer. If we don't find anything in here that links him to the kidnappings … I hate to say it, but we might be back at square one."

"Oh, we'll find something all right. I'm sure of it," Sally said. "Nordstrom thought he was safe, and he didn't see this raid coming at all. He hasn't had time to hide anything or get rid of any evidence."

They got busy searching the place, tearing it apart. Sally was praying for a discovery like the one they had made in French's apartment, where they had found the action figure belonging to one of the kidnapped boys. Or, if they couldn't find anything like that, she was at least hopeful there would be something that would link Nordstrom to French and Drake.

However, as positive and as hopeful as Sally felt, as the day went on, her hope began to fade, and her frustration started to grow. She had been utterly convinced this operation would yield a game-changing result—if not the discovery of the location of the missing children, then at least some sort of proof that Nordstrom was linked to the kidnappings. However, aside from his obvious penchant for using cocaine, there was no evidence that Nordstrom was involved in any sort of criminal activity.

As for the identity of Nordstrom's mysterious friend who had visited him late at night during Sally's unauthorized surveillance operation, there was simply no trace of the man. There was nothing at all in the house, not a single thing from which they could glean his identity or anything about him. Sally cursed herself for not putting the tracker on the man's vehicle instead of Nordstrom's. Then again, she thought, if she had done that, they wouldn't have discovered that Nordstrom was buying cocaine from a dealer downtown, and they wouldn't have been able to conduct this search.

Although it seemed like they were at least coming closer to catching Charlie French, the other key suspect, Julian Drake—the main suspect in the aquarium kidnapping—appeared to have simply vanished into thin air, somehow teleporting himself to the other side of the planet. There was nothing in Nordstrom's house that gave them any clues to the whereabouts of Drake and nothing that proved that Nordstrom knew him. This was also the case with French—they were not able to discover anything at all that proved that Nordstrom had any connection with the fugitive.

After a few hours of exhaustive searching, Sally, Haxton, and Kosinski all took a break.

"I haven't found a damn thing," Kosinski said. "Aside from a line of coke here and there, this guy's place is as clean as a whistle. There's nothing linking him to the kidnappings, not a single thing."

"Tell me about it," Haxton muttered, shaking his head. "We've been tearing this place apart for hours now, and there's just nothing … nothing at all."

Sally was the most frustrated and disappointed of all of them. She had been so convinced that this operation would yield a major discovery, a huge breakthrough in the case. Yet, it had turned out to be a huge disappointment. She had nothing to say; the look of frustration and defeat on her face said it all.

"What about the guy's work?" Kosinski said. "Let's not

give up hope yet. We still need to go search his business premises, right?"

"The Thor's Hammer depot," Haxton said.

Kosinski chuckled. "That name always gets me, man. Who does this guy think he is calling his stupid delivery company 'Thor's Hammer' anyway? What a joke."

"It's probably down to his Scandinavian roots," Sally said. "His last name, Nordstrom, it's either Norwegian or Swedish. Either way, it's a reference to his Viking ancestors and their mythology, not the Marvel superhero character."

"Ah ... yeah, I guess I should have noticed that with his name," Kosinski said sheepishly. "Still, I think it's a dumb name for a delivery company. Anyway, there might be something valuable there. I mean, didn't you say things were kinda suspicious there every time you two visited, Sally?"

"There was this terrible noise that seemed to mysteriously start every time we showed up, yes," Sally said. "It seemed very suspicious to me."

"Suspicious it was, yeah," Haxton said, "but I'm afraid we can't search the premises at the depot, not with the warrant we currently have. We need to have evidence to charge him with a much more serious crime than drug possession in order to get a warrant approved to search his business premises."

"Then we're probably not gonna find anything tying this asshole to the kidnappings," Kosinski said, his shoulders slumping with disappointment.

Everyone fell silent at this point. There was nothing

much to say about what seemed to be the failure of the operation.

While contemplating this failure, though, Sally glanced up at the security camera and remembered that Nordstrom had given them footage from inside his house to prove his alibi—these cameras rolled twenty-four-seven, and Sally was certain they had to have caught the face of Nordstrom's mysterious friend on them.

"There!" she said, feeling a fresh sense of hope surging through her as she pointed up at the security camera, mounted in the corner of the ceiling of the living room, where the three of them were standing. "The guy who visited Nordstrom last night—these cameras must have caught his face! Nordstrom used footage from these cameras to prove he was at home the whole time, and now we can use them to prove he's guilty."

"Why the hell didn't we think of that before?" Kosinski gasped. "Where's the feed? How do we access the footage?"

"It'll be linked to Nordstrom's computer," Sally said. "But we're not going to be able to get into that without his password."

"Can we compel him to give it to us?" Kosinski asked.

Haxton shook his head. "Getting into his phone or computer isn't covered under this search warrant; it'd only be part of it if he was being charged with something a lot more serious. But we can demand that he shows us the footage to prove his innocence. If he refuses, we can hold him longer and maybe get a more thorough warrant —including permission to access his phone and computer, and possibly his business premises, too—authorized. Either way, it's a win for us. Well done, Sally. I can't believe we overlooked the whole security camera thing."

Kosinski chuckled. "That son of a bitch Nordstrom

"Call the guys at the station, get them to talk to Nordstrom about this," Sally said. "Meanwhile, I'm going to—"

Before Sally could complete this sentence, Haxton's phone started to ring. He held up his hand, gesturing for the others to be silent so he could hear whoever was calling, and then he answered the call.

They couldn't hear what was said, but they could see Haxton's facial expression changing drastically. It was clear that some shocking news was being delivered.

"All right," he finally said. "I understand … thanks for letting me know."

With his jaw set tight and his face grim, he shoved his phone back into his pocket and let out a long, slow sigh while shaking his head.

"What's going on?" Sally asked. "Who was that?"

"That was a cop from Albuquerque," Haxton said. "They found French."

"Shit, well, isn't that great news?" Kosinski blurted out. "We got one of the main suspects!"

"He's dead," Haxton said. "They found him in an alley downtown … bullet to the back of the head."

33

Sally felt as if someone had just punched her in the gut. The news that French—one of the prime suspects and someone who could have led them to the missing children as well as provided evidence to prove Nordstrom's involvement—had been murdered was devastating.

"Shit … now what are we gonna do?" Kosinski muttered. "Next thing we know, Julian Drake will turn up dead, too, and then we've got nothing—no evidence linking Nordstrom to anything except snorting a few lines of coke."

"I'm sure it was Nordstrom's friend who did this," Sally said. "He and Nordstrom must have found out that French was about to get caught. The friend—whoever the hell this guy is—must have arranged to meet up with French, probably on the pretense of helping to get him across the border into Mexico. But instead, he gave him a bullet to the back of the skull to silence him permanently."

"You're sure it was Nordstrom's buddy who did this? I mean, he would have had to drive a long way to have done it."

"Who says he drove there?" Sally said. "We don't know who this guy is. Without any hint of who he might be, no law enforcement agents are looking for him. He could easily have flown there, rented a car, done the deed, and then he might already be on his way back here. Hell, or anywhere."

"Let me call the station, see what Nordstrom said when they asked him to show us the security camera footage from his house last night," Haxton said.

He got out his phone and dialed the station. Sally and Kosinski waited with bated breath for the news about Nordstrom. They both began to grow more hopeful as they observed Haxton's facial expression changing as he listened and nodded. As the person on the other end of the line was speaking, Haxton got out his notepad and scribbled something down. "Uh-huh … uh huh, got it … thanks," he said and then shoved the phone back into his pocket.

"Well?" Kosinski asked. "What did they say?"

"Nordstrom is cooperating. He's given us the password to his computer here, which is linked to his security camera system."

Sally wasn't pleased about this—to her, it indicated that Nordstrom knew there was nothing on the security camera footage that they could use. "Let's not get our hopes up," she muttered. "He wouldn't have been so eager to cooperate if there was anything on there that would get him into trouble."

"We'd better check it out anyway," Haxton said.

They went into Nordstrom's study, and Haxton sat down at the desk and logged onto Nordstrom's computer using the password he had willingly provided. Sally immediately thought it was odd that there seemed to be so few items on his Windows desktop.

"He's probably got another computer he uses for illicit activities," she said. "That's why he didn't care about giving us the password to this one."

"Well, let's take a look anyway," Haxton said. "Here's the icon for the security system."

Haxton clicked on the icon and opened the link. It was easy enough to navigate to the camera feed, so he did that and sought out the footage from the previous night.

"When did you say his buddy got here?" Haxton said.

"It was pretty late, but it was before midnight."

"We'll go back to around ten o'clock then," Haxton said.

There were multiple video feeds, and Haxton brought all of them up on the screen simultaneously. The three cops sat and paid close attention to the videos playing in all four boxes. For a while, they watched as Nordstrom did little more than sit on his sofa and scroll idly through social media feeds on his phone. After an hour of this, however, he got up.

"This is it," Sally said. "This must be when his friend came over. Let's see what this guy looks like."

The security cameras didn't cover the entirety of the

house, only the main rooms. They watched as Nordstrom appeared to walk toward the front door, but then, at the moment when it seemed as if he was about to open the front door, a moth flew in front of the camera and settled on the lens, blocking it completely. After a few seconds, the moth flew away … and Nordstrom was standing near the front door alone. He was talking, but these cameras only recorded video footage, not sound, and it seemed as if he might be talking on the phone rather than to another person. In any case, there was no other person to be seen.

"What the hell?" Sally murmured, staring at the screen in disbelief.

"You, uh, you definitely saw another person come in here last night, right?" Haxton asked.

"I'm one hundred percent sure of it," Sally said. "This guy, whoever he was, parked his car in Nordstrom's driveway, walked past me while I was hiding under Nordstrom's car, and then entered Nordstrom's house. I saw two bodies on the thermal imaging camera—two separate bodies—and I heard two different voices with the audio device."

"This camera, though, is showing us something very different," Haxton said. "It looks like Nordstrom is alone."

"The other guy might be … I don't know, standing in that closet that's just out of view of the camera," Sally said.

"Why would the guy stand in a closet?" Kosinski asked. "That'd be pretty weird."

"I don't know!" Sally snapped. "Maybe because he knew it was a spot the camera couldn't see!"

"All right, all right, calm down here, Sally," Haxton said.

"Well, it sounds like Kosinski is trying to imply that I'm crazy or something," Sally said.

"Hey, hey, I didn't say anything like that," Kosinski said defensively. "I'm just saying it's weird that a guy would go to his buddy's house and then stand in a freakin' *closet* while he's talking to him, okay? Because that *is* weird … very weird."

"Relax, I'm sure we'll see the guy when he leaves the house," Haxton said. "Even if it's a brief glimpse. These cameras cover the front and back doors, and although a stupid moth flew in front of the camera at the exact moment that this guy entered the house, the odds of that happening again are higher than those of winning the damn lottery. Just hang on, you two, we'll see this guy. Sally, you said he came out of the house after a while and drove away, yeah?"

"I guess he did, but I left before he did to avoid being caught snooping around out there."

"Ah … so this guy could have stuck around for Nordstrom's little coke party later in the evening. Let's hope he did because then we'll see his face nice and clear on at least one of these cameras."

They continued to closely scrutinize the footage. Nordstrom walked around for a while, and at one stage, walked out the back door, staying out in the backyard for a while before re-entering the house. After that, he returned to the sofa for a while, then made a phone call and left the house. He was out for around an hour, and then when he returned, he did some lines of cocaine on his coffee table. Then seemed to put on some music and dance for two hours before wandering off to take a shower and then go to bed.

And through the entire footage—all four cameras—there wasn't a single shot of anyone else in the house.

"Sally ... either this other guy stayed in the closet the entire night and somehow managed to teleport himself out of the house in the morning," Haxton said slowly, "or ... there never was another guy."

Sally was angry, but she was also confused. She didn't see how this could be possible. She had seen the other car pulling up, she had heard the man, seen his feet and legs as he walked past the car she had been hiding under. She had seen two people on the thermal imaging camera and had heard two distinct voices talking.

Yet there was nothing on the cameras, nothing at all.

"Please don't take this the wrong way, Sally," Haxton said softly, "but you did—you *do*—have a concussion from what happened the other night. Concussions, even mild ones, can sometimes cause hallucinations."

"He's right, Sally," Kosinski said. "This one time, I slipped on some ice and hit my head so hard that I blacked out. For the next few days, I could swear I kept seeing Michael Jackson following me around ... yes, the dead pop star, *that* Michael Jackson."

"I'm not crazy," Sally murmured, staring at the screen with eyes that were wide with both shock and disbelief. "I didn't hallucinate that stuff."

"Nobody's saying you're crazy, Sally," Haxton said. "It's

just that … you know, with a head injury, sometimes … sometimes people see things that seem so very, very real to them, but in reality, those things aren't there. It's nothing to be ashamed of; it can happen to anyone."

Sally wanted to say something, wanted to have an angry comeback … but she couldn't. Indeed, she was even starting to doubt herself at this point. Maybe Haxton and Kosinski were right. Maybe her concussion had caused her to hallucinate. Maybe there never had been a second person here at all, and it was all in her head…

"I … I think I need to go home," Sally said. "Yeah … I need to go home and rest for a while."

"We've done about all we can here," Haxton said. "We've torn this place apart, we've checked the camera footage through the whole night, and we haven't found a single thing that shows that Nordstrom did anything illegal besides purchasing and consuming cocaine. I'm sorry, Sally, but I think this is a dead end. I think, as much of a prick as he is, Nordstrom might not be involved."

"What about Aling's testimony?" Sally asked. She now felt like she was grasping at straws. The entire case seemed to be falling to pieces.

"What about it?" Haxton said. "I know you believe him. I know you *want to* believe him, but he has no evidence to back up his claims that Nordstrom told him to do all that stuff. Basically, it's his word against Nordstrom's, and you know that won't hold up in court."

"But I … I *know* Aling wasn't lying," Sally murmured, feeling even more doubtful about everything now.

"You think he wasn't lying," Haxton said. "There's no

way to prove beyond a shadow of a doubt that he wasn't. Not without hard evidence. And he apparently threw that hard evidence into a river, so I don't know how you plan on proving anything."

"I think maybe you should do like you just said, Sally," Kosinski said sympathetically, "and go home and take a rest. Let Gareth and me wrap up things here. We'll take care of it. Don't worry about it. You just … get some much-needed rest."

Sally nodded slowly. She felt defeated and crushed and felt further than ever from finding and saving the three missing boys. How could this be possible? Had she really hallucinated that entire episode? Was her sixth sense so completely wrong about both Aling and Nordstrom? It certainly felt that way, and she felt totally lost and awash with confusion.

"All right," she said, staring at the floor, feeling as if her world was collapsing all around her. "I'll go home. I'll … I'll see you guys later."

As she was walking out of the house, though, Haxton got another phone call. And after he had finished talking to the person on the other end of the line, he raced out of the house and stopped Sally before she got into her car.

"Gareth, what's wrong?" she asked.

"You're not gonna believe this," he said breathlessly, "but another child has been kidnapped."

"*Y*ou gotta be kidding me," Sally gasped. "When?"

"An hour ago, from the ice rink in the downtown mall," Haxton answered. "It was a similar story to the movie theater thing. The kid went to the bathroom, didn't come back, and when they went to look for him fifteen minutes later, he was gone. Eight-year-old boy, by the way."

"I can't believe this," Sally murmured, shaking her head.

"It proves one thing," Haxton said. "Nordstrom couldn't have had anything to do with it since we've had him in custody all day, and he hasn't had a phone on him or anything he could have used to communicate with. And obviously, French, being in New Mexico, and, well, dead, couldn't have had anything to do with it either."

"But then Aling couldn't have done it, either," Sally said. "He's also still in custody."

"That's the thing," Haxton said with a sigh. "I thought Aling was still in custody, but it turns out he was released on bail last night. And since being released, nobody's been able to track him down."

Sally felt as if another terrible blow had been struck against her. Had she been so utterly wrong about Aling? Had he been the culprit all along? Perhaps, she thought, he was an incredibly skilled liar—just as Haxton had suggested. Maybe he had completely fooled her. Maybe her sixth sense, her gut instinct, simply wasn't nearly as accurate as she had once thought it was.

"Who's at the scene?" Sally asked. "Are there witnesses? Security camera footage, anything?"

"Some officers are at the ice rink, yeah, but I'm not sure who, exactly. Look, you said it yourself, you need to go home and get some rest. Kosinski and I will handle this. We'll go down there now and check things out. Don't worry about it. We'll be as thorough as we can possibly be, trust me."

Usually, Sally would have argued that she was perfectly capable of handling the situation and would have insisted on participating in the investigation, but now, feeling completely defeated and deflated, all she could do was nod weakly, doing her best not to break down and cry.

"All right," she said to Haxton. "All right, you and Kosinski can handle this."

"Get some rest, Sally, and call me if you need anything," Haxton said, giving Sally's shoulder a sympathetic squeeze.

Sally drove home in a daze. Nothing felt real; it seemed as if she was drifting through some sort of waking dream. She had heard about the delayed onset of symptoms from a concussion. Was that what she was feeling?

"I can't believe I was so wrong about everything," Sally murmured to herself as she drove. "I just … I can't believe it. I was so sure, so certain, and now it turns out I wasn't only wrong, I may have hallucinated the entire thing."

While she felt bad about her own failings, she felt even worse for the kidnapped children. With the latest series of revelations in the case, they were back to square one, and now the hope of finding the kidnapped children alive had dwindled to almost zero. Thinking of her own son, Derek, made Sally even more acutely aware of the terrible plight of the poor children who had been abducted, and she could no longer hold back the tears. She pulled over to the side of the road and wept bitterly.

Sally had never been one to dwell on defeat and failure, though, and after she had allowed her sadness and disappointment to pass, they were replaced with a new, fresh sense of courage and determination.

She remembered an occasion on which something similar had happened—she had been so certain about a particular suspect and his guilt, yet all the evidence seemed to have pointed to the guilty party being someone else. And indeed, her fellow officers had been convinced that the suspect Sally had been pursuing was not guilty. Yet she had simply known he was; her gut instinct had told her he had to be, and she had persisted in investigating him, even though to everyone else this had seemed like folly.

And in the end, they had all been proven wrong, and Sally had been proven right, against all odds.

"I didn't hallucinate that stuff," she said determinedly to herself, gripping the steering wheel tight, her jaw clenched, every muscle in her body taut, her eyes staring straight ahead with an iron-hard gaze. "I don't know what tricks Nordstrom pulled with his security cameras, but I know there was another person in his house that night. And I know he's involved in these kidnappings somehow ... and I'm going to prove it."

She drove home, feeling renewed and refreshed. She had stared defeat and failure in the face and had almost succumbed to it, but now, now she was ready to attack this case with a new sense of purpose and vigor.

The answer to Nordstrom's dark secrets lay not in his house but at his business. She remembered the rusty old van parked in a dark corner of the warehouse, with all its doors welded shut. And she recalled how, when she and Haxton had gone to investigate the warehouse, the skull-rattling "broken compressor" noise had started and persisted, and how the same racket had shaken the walls of the building pretty much every time they had gone there.

It wasn't a coincidence. She was sure of that.

"The answer is in that warehouse," Sally said to herself, bringing up the warehouse on Google maps and taking a close look at the area around it. "I'm sure of it."

There was no way that she and her fellow police officers would be issued a warrant to search the warehouse, not now, with the latest developments in the case. However, Sally hadn't allowed the lack of a warrant to prevent her from conducting an investigation before, and she wasn't about to let it happen now.

A plan was forming in Sally's mind, and soon she was ready to take the first step in putting that plan into action.

She walked out of her house—which was still being watched over by two police officers, who gave her a friendly nod from their cruiser, to which she responded with a smile and a wave—and headed over to her neighbor's house and rang the doorbell.

Her neighbor—a sweet, elderly woman named Mrs. Tomlinson—came shuffling through the house to answer the door. She beamed out a friendly smile when she saw Sally standing there.

"Why hello, Sally, it's lovely to see you! How's that special little boy of yours? I haven't seen him playing in the yard these past few days. And why are those policemen parked in your driveway? There seems to be a police car there every night now. It's got me a little worried, I have to say."

"Never fear, Mrs. Tomlinson. There's nothing to be worried about," Sally said. "It's just a case I'm working on. I need some extra help. That's why my fellow cops are always there. And Derek's staying with his father for a while. That's why you haven't seen him in the yard."

"Ah, I see, I see," Mrs. Tomlinson said, the smile never fading from her cheerful face. "Well, what can I do for you today, Sally?"

"I was wondering if I could use your phone to make a quick call?" Sally asked. "I seem to have lost my cellphone, and it's a pretty urgent matter."

"Of course, of course, come on in," Mrs. Tomlinson said. "The phone's in the kitchen. Go ahead and talk as long as you need to. I'll be in the living room if you need me."

"Thanks so much, Mrs. Tomlinson," Sally said.

She went to the kitchen, waited until her elderly neighbor was out of earshot, and then dialed the number she had written on the back of her hand—the number for the Thor's Hammer depot.

A familiar voice—that of Nordstrom's pretty young secretary—came through on the other end of the line. "Hello, Thor's Hammer Deliveries. How can I help you?"

Sally disguised her voice, putting on an accent. "Hello, I was just wondering what time the depot closes today?"

"We close here at five pm. Is there anything else I can help you with?"

"No, thank you," Sally said, and she put down the phone. "All right," she whispered to herself. "Tonight then … tonight we do this."

35

*I*f Sally felt a little like a criminal, it was because she was about to break the law. She justified her upcoming actions with the fact that she was doing it to save the kidnapped children, but the fact was she was about to commit a crime, one that could land her in serious trouble if she got caught.

Dressed all in black, with a black balaclava covering her head and face, too, she observed the Thor's Hammer depot through her night vision binoculars. From her vantage point—the roof of a nearby motor workshop, which was closed for the weekend, and which had been easy to break into—Sally had a good view of the depot. It was early evening, and the last vehicle had left the parking lot an hour earlier, and since then, she hadn't seen any evidence of anyone's presence there.

There were security cameras, of course, and Sally figured there was a good chance she would get caught on one of them. However, since she was completely disguised, she wasn't worried about later being identified, and since she was a cop herself, she knew nobody was going to be calling in the forensics department to search for stray hairs or other DNA evidence for a crime as relatively minor as illegally entering business premises and sneaking around.

Now that she was sure the coast was clear, she climbed down off the workshop roof and made her way across the street to the Thor's Hammer premises. A tall steel fence surrounded the depot, and it would be difficult, if not impossible, to scale without a ladder, but on Google maps, Sally had noticed there was a large tree next to the fence at the back. She'd brought a short length of rope with her, and when she got around to the rear of the property, she was pleased to see that the tree would be easy to get into.

Moving silently and stealthily through the darkness, she climbed up into the tree, then tied the rope around a study bough that hung over the depot premises. She gave the rope a few tugs to test it, and then, when she was confident she had tied a sturdy enough knot, she began lowering herself down the length.

It wasn't too difficult a climb, and soon enough, she was on the ground, inside the depot. Even though she had observed the place for an hour and had made completely certain there was nobody there, she waited in the thick patch of dark shadow beneath the tree for a minute or two before she moved.

Her heart was pounding in her chest, and her nerves were tingling, and all her senses were on full alert. She felt as if she could have heard a pin dropping from a mile away. The sky above was clear and starry, and there was no moon, so the ambient light was low and dark, which worked in Sally's favor.

Buzzing with adrenalin, she raced across the large open area between the back fence and the warehouse, a run that seemed to take forever, and then, finally, she got to the warehouse. The main entrance, through which the trucks and vans entered, was locked and secured with a heavy padlock and chain.

However, Sally knew there was a side door to the warehouse—she had seen it when she and Haxton had searched the place. Keeping to the shadows, even though she was sure there wasn't anyone around, Sally went around to the side door.

In the eyes of the law, she had been guilty of nothing more than trespassing up to this point. Now, however, she was about to add another charge to her sheet: breaking and entering.

She took a long crowbar out of her black backpack. Being a cop, one learned about the many methods criminals used to get into places they weren't supposed to, and Sally had learned that many door locks, aside from the very sturdiest ones, could be overcome by simple force and leverage—a principle everyone learned about in basic physics.

She jammed one end of the crowbar between the door and the frame, right where the doorknob was, and then threw all of her weight into the other end of the crowbar, pushing hard on it until she heard the sharp crack of wood breaking.

The door swung open, but as it did, a piercing wail screamed out of the warehouse, its terrifying volume piercing Sally's ears as if a torturer was drilling through her ears with jagged drill bits. The unexpected fright of it almost gave her a heart attack. This was something she hadn't planned for at all: the warehouse had a burglar alarm, and she had just set it off.

"Shit!" she gasped, her voice completely inaudible over the screeching howl of the burglar alarm.

Her first instinct was to bolt, to sprint back to the rope and scramble up it into the tree to escape and freedom, but despite the horrendous screaming of the alarm, Sally forced herself to remain calm.

As a cop, she knew that it usually took even the best security companies a couple minutes to respond to an alarm. As terrifying as the sound was, she had maybe two or three minutes to play with—if she moved fast, she could accomplish what she needed to and be off the premises by the time the security people arrived.

There was one place in the warehouse that she wanted to investigate more than any other spot—the mysterious welded-shut van. She flipped on her headlamp—there was no point in trying to be stealthy now, and even though the cameras would pick her up, they wouldn't be able to see her face due to the balaclava—and raced through the warehouse, adrenalin surging through her body.

She got to the van and hastily tried all of the doors, but every single one of them was welded shut. Shining her headlamp through the dusty windscreen, she saw that the rear compartment was completely separated from the driver's seat by a solid metal section.

Dropping to her knees, she looked under the van and saw that the entire view of the underside was blocked all around the van by sandbags stacked around it on all sides.

She could barely hear herself think over the horrendous screaming of the alarm siren, but she thumped on the side of the van with her fists.

"Hello!" she yelled, her own voice almost lost in the chaotic screaming of the alarm, which was echoing madly through the huge warehouse. "Is anyone in there?"

Then her heart almost stopped—she heard a child's voice, faint and barely audible, calling out from inside the van.

Or did she? Was her mind playing tricks on her? Was this the concussion causing her to hallucinate again?

Painfully aware of the fact that her time was running out, she dropped to the floor and began frantically pulling the sandbags out from under the van. When she had pulled two out, she shone her headlamp under the van ... and instead of seeing space there, as one would expect to see under any vehicle, there was a solid wall of steel. The sandbags were there to cover this up from the eyes of anyone looking at the van.

"Oh my God," Sally gasped. "There's some sort of secret compartment here ... there's a secret compartment under the van!"

She scrambled to pull more of the sandbags away from the underside of the van, but then, suddenly, all the lights in the warehouse came on.

"You! Stop what you're doing and put your hands where I can see 'em!" a raspy male voice yelled aggressively.

Sally froze, and the blood in her veins felt as if it were turning to ice.

"Turn around and face me, and put your hands behind your head!" the security man roared. "Do it, or I swear to God I'll shoot!"

Sally heard the sound of combat boots running through the warehouse toward her. She raised her hands above her head and turned around slowly to face the men. She saw that there were three security guards, one armed with a shotgun and two armed with pistols, running toward her. All three of them had their guns aimed at her.

"It's okay," she said slowly. "I'm a police officer, I'm a cop, and I'm here—"

"Shut your fucking mouth!" one of the men roared. "I'm not interested in your bullshit or your lies! Get on your knees, keep your hands behind your head, do it!"

A sense of both fear and desperation grasped Sally with an icy grip. "There are kidnapped children in this van!" she yelled. "I'm a cop! I'm trying to find kidnapped children!"

"Sure you are," the man with the shotgun growled sarcastically. "Shut your fucking mouth now before we decide to smash some of your fucking teeth out."

Two of the guards reached her. They shoved her onto the ground, forced her arms behind her back, and hand-cuffed her wrists.

"Please!" Sally begged. "You don't understand, this van, there are—"

"I said shut up, you crazy bitch!" one security guard yelled. "What the fuck is wrong with you? Jake, Dylan, get her out to the car and lock her up in the back until the cops get here."

Now that she was handcuffed, the men pulled Sally back onto her feet. She opened her mouth to protest, but the man with the shotgun slammed the butt of the firearm into her solar plexus, knocking the air out of her lungs and causing her knees to crumble beneath her.

Gasping for breath and feeling as if she was about to pass out, Sally was dragged ignominiously out of the warehouse and locked in the back of one of the security company's cars.

Her unauthorized investigation was over … and now, on top of that, she was also a felon in the eyes of the law.

36

"I want her locked up in a mental institution," Nordstrom growled, glaring at Sally, who was sitting teary-eyed in the back of a police cruiser.

Nordstrom, who had come to the depot as soon as the security company had informed him of the break-in, was talking to Haxton, who was one of the officers who had responded to the security company's call to the police to report the capture of a suspect.

"You're in no position to be making demands, Nordstrom," Haxton growled.

"That psychotic bitch is schizophrenic!" Nordstrom yelled. "She belongs in the fucking looney bin, with her conspiracy theories about me and my warehouse!"

"Why don't you let me take a look inside then if this theory is so crazy?" Haxton asked coolly, his eyes steely.

"Get a fucking warrant, then you can take as long and as thorough a look as you want," Nordstrom spat. "But until then, nobody except my employees is allowed inside my warehouse. I'm sick of this bullshit, these lies about me, sick of it! That crazy skank crossed a line tonight. She crossed a fucking line! I want her locked up! And you can *bet*, Detective, you can fucking *bet* on the fact that you people will be hearing from my lawyers for this little stunt. They're going to make sure that psycho sees prison time for this. I promise you that, Detective, she's going to see prison time for this bullshit!"

Haxton was bristling with anger at Nordstrom's attitude, but he realized that he didn't have a leg to stand on, at least in the eyes of the law. Now that Sally had crossed this line, Nordstrom had every right to refuse them entry to his warehouse unless they had a search warrant.

"She won't bother you again," Haxton muttered, before turning around and walking away, his barely suppressed rage plainly visible in the white-knuckled balling of his fists at his sides.

"She'd better not!" Nordstrom yelled behind him. "My lawyers will come after all of you if she sets foot on my property again!"

Haxton went and sat in the driver's seat of the cruiser in which Sally was being held. He looked through the steel mesh at her and shook his head slowly, letting out a long, sad sigh of disappointment.

"I can't believe you did this, Sally," he said. "I never thought you'd be on the other side of this mesh, sitting in the back of a cruiser in handcuffs. I never thought I'd see this day."

"Those children are in there, Gareth," Sally insisted, tears rimming her eyes, her hands trembling. "There's a secret compartment in that old van, it's hidden by sand-bags, and I-I heard a child's voice, I—"

"You heard a child's voice over a siren that's louder than a guitar amp at a heavy metal concert? Sally … I don't know what happened to you when that truck smashed into your car, but ever since then … I don't know. I think this concussion is worse than the doctor thought it was. You're acting crazy. You're acting obsessed, being completely illogical. You've lost touch with reality, Sally. I hate to say it, but you have. I wanna help you, really, I do, but you've put me in one hell of a position here. Nordstrom called the press, and those vultures are all over it. If he hadn't done that, maybe, just maybe, I could have let you off the hook. But now, with the media watching us like hawks, I can't do that. If I let you off, it'll cause a shitstorm like nothing this department has seen."

"Wh-what are you saying, Gareth?" Sally gasped.

"I'm not only going to have to charge you, but I'm also going to have to … to fire you. I'm sorry, Sally, but you crossed a line here tonight. God, I wish you hadn't, and I wish I didn't have to do this, but there's no way around it. I'm going to have to let you go."

Sally was too shocked to respond. But more than that, she was devastated by how much of a catastrophe it all was. She was sure the children were there, imprisoned inside that old van with its secret compartment, a mere hundred yards away from where they were now. Yet nobody would believe her; everyone thought she was crazy now, even Haxton. They all thought that she had lost her mind … and indeed, she was starting to wonder whether she may have lost her mind.

"All I can do now is damage control," Haxton continued. "I'm sorry, Sally … I wish there was something else I could do, but there just … there isn't."

"I … I understand, Gareth," she murmured hoarsely, fighting back a flood of tears.

"Look, there's, uh, there's maybe something we can do to maybe lessen the impact of all of this," Haxton said. "If you go to the doctor, tell him you've been hallucinating, seeing all sorts of things, maybe having migraines or something—we could at least get you out of having to do jail time if all this erratic behavior could be put down to the concussion being more serious than the doc initially thought."

"You … you want me to pretend that I've been seeing things?" Sally asked.

"Well, you *have* been seeing things and hearing things that aren't there Sally," Haxton said. "I mean, how else do you explain all of this? We looked through that security camera footage from Nordstrom's place together. There was nobody else there! We all saw it. But you insisted there was a second person there, even though the evidence was clearly pointing to the fact that he was alone all night. And now this, thinking that the kids are locked up in this warehouse, inside some secret compartment in a rusty, old, broken-down van in there? Sally, you have to be able to see how insane this all sounds."

"So you think I'm crazy, Gareth? And you want me to

go to a doctor and tell him that I think I've gone crazy, too?"

"I'm not saying you're crazy. Look, all sorts of weird shit happens when you get a bad head injury. You heard what Kosinski said about his own head injury and seeing stuff that wasn't there. It doesn't mean you're crazy. It just means you suffered some head trauma that might be affecting the way your mind works. That's all, seriously. Please, just do this, Sally. For your own sake."

She bowed her head, sobbing softly, and nodded. "Fine … I'll do it. I'll see a doctor."

Another cop came and knocked on the driver's door, and Haxton rolled down the window. "I need to take her downtown for processing now, sir," the cop said to Haxton.

Haxton nodded grimly. Then he turned to Sally. "It's time to go now, Sally. I'm sorry … But you know what's coming next. It has to be done, and there's no way around it, I'm afraid."

Sally nodded, sniffing and sobbing. Haxton got out of the cruiser, and the other cop got in. Then he drove off, heading for the police station, where he would fingerprint her, take her mugshot, process her, and put her in a cell.

Sally watched Haxton through the passenger window as they drove away. He looked defeated, crumpled up like an old handkerchief. More than anything, he looked broken.

And that, as Sally was driven away to be processed and thrown in a cell, was exactly how she felt, too.

37

Sally's ex-husband, Simon, came to bail her out later that evening. He could barely even make eye contact with her as they walked out of the station together.

"Where's Derek?" Sally asked softly. Her eyes were red from all the crying, and she was only barely able to fight back tears.

"Staying with my parents," Simon said.

"Did you tell him what I did?"

Simon sighed and shook his head. "No. I didn't tell my parents, either. But seriously, Sally, what the hell is going on? Why on Earth did you do this?"

"I just … I was following a lead, Simon, a really solid lead—"

"That you couldn't pursue through official channels? A lead that you had to pursue by breaking into someone's business like a burglar?"

"Simon, thank you for bailing me out and everything. I really appreciate it, but I just, I really don't want to argue about this right now. If you could please just take me home and let me rest … that's all I want right now."

"You *are* going to see the doctor tomorrow about this concussion and these hallucinations, right?" Simon asked. "I'll drive you there. But seriously, you *have to* go. Gareth told me—"

"I know what Gareth said," Sally said. "And yes, I'll go."

"You'd better pack a bag in the morning then. They'll probably want to keep you there for observation for a few days."

"I understand that. Don't worry, I'll be ready. Thank you for the offer of a ride, by the way."

"Well, in your condition, you shouldn't be driving," Simon said. "I'm just doing what any decent person would do in this situation."

"And I truly appreciate that, seriously, I do," Sally said. "But could we … not talk anymore on the drive home? I … I need some quiet time, and I just … after everything that's happened, I don't have the energy to talk about this anymore."

"All right," Simon said. He was still upset, of course, and there were plenty of other things he wanted to say to Sally about what she had done, but he realized those things would only make the situation worse, so he held his tongue.

They drove to Sally's place in silence, and the only words that passed between them were when she said farewell to him at the end of the journey. The cops in the cruiser in her driveway watched her get out of the car, but this time there were no smiles or waves when she walked past them … only looks of pity and disappointment.

As Sally unlocked her front door, a terrible realization hit her with the full force of a viciously swung sledgehammer. This was the lowest point she'd ever been at in her life. She had completely screwed up the kidnapping case, had destroyed her own reputation, and got herself fired. Everyone thought she had brain damage. Indeed, she was almost convinced that she did have brain damage.

Almost…

The next morning Simon showed up at nine, the time they had agreed on to visit the doctor. However, Sally wasn't waiting on the porch, as she had said she would be. Simon hadn't gotten much sleep the night before, and he was already in a bad mood. Sally's tardiness only served to annoy him further.

"I swear to God if she wasn't the mother of my boy," he muttered to himself as he got out of his car and marched up to the front door, where he rang the doorbell repeatedly. "Sally! What are you doing? It's already five after nine; we're gonna be late!"

There was no response, so he rang the doorbell a few more times.

"Sally! Hurry up, dammit! Seriously, you're gonna miss your appointment! I don't wanna have to drive like a maniac just to get you there on time!"

Since there was no response, he got out his phone and

dialed her. However, instead of ringing, it went straight to voicemail. Now, instead of plain anger, a different emotion began to creep into Simon's head—worry. Sally did have a head injury, after all, and it wasn't unheard of for people who had received a hard blow to the head to seem perfectly healthy for a few days but then suddenly die.

With worry rising steadily within him, Simon strode briskly over to the cop car parked in Sally's drive. One of the cops inside rolled down the window to talk to him.

"Hey, pal, you're Sally's ex-husband, right?" the cop asked with a friendly smile.

"Yeah. So, I was supposed to take her to the doctor now, but she's not answering the door, and her phone's going straight to voicemail. Has she left the house or something? Have you seen anything?"

The cop shook his head. "We haven't seen anyone enter or exit the place. We thought she was still sleeping; nobody's opened the drapes or the windows, and we didn't see any lights come on in the house before the sun came up or anything."

"Shit," Simon muttered, the worry within him now almost reaching panic-inducing levels. He ran over to the door and tried it, and he found it was locked.

He ran around to the backyard, climbing over the four-foot wooden fence that separated the backyard from the front section of the house. He went straight to the back door, and when he turned the door handle, it was open.

Dreading what he might find inside, he ventured into

the house, which was gloomy on account of all the drapes being shut. The place was a bit of a mess; there were dishes piled up in the sink and dirty takeout containers on the counter, and a few of Derek's toys scattered across the floor. It wasn't that Sally was a slob; she'd been working so relentlessly on the kidnapping case that she'd barely had any time to keep the place clean. And with Derek not being around and her being here on her own, keeping the place spotless wasn't high up on her list of priorities.

Simon went straight to the bedroom, stopping to check the bathroom on the way there. She wasn't in the bathroom, and that made his worry levels shoot up even higher. He practically sprinted into the bedroom, where he was expecting to see her lying in bed … hopefully just asleep and not dead. He desperately prayed.

Yet the moment he stepped into the bedroom, he saw at once that the bed was empty. He stopped and stared in confusion at the unmade bed for a few moments.

"What the hell?"

He dashed out of the bedroom and hastily searched the rest of the house, calling Sally's name as he did. There was no response from anywhere, and it quickly became obvious that she was gone.

There was one last thing Simon needed to check to confirm a new suspicion that was growing in his mind. He hurried back to the bedroom and opened the top drawer of the left-hand bedside table. This was where Sally always kept her .38 Special revolver—her privately owned firearm, not her police-issue pistol—which she had been forced to hand in along with her badge when she had been so ignominiously fired the previous evening.

The revolver was missing.

"Oh, shit," Simon murmured, the blood draining from his face.

38

"**W**hat do you mean she's *gone?*" Haxton demanded, his voice sounding even more hoarse and gravelly over the radio than it did in person.

"I'm sorry, sir, but she must have sneaked out," answered the junior officer, one of the cops who had been stationed in the cruiser outside Sally's house.

Simon and the other cop were standing outside the cruiser, looking anxious and worried as the man communicated with Haxton.

"Sneaked out?" Haxton yelled. "You morons were supposed to be watching her!"

"We were, I mean, we did watch her, sir, but we were posted here to, uh, prevent threats from getting to her, not to—"

"Don't argue with me, you idiot!" Haxton snapped. "Shit … so she's on the loose with a gun and a head injury that's completely warped her perception of reality. This is bad…. This is *really* bad."

"I think she might be going after Nordstrom, sir," the cop suggested. "I mean, she *was* completely convinced that he was the kidnapper, right?"

"Yeah, yeah, I think you may be right," Haxton muttered, still angry but beginning to calm down. "I'll send units to his residence and his business right away. The media shitstorm around the whole unhinged break-in thing is going to be bad enough, but if she really loses her mind and murders him ... my God, it'll be the end of this department. Our name will get dragged through the mud, not just in the national media, but probably the fucking international media as well. My God, we have to stop her before she does something truly insane. You two stay there, call me the instant you see her if she comes back there! I'll put out a statewide alert, and I'll put out a citywide APB on her. We *have to* stop her ... we *have to.*"

"Got it, sir."

"Simon, can you hear me?" Haxton asked, the police radio adding a crunchy crackle to his voice.

The cop handed Simon the radio receiver so he could respond.

"I can hear you, Gareth," Simon said. He and Haxton were on good terms, having spent quite a lot of time together back when Simon had been married to Sally.

"She knows where Derek is, right?" Haxton asked.

"Yeah, she knows he's with my parents right now."

"Get him somewhere else," Haxton said. "After she tries to take out Nordstrom, she's probably going to try to get to Derek—"

"Whatever she's planning to do today, Gareth, I know

that she'd never, ever hurt Derek," Simon said. "Our son means more to her than life itself. Even with the head injury and the confusion and hallucinations, I know she would never, ever harm our son."

"I know that, too, and I wasn't going to suggest that she would do that," Haxton said. "But she likely knows that she's going to be a wanted fugitive, so she'll probably want to take Derek with her to wherever she's planning on running to. Get him somewhere safe, but I need you and your parents to communicate with each other as if he's still with them. You what a good detective she is. She'll track you, listen in on your calls, and figure he's still there. She'll probably try to sneak into your parents' place to pick up Derek—we could catch her when she does this."

"Ah, okay, okay, I'll do that."

"Good. Don't tell anyone where you're taking him, not even me. Just make sure he's safe," Haxton said.

"Got it."

"That's it!" Haxton barked. "Now I'm heading out to track down this crazy woman to stop her before she does anything truly insane, something that'll get our names splashed all over the pages of international news!"

"*Y*ou're sure you weren't followed here?" the man asked Nordstrom as the two of them walked along the pier.

"You know me, I'm no idiot. I drove into town, parked at the downtown mall, then walked half an hour to the Greyhound office, taking the most complicated route I could, and got my ticket here. And you picked me up from the Greyhound stop, Erik. Did you see anyone suspicious there?"

"No."

"Then quit being so paranoid," Nordstrom muttered.

"The merchandise has become a liability now," the man named Erik said as they continued along the pier, with a pleasant background sound being provided by the ocean waves lapping gently against the hulls of the many boats moored there. The sun was setting, lighting up the crests of the waves in tones of orange and red. "I didn't want to do this ... but we have no choice."

"You think I wanted it, either?" Nordstrom snapped. "God, we worked so fucking hard on this ... and the buyers were ready to transfer the ten million into my Swiss account. Now we have to dump it all at sea, and we get nothing. Fucking nothing! Makes me sick."

"Better than getting multiple life sentences, I can tell you that," Erik muttered. "That crazy bitch almost had us busted ... almost."

"Yeah, well, in the end, she didn't. And now, whenever her cop buddies find her, she's going to be committed to a fucking lunatic asylum. A couple hours ago, I spoke to her partner, that Haxton guy. He's got every unit in the city looking for her."

"Even better for us," Erik said with a dark smile. "Nobody's going to take much notice when we dispose of the merchandise."

"Even so, we need to be careful. We need to be out at least ten miles off the coast before we sink 'em to the bottom of the ocean."

"Agreed," Erik said as they reached his sailboat, a medium-sized vessel capable of being crewed by two men. "Well, here we are. Let's get this over with. We can try again next year when all the hype about this case has died down. The buyer will still be willing to pay at that time, I'm sure."

"He will. He's always hungry for more of them."

The men entered the sailboat and cast off the mooring ropes as they prepared to sail out of the harbor and into the open sea.

"Go down to the hold and check on the merchandise,"

Erik said to Nordstrom. "I mean, it's not as if anyone can hear them scream out there, but I don't want my sailing excursion to be disturbed by the sound of—"

A sudden, loud thump that came from the deck above the men cut off Erik's words.

"What the hell was that?" Nordstrom gasped.

Before Erik could answer, they heard the sound of footsteps charging down the stairs. Erik dashed across the room to where a shotgun was mounted on the wall, but before he could grab the firearm, a young man dressed in a gray trench coat burst through the door and leveled his revolver at the men. Erik froze, as did Nordstrom.

He wore aviator sunglasses and had a thick black goatee, so his face was obscured. However, when he opened his mouth to speak, both men realized that the "man" wasn't a man but a woman in disguise.

"Don't fucking move," a familiar female voice said. "Both of you, hands behind your heads. Get on your knees."

"Lawson?" Nordstrom gasped, his jaw hanging open with disbelief. "How the fuck?"

Sally took off her glasses, yanked the black wig off her head, and peeled off the fake goatee, which she tossed aside. "I put a GPS tracker on your car a while ago, Nordstrom," she said. "I followed you to the mall in a rented car, and then I tracked you on foot to the ticket office. As for the costume, this was something I had left over from a drug sting operation a few years ago. It clearly worked well enough for you to not notice when I got on the same Greyhound."

"You're insane, you fucking bitch," Nordstrom snarled. But in his words, there was a crippling fear, a true terror.

"Wrong," she said. "And now, seeing you two together like this ... well, it's like you're standing next to a mirror, isn't it, Karl Nordstrom ... or, should I say, Karl Magnus, standing there with your identical twin, Erik Magnus."

Both men—who were indeed identical twins and who looked so similar that it was almost impossible to tell them apart—gasped with surprise.

"How the fuck did you—"

"A little thing called 'deep research,' Karl," Sally said calmly. "You went to great pains to disguise the fact that you had legally changed your name when you were eighteen, and you did everything you could to hide the ties you had to your own family ... your twin brother. But some things just can't be buried, not permanently. It took me a lot of digging, believe me ... a lot of effort, and I had to call in a big favor with an old friend at the FBI to finally unearth the truth, but when I did, when it all came out, it finally made sense. I finally understood how you were able to fool everyone."

Erik, who now knew the game was up, lunged across the room, trying to grab the shotgun off the wall. The thunderclap of a gunshot boomed across the room, and Erik fell to the floor, screaming and clutching his thigh, from which blood began to ooze.

"I'll put the next one in your gut, Erik, and you'll die in slow agony," Sally said coldly. "I suggest you keep still. And that goes for you, too, Karl. Unless you'd like hot lead implant in your thigh, too, I suggest you get on your knees."

From down below in the hold came the muffled sound of a child's scream.

"So that's where you kept them, huh?" Sally asked. "The kidnapped children, locked up in this boat ... I was wrong about the secret compartment in the van in the warehouse. I know that now. But I wasn't *completely* wrong about it, was I? Because that was where you were keeping Julian Drake, who you framed by paying him to carry out a large duffel bag full of old clothes from the aquarium on the day one of the boys was kidnapped there. And then, when he had served your purpose, you locked him up in that van, intending to kill him and dump his body as soon as our attention was off you guys. But French, he was part of your sick little operation, wasn't he?"

"I ain't saying a fucking thing," Nordstrom—or, rather, Karl Magnus—spat.

Sally chuckled humorlessly. "He was, I know that now. You and your twin brother paid him to hack into those security camera systems and loop the footage so you wouldn't be caught on camera. Then you helped French escape when we came after him. Of course, when we got close to actually catching him, you had to take drastic action before he sang and blew the lid on your little kidnapping scheme ... so you, Erik, went down to Albuquerque and put a bullet in the back of his head."

"You have no way of proving that," Erik gasped, grimacing with pain as he gripped his bleeding thigh.

"But just in case you did get caught on camera, you had a fall guy: Peter Aling. You, Erik, dressed up like him every time you kidnapped a child. The thing that made this obvious to me was the fact that witnesses always described the kidnapper as being around average height, whereas Aling is actually over six feet. You two, though, are average height, and it's easy enough to put on a long blond wig to look like Aling. When Aling tried to confess, you made him disappear as soon as he was let out on bail. Even though he had no real evidence against you, since you made him throw his phone into the river, he was a liability. I suspect we'll find him locked up in that soundproof welded-shut van in the warehouse, where you were keeping him to dispose of him along with Julian Drake after you'd disposed of the kidnapped children."

"You … you fucking slut, you whore," Karl snarled. There was nothing else he could say; Sally had figured out their whole scheme.

"And then, to really solidify things and turn my own people against me because you knew how close I was getting to exposing everything, you went and openly bought drugs where you knew you'd be caught, Karl. That gave us an excuse to get a warrant to take you in and hold you downtown—which is exactly what you wanted us to do. With French conveniently dead, and you downtown at the station, Erik here went and kidnapped another child from the ice rink, once again wearing the Peter Aling disguise. That 'proved' that you were totally innocent, Karl, since nobody knew about the existence of your identical twin. And the fact that Erik is your identical twin made it possible to fool everyone."

"You think you know it all, huh?" Karl snarled.

"You knew I was watching you that night," Sally said calmly. "That's why you called Erik to come to your place. And by the way, Erik, in addition to the sedan registered in your name, I know you also have a black Ford F-150 registered in your name ... the same truck that was used in the attempt to kill me. The attempt by *you two* to murder me."

"You bitch!" Karl roared, enraged but helpless to do anything.

"So, you got your twin brother to come over and visit. He did stand in the closet and talk to you so that both of you weren't on camera at the same time, and you made sure you were both wearing the exact same outfit. He left via the backdoor, and you climbed out of a window in one room that wasn't covered by a camera, then walked back in through the backdoor as if you were returning from being outside. Meanwhile, Erik went through the neighbor's yard, got back to his car, and left. That little stunt made everyone think I had brain damage because I was so sure that there were two people in your house while it looked like you were alone. You're smart, Karl, and you are, too, Erik ... but you're both complete psychos. And this right here ... this is the end of the road for both of you. You're both going to spend the rest of your lives in prison."

And in the background, all of them could hear the wail

of sirens approaching the harbor. Sally was right. It was all over for the brothers, and soon the kidnapped children would finally be free and reunited with their families.

EPILOGUE

"I still can't tell you how sorry I am for ever doubting you," Haxton said to Sally, shaking his head and sighing sadly. "I feel like such a jerk for telling everyone you were crazy … for insisting you were crazy myself."

"I already told you, Gareth, I don't hold it against you," Sally said with a smile. "How could I? Those scumbag brothers were—and I hate to admit this, but it's true—geniuses. They almost got away with the whole thing because they planned it so very, very well. And if I didn't have a big favor to call in with my buddy at the FBI, we never would have even discovered that Karl had a former identity and an identical twin. And without the discovery of his identical twin…"

"Those kids would be at the bottom of the ocean in a steel cage, Drake and Aling, too, and you'd be unjustly locked up in an insane asylum. And we almost fell for it, all of us."

"But we didn't, Gareth. We didn't. I never gave up on my gut feeling about Nordstrom and thank God I didn't."

Haxton nodded. "Thank God you didn't. Thanks to you, all the kids are back home with their parents, and Drake and Aling weren't murdered."

"How is Drake, anyway?" Sally asked. "He was almost dead of starvation when you guys pulled him out of that welded-shut van."

"Last I heard, the doctors said he was on his way to a full recovery. He'll be fine. He's a jerk and a bit of a creep, but he wasn't a kidnapper."

"Nope. Only the Magnus brothers were, and French, since he was an accessory with his hacking of the security camera systems."

"Well, French got what he deserved," Haxton said, "and Karl and Erik Magnus will, too. There's no way they're not going to spend the rest of their miserable lives in prison."

"Speaking of that," Sally said, "the case isn't totally closed yet … because now that we've finally identified and tracked down the billionaire buyer of the kidnapped children, it's time to arrest him and wrap up this whole thing. The evidence against him is so watertight that not even the best lawyer on Earth can keep that scumbag from spending the rest of his days in a prison cell. Let's go, Gareth, let's go get him!"

Made in the USA
Monee, IL
11 April 2022

94596957R00167